John Berry Alden, And others

# The Poetical Speaker

A Miscellany Gathered from Original and Classic Sources

John Berry Alden,  And others

**The Poetical Speaker**
*A Miscellany Gathered from Original and Classic Sources*

ISBN/EAN: 9783337061883

Printed in Europe, USA, Canada, Australia, Japan

Cover: Foto ©Andreas Hilbeck / pixelio.de

More available books at **www.hansebooks.com**

# THE
# POETICAL SPEAKER

A MISCELLANY

GATHERED FROM ORIGINAL AND
CLASSIC SOURCES

COMPILED BY

## JOHN B. ALDEN

NEW YORK
JOHN B. ALDEN, PUBLISHER
1890

# CONTENTS.

Contents.

# THE POETICAL SPEAKER.

## THE BABY.

**Where** did you come from, **baby dear?**
**Out of the** everywhere into **the here.**

Where did you get your eyes so blue?
Out of the sky as I came through.

**What makes the** light **in them** sparkle **and**
 spin?
**Some** of **the** starry spikes left in.

Where did you get **that** little tear?
I found it waiting when I got here.

What makes your forehead so smooth **and**
 high?
**A** soft hand stroked it as I went by.

**What** makes your cheek like a warm white
 rose?
Something better than any **one** knows.

**Whence** that three-cornered smile of bliss?
Three angels gave me at once a kiss.

Where did **you** get that pearly ear?
God spoke, and it came out to hear.

**Where** did you get those arms and hands?
**Love** made itself into hooks and bands.

Feet, whence did you come, darling things?
From the same box as the cherub's wings.

How did they all just come to be you?
God thought about me, and so I grew.

But how did you come to us, you dear?
God thought of *you*, and so I am here.

GEORGE MacDONALD.

---

## TRUST IN GOD.

Courage, brother! do not stumble,
  Though thy path be dark as night;
There's a star to guide the humble:
  "Trust in God, and do the right."

Let the road be rough and dreary,
  And its end far out of sight,
Foot it bravely!  Strong or weary,
  "Trust in God, and do the right."

Perish policy and cunning!
  Perish all that fears the light!
Whether losing, whether winning,
  "Trust in God, and do the right."

Trust no party, sect or faction ;
  Trust no leaders in the fight;
But in every word and action,
  "Trust in God, and do the right."

Trust no lovely forms of passion :
  Fiends may look like angels bright;
Trust no custom, school, or fashion,
  "Trust in God, and do the right."

Simple rule and safest guiding,
  Inward peace and inward might,

Star upon our path abiding,
  "Trust in God, and do the right."

Some will hate thee, some will love thee,
  Some will flatter, some will slight;
Cease from man, and look above thee,
  "Trust in God, and do the right."

NORMAN MACLEOD.

---

## THE GREEDY FOX.

On a winter's night,
  As the moon shone bright,
Two foxes went out for prey;
  As they trotted along,
  With frolic and song
They cheered their weary way.

  Through the wood they went,
  But they could not scent
A rabbit or goose astray;
  But at length they came
  To some better game,
In a farmer's barn by the way.

  On a roost there sat
  Some chickens, as fat
As foxes could wish for their dinners;
  So the prowlers found
  A hole by the ground,
And they both went in, the sinners!

  They both went in,
  With a squeeze and a grin,
And the chickens were quickly killed;
  And one of them lunched,
  And feasted, and munched,
Till his stomach was fairly filled.

The other, more wise,
Looked about with both eyes,
And hardly would eat at all;
For as he came in,
With a squeeze and a grin,
He remarked that the hole was small;

And, the cunning elf,
He said to himself,
"If I eat too much, it's plain,
As the hole is small,
I shall stick in the wall,
And never get out again."

Thus matters went on
Till the night was gone,
And the farmer came out with a pole;
The foxes both flew,
And one went through,
But the greedy one stuck in the hole.

In the hole he stuck,
So full was his pluck
Of the chickens he had been eating—
He could not get out,
Or turn about,
And so he was killed by beating.

ANONYMOUS.

## THE GRAY SWAN.

"O, tell me, sailor, tell me true,
Is my little lad, my Elihu,
A-sailing with your ship?"
The sailor's eyes were dim with dew:
"Your little lad, your Elihu?"
He said with trembling lip:
"What little lad?  What ship?"

"What little lad ? as if there *could* **be**
  Another such a one as he !
    What little lad, do you say ?
Why, Elihu, **that took** to the sea
The moment I put him off my knee !
    It was just the other day
    The Gray Swan sailed away !"

"**The** other day ? "—the sailor's eyes
  Stood open with a great surprise,—
    "The other day ? the Swan ?"
His heart began in his throat to rise.
"**Ay, ay,** sir ! here in the cupboard lies
    The jacket he had on !"
  "**A**nd so your lad **is gone ?**

"But, my good mother, **do you know**
  All this was twenty years ago ?
    *I* **stood** on the Gray Swan**'s deck,**
And to that lad I saw you throw,
Taking it off, **as it** might be, so !
    The kerchief from your neck."
  " Ay, and he'll bring it back !"

" And **did** the little lawless lad,
  That has made you sick and made you sad,
    **Sail** with the Gray Swan's crew ?"
"**La**wless !  The man is going mad !
  **The** best **boy** ever mother had ;—
    Be sure he sailed **with the crew !**
    **W**hat would you have him do ?"

" And he has never written **line,**
  Nor sent you word, nor made you sign,
    To say he was alive ?"
" Hold ! if 'twas **wrong,** the wrong was mine ;
  Besides, he may be in the brine ;
    And could he write from the grave ?
    Tut, man !  What would you have ?"

  " Gone, twenty years,—a long, long cruise !
   'Twas wicked thus your love to abuse !
    But if the lad still live,
  And come back home, think you, you can
  Forgive him ? "—" Miserable man !
   You're mad as the sea,—you rave.
   What have I to forgive ? "

   The sailor twitched his shirt so blue,
  And from within his bosom drew
   The kerchief. She was wild.
  " O God, my Father ! is it true ?
   My little lad, my Elihu !
   My blessed boy, my child !
   My dead, my living child ! "

ALICE CARY.

-----

## THE ANT AND THE CRICKET.

A silly young Cricket, accustomed to sing
Through the warm, sunny months of gay summer
  and spring,
Began to complain, when he found that at home
His cupboard was empty, and winter had come.
   Not a crumb to be found
   On the snow-covered ground,
   Not a flower could he see ;
   Not a leaf on a tree :
" O, what will become," says the Cricket, " of
  me ? "

At last, by starvation and famine made bold,
All dripping with wet, and all trembling with
  cold,
Away he set off to a miserly Ant,
To see if, to keep him alive, he would grant
   Him shelter from rain,—
   A mouthful of grain.

He wished only to borrow,
   He'd repay it to-morrow;
If not, he must die of starvation and sorrow.

Says the Ant to the Cricket, " I'm your servant
   and friend,
**But** we Ants never borrow, we Ants never lend.
**But** tell me, dear sir, did you lay nothing by
**When** the weather was warm?" Said the
   Cricket,
     " Not I !
    My heart was so light,
    That I sang day and night,
    For all nature looked gay."
    " You *sang*, sir, you say ?
Go, then," says the Ant, " and *dance* winter
   away."
Thus ending, he hastily lifted the wicket,
And **out of** the door turned the poor little
   Cricket.

Though this is a fable, the *moral* is good :
If you live without work, you must go without
   food.

ANONYMOUS.

---

## ROLL CALL.

" Corporal Green !" the Orderly cried ;
  " Here !" was the answer loud and clear,
  From the lips of the soldier who stood near;—
And " Here !" was the word the next replied.

" Cyrus Drew !"—then a silence fell—
  This time no answer followed the call;
  Only his rear-man had seen him fall,
Killed or wounded, he could not tell.

There they stood in the failing light,
  These men of battle, with grave, dark looks,

As plain to be read as open books,
While slowly gathered the shades of night.

The fern **on the** hill-sides was splashed with
      blood,
      And down **in** the corn where the poppies
          grew
      Were redder stains than the poppies **knew**;
And crimson-dyed was the river's flood.

**For** the **foe had crossed** from the other side
      That **day**, in the face of a murderous fire
      That swept them down in its terrible ire—
**And** their life-blood went to color **the tide.**

" Herbert Kline ! "   At the call there came
      Two stalwart soldiers into the **line**,
      **Bearing** between them this Herbert Kline,
Wounded and bleeding, to answer his name.

" Ezra Kerr ! "—and a voice answered, " Here ! "
      " Hiram Kerr ! "—but no man replied.
      They were brothers, these two ; the sad winds
          sighed,
And a shudder **crept** through the corn-**field** near.

" Ephraim Deane ! "— then a soldier spoke :
      " Deane carried our regiment's colors," he said;
      " Where our ensign was shot I left him **dead,**
**Just** after the enemy wavered and broke.

" Close to the road-side his body lies ;
      I paused **a** moment and gave him drink ;
      He murmured his mother's name, I think,
And **Death** came with it, and closed his eyes."

'Twas a victory ; yes, but it cost us dear—
      For that company's roll, when called at night,
      Of a *hundred* men who went into the fight,
Numbered but *twenty* that answered " Here ! "
N. G. SHEPHERD.

## THE MILLER OF DEE.

The moon was afloat,
Like a golden boat
On the sea-blue depths of the sky,
When the miller of Dee,
With his children three,
On his fat, red horse, rode by.

" Whither away, O miller of Dee ?
Whither away so late ? "
Asked the tollman old, with cough and sneeze,
As he passed the big toll-gate.

But the miller answered him never a word,
Never a word spake he.
He paid his toll, and he spurred his horse,
And rode on with his children three.

" He's afraid to tell ! " quoth the old tollman,
" He's ashamed to tell ! " quoth he.
" But I'll follow you up and find out where
You are going, O miller of Dee ! "

The moon was afloat,
Like a golden boat
Nearing the shore of the sky,
When, with cough and wheeze,
And hands on his knees,
The old tollman passed by.

" Whither away, O tollman old ?
Whither away so fast ? "
Cried the milkmaid who stood at the farm-
yard bars
When the tollman old crept past.

The tollman answered her never a word ;
Never a word spake he.
Scant breath had he at the best to chase
After the miller of Dee.

    "He won't tell where!"
    Said the milkmaid fair,
"But *I'll* find out!" cried she.
    And away from the farm,
    With her pail on her arm,
She followed the miller of Dee.

The parson stood in his cap and gown,
    Under the old oak tree.
"And whither away with your pail of milk,
    My pretty milkmaid?" said he;
But she hurried on with her brimming pail,
    And never a word spake she.

"She won't tell where!" the parson cried,
    "Its my duty to know," said he.
And he followed the maid who followed the
    man
    Who followed the miller of Dee.

After the parson, came his wife,
    The sexton he came next.
After the sexton the constable came,
    Troubled and sore perplext.
After the constable, two ragged boys,
    To see what the fun would be;
And a little black dog, with only one eye,
Was the last of the nine who, with groan and
    sigh,
    Followed the miller of Dee.

    Night had anchored the moon,
    Not a moment too soon,
      Under the lee of the sky;
    For the wind it blew,
    And the rain fell, too,
      And the river of Dee ran high.

He forded the river, he climbed the hill,
    He and his children three;

But wherever he went they followed him still,
  That wicked miller of Dee!

Just as the clock struck the hour of twelve,
  The miller reached home again ;
And when he dismounted and turned—behold!
Those who had followed him over the wold
  Came up in the pouring rain.

Splashed and spattered from head to foot,
  Muddy and wet and draggled,
Over the hill and up to the mill,
  That wet company straggled.

They all stopped short ; and then out spake
  The parson, and thus spake he :
" What do you mean by your conduct to-night,
  You wretched miller of Dee ? "

" I went for a ride, a nice cool ride,
  I and my children three ;
For I took them along, as I always do,"
  Answered the miller of Dee.

" But you, my friends, I would like to know,
  Why you followed me all the way ? "
They looked at each other—" We were out for
    a walk,
  A nice cool walk ! " said they.

Eva L. Ogden.

---

## WHO STOLE THE BIRD'S NEST ?

To whit ! To whit ! To whee !  Will you listen
    to me ?
Who stole four eggs I laid, and the nice nest I
    made ?

Not I, said the cow, Moo-oo! Such a thing I'd
 never do.
I gave you a wisp of hay, but didn't take your
 nest away.
Not I, said the cow, Moo-oo! Such a thing I'd
 never do.

To whit! To whit! To whee! Will you listen
 to me?
Who stole four eggs I laid, and the nice nest I
 made?

Bobolink! Bobolink! Now what do you think?
Who stole a nest away from the plum tree to-
 day?

Not I, said the dog, Bow-wow! I wouldn't be
 so mean, I vow.
I gave hairs the nest to make, but the nest I
 did not take.
Not I, said the dog, Bow-wow! I wouldn't be
 so mean, I vow.

To whit! To whit! To whee! Will you listen
 to me?
Who stole four eggs I laid, and the nice nest I
 made?

Coo-oo! Coo-oo! Coo-oo! Let me speak a word
 too.
Who stole that pretty nest from little yellow-
 breast?

Not I, said the sheep. Oh, no, I wouldn't treat
 a poor bird so.
I gave wool the nest to line, but the nest was
 none of mine.
Baa, baa! said the sheep. Oh, no, I wouldn't
 treat a poor bird so.

To whit! To whit! To whee!  Will you listen
    to me?
**Who** stole four eggs I laid, and the nice nest **I**
    made?

Caw! **caw**! cried the crow, I should like to know
What thief took away a bird's nest to-day.

Cluck! cluck! said the hen, don't ask me again!
Why, I haven't a chick would do such a trick.
We all gave her a feather, and she wove them
    together.
I'd scorn to intrude on her and her brood.
Cluck! cluck! **said the hen, don't ask** me again.

Chirr-a-wirr!  Chirr-a-wirr! **We** will **make a**
    great stir!
Let us **find out his** name and all cry, For shame!

I would not rob a bird, said little Mary Green;
I think **I** never heard of anything so mean.

'Tis very cruel, too, said little Alice Neal;
I wonder if **he** knew how **sad the bird would**
    **feel?**

**A** little boy hung down his head and went and
    hid behind the bed;
For he stole that pretty nest from poor little yel-
    low-breast;
And he fel**t so** full of shame, he didn't like to
    tell his name.

LYDIA MARIA **CHILD.**

---

## GET UP.

Whose voice is it **that** rings so clear,
The first in the morning that we hear?
"Up! up!" it says.  "An hour or more
**I have** been crowing **away at** the door.

The horse has gone with the boy to plow ;
Sarah has started to milk the cow ;
Sure there is plenty for all to do,
And all are up, my young friend, but you."

"Up ! up !" cries the busy sun ;
" Is there not work enough to be done ?
Are there no lessons to learn, I pray,
That you should be dozing the time away ?
Who would give light to all below,
If I were idly to slumber so ?
What would become of the hay and corn,
Did I thus waste the precious morn ?"

"Up ! up !" cries the buzzing Bee ;
" There's work for you as well as for me ;
Oh how I prize the morning hour,
Gathering sweets from the dewy flower !
Quick comes on the scorching noon,
And the sombre night will follow soon.
Say, shall it chide for idle hours,
For time misused and for wasted powers ?"

ANONYMOUS.

## THE MIMIC.

A mimic I knew, who, to give him his due,
Was exceeded by none, and was equaled by few.
He could bark like a dog ; he could grunt like a
    hog ;
Nay, I really believe he could croak like a frog.

Then, as for a bird, you may trust to my word,
'Twas the best imitation that ever you heard :
It must be confessed that he copied birds best :
You'd have thought he had lived all his life in a
    nest.

It happened one day, that he came in the way
Of a sportsman—an excellent marksman, they
    say ;

And near a stone wall, with his little bird-call,
The mimic attempted to imitate all.

So well did he do it, the birds all flew to it;
But, ah! he had certainly reason to rue it.
It turned out no fun, for the man **with** the gun,
Who was seeking for partridges, **took** him for
    **one.**

He was shot **in** the side, and **he** feelingly cried,
A moment or so ere he fainted and died:
" Who for others prepare a trap should beware
**They** do not themselves fall **into** the snare."

ANONYMOUS.

---

## LITTLE MAY'S ANSWER.

" Now where **are** you going, little May, little
    May ? "
  I said to our wee bonny baby ;
For her little feet pattered so briskly that day,
So fast and so far did they bear her away,
  I thought she would lose herself, maybe.

**" For** birds' nests I'm going." our baby replied ;
  " There are lots of nice birdies all round ;
Tom says they have nests in the grass where they
    hide
Their **little** young birdies.   **He** said if I tried,
  I could find them right down on the ground."

" The prairie **is** wide, little May, little May,
  And the grass is as high **as** your head ;
There are snakes in it, too—ugly snakes—so they
    say ;
I'm afraid you'll be lost if you wander away—
  Come back **and** pick roses instead."

" Why, God will take care of me—don't be
    afraid ! "
  **Now what** could I say ? 'twas my teaching ;

I caught up and carried the dear little maid
To a moss-covered stone, 'neath the willow's
    thick shade,
  And said, "There! you've a pulpit to preach in."
                          ANONYMOUS.

## AN ELEGY ON THE GLORY OF HER SEX, MRS. MARY BLAIZE.

Good people all, with one accord,
  Lament for Madam Blaize,
Who never wanted a good word—
  From those who spoke her praise.

The needy seldom passed her door,
  And always found her kind;
She freely lent to all the poor,—
  Who left a pledge behind.

She strove the neighborhood to please
  With manners wondrous winning;
And never followed wicked ways,—
  Unless when she was sinning.

At church, in silks and satins new,
  With hoop of monstrous size;
She never slumbered in her pew,—
  But when she shut her eyes.

Her love was sought, I do aver,
  By twenty beaux and more;
The king himself has followed her,—
  When she has walk'd before.

Now her wealth and finery fled,
  Her hangers on cut short all;
The doctors found, when she was dead,
  Her last disorder mortal.

Let us lament in sorrow sore,
  For Kent-street well may say,
That had she lived a twelvemonth more,—
  She had not died to-day.
                        GOLDSMITH.

## GOOD-NIGHT **AND** GOOD-MORNING.

A fair little girl sat under a tree,
Sewing as long as her eyes could see;
Then smoothed her work and folded it right,
And said, "Dear work, good-night! good-
   night!"

Then a number of rooks came over her head,
Crying. "Caw! caw!" on their way to bed;
She said, as she watched their curious flight,
"Little black things, good-night! good-night!"

The horses neighed, and the oxen lowed,
The sheep's "Baa! baa!" came over the road;
All seeming to say, with a quiet delight,
"Good little **girl**, good-night! good-night!"

She did not **say** to the sun "Good-night!"
Though she saw him there, like a ball of light;
For she knew that he had God's time to keep
**All** over the world and never could sleep.

The tall pink foxglove bowed his head;
The violets curtseyed and went to bed;
And good little Lucy tied up her hair,
And said, on her knees, her favorite prayer.

And while **on** her pillow she softly lay,
She knew **nothing** more till again it was day,
And all things said to the beautiful sun,
"Good-morning! good-morning! our work is
   **begun!**"

LORD HOUGHTON.

---

## THE THREE SONS.

I have a son, a little son, a boy just five years
   old,
With eyes of thoughtful earnestness and mind
   **of gentle** mold.

They tell me that unusual grace in all his ways
    appears,
That my child is grave and wise of heart beyond
    his childish years.
I cannot say how this may be—I know his face
    is fair,
And yet his chiefest comeliness is his sweet and
    serious air.
I know his heart is kind and fond, I know he
    loveth me ;
But loveth yet his mother more with grateful
    fervency.
Strange questions does he ask of me when we to-
    gether walk ;
He scarcely thinks as children think, or talks as
    children talk.
Nor cares he much for childish sports—dotes not
    on bat or ball ;
But looks on manhood's ways and works, and
    aptly mimics all.

I have a son, a second son, a simple child of
    three ;
I'll not declare how bright and fair his little fea-
    tures be ;
How silver sweet those tones of his as he prattles
    on my knee.
I do not think his light blue eye is like his
    brother's, keen,
Nor his brow so full of childish thought as his
    hath ever been ;
But his little heart's a fountain pure of kind and
    tender feeling,
And his every look's a gleam of light, rich depths
    of love revealing.
When he walks with me, the country folk, who
    pass us in the street,
Will turn in joy and bless my boy, he looks so
    mild and sweet.

A playfellow is he to all, and yet, with cheerful
    tone,
Will sing his little song of love when left to
    sport alone.

I have a son, a third sweet son; his age I cannot
    tell,
For they reckon not by years or months where
    he is gone to dwell.
To us for fourteen anxious months his infant
    smiles were given,
And then he bade farewell to earth and went to
    live in heaven.
I cannot tell what form is his, what look he
    weareth now,
Nor guess how bright a glory crowns his shining
    seraph brow.
The thoughts that fill his sinless soul, the bliss
    which he doth feel,
Are numbered with the secret things which God
    will not reveal.
I know the angels fold him close beneath their
    glittering wings,
And soothe him with a song that breathes of
    heaven's divinest things.
I know that we shall meet our babe (his mother
    dear and I)
When God for aye shall wipe away all tears from
    every eye.

MOULTRIE.

---

## WHEN THE COWS COME HOME.

    With klingle, klangle, klingle,
    Far down the dusky dingle,
    The cows are coming home;
Now sweet and clear, and faint and low,
The airy tinklings come and go,
Like chimings from a far-off tower
Or patterings of an April shower

That make the daisies grow ;
  Ko-ling, ko-lang, ko-lingle-lingle,
  Far down the dark'ning dingle,
  The cows come slowly home ;
And old-time friend, and twilight plays,
And starry nights and sunny days,
Come trooping up the misty ways,
  When the cows come home.

  With jingle, jangle, jingle,
  Soft tones that sweetly mingle,
  The cows are coming home ;
Malvine, and Pearl, and Florimel,
De Kamp, Red Rose, and Gretchen Schell,
Queen Bess, and Sylph, and Spangled Sue—
Across the fields I hear her " loo-oo,"
  And clang her silver bell ;
  Go-ling, go-lang, go-lingle-lingle,
  With faint, far sounds that mingle,
  The cows come slowly home ;
And mother-song of long gone years,
And baby joys and childish fears,
And youthful hopes and youthful tears,
  When the cows come home.

  With ringle, rangle, ringle,
  By twos, and threes, and single,
  The cows are coming home ;
Thro' violet air we see the town,
And the Summer sun a-sliding down,
And the maple in the hazel glade
Throws down the path a longer shade,
  And the hills are growing brown ;
  To-ring, to-rang, to-ringle-ringle,
  By threes, and fours, and single,
  The cows come slowly home ;
The same sweet sound of wordless psalm,
The same sweet June-day rest and calm,
The same sweet smell of buds and balm,
  When the cows come home.

With tingle, tangle, tingle,
Thro' **fern** and periwinkle,
The cows are coming home;
**A-loitering** in the checkered stream,
Where the **sun**-rays glance and gleam,
Clarine, Peach-bloom, and Phœbe Phillis
Stand knee-deep in the creamy lilies,
  **In a dro**wsy dream;
  **To-link,** to-lank, to-linkle-linkle,
  O'er banks with buttercups a-twinkle,
  The **cows** come slowly home;
And up thro' Memory's deep ravine
Come the brook's old song and its old-time
    **sheen,**
And the crescent of **the silver** Queen,
  When the cows come home.

  **With klingle,** klangle, klingle,
  **With** " loo-oo," and " moo-oo," and jingle,
  The cows are coming home;
And over there on Merlin hill,
Sounds the plaintive cry of the whip-poor-will
And the dew-drops lie on the tangled vines,
And over **the** poplars Venus shines,
  And over the silent mill.
  Ko-ling, ko-lang, ko-lingle-lingle,
  With ting-a-ling and jingle,
  The cows come slowly home.
Let down the bars; **let in the** train
Of long-gone songs, and flowers, and rain,
For dear old times **come** back again,
  **W**hen the cows come home.

ANONYMOUS.

---

## BATTLE OF HOHENLINDEN.

On Linden, when the sun was low,
All bloodless lay the untrodden snow,
And dark as winter was the flow
  **Of Iser,** rolling rapidly.

But Linden saw another sight,
When the drum beat, at dead of night,
Commanding fires of death to light
   The darkness of her scenery.

By torch and trumpet fast arrayed,
Each horseman drew his battle-blade,
And furious every charger neighed,
   To join the dreadful revelry.

Then shook the hills with thunder riven,
Then rushed the steed to battle driven,
And, louder than the bolts of Heaven,
   Far flashed the red artillery.

But redder yet that light shall glow,
On Linden's hills of stained snow,
And bloodier yet the torrent flow
   Of Iser, rolling rapidly.

'Tis morn, but scarce yon level sun
Can pierce the war-clouds, rolling dun,
Where furious Frank and fiery Hun
   Shout in their sulphurous canopy.

The combat deepens.  On, ye brave,
Who rush to glory, or the grave!
Wave Munich, all thy banners wave,
   And charge with all thy chivalry!

Few, few shall part where many meet!
The snow shall be their winding-sheet;
And every turf beneath their feet
   Shall be a soldier's sepulchre.

CAMPBELL.

---

### WHAT THE MOTHER HEARD.

As I walked over the hills one day,
I listened and heard a mother-sheep say:
" In all the green world there is nothing so sweet

As my little lammie with his nimble feet;
With his eyes so bright and his wool so white,
Oh, he is my darling, my heart's delight!
The robin, he that sings in the tree,
Dearly may dote on his darlings four,
But I love my one little lambkin more."
So the mother-sheep and the little one
Side by side lay down in the sun,
And they went to sleep on the hillside warm,
While my little lammie lies here on my arm.

I went to the kitchen, and what did I see
But the old gray cat, with her kittens three?
I heard her whispering soft; said she:
" My kittens, with tails so cunningly curled,
Are the prettiest things there can be in the
    world.
The bird in the tree, and the old ewe, she
May love their babies exceedingly;
But I love my kittens with all my might,
I love them at morning, at noon and night;
So I'll take them all up, the kittens I love,
And we'll lie down together beneath the warm
    stove."
So the kittens lie under the stove so warm,
While my little darling lies here on my arm.

I went to the yard, and I saw the old hen
Go clucking about with her chickens ten;
And she clucked, and she scratched, and she
    bristled away,
And what do you think I heard the hen say?
I heard her say, " The sun never did shine
On anything like to these chickens of mine;
You may hunt the full moon, and the stars, if
    you please,
But you never will find ten such chickens as
    these.
The cat loves her kittens, the ewe loves her lamb,
But they know not what a proud mother I am;

For lambs or for kittens I won't part with these,
Though the sheep and the cat should go down on
  their knees.
My dear downy darlings, my sweet little things,
Come, nestle now cosily under my wings."
So the hen said, and the chickens all sped
As fast as they could to their warm feather-bed;
And there let them lie, on their feathers so warm,
While my little chicken lies here on my arm.

Mrs. Carter.

## MR. NOBODY.

I know a funny little man, as quiet as a mouse,
Who yet the mischief does that's done in every-
  body's house :
There's no one ever sees his face, and yet we all
  agree
That every plate we break was cracked by Mr.
  Nobody.

'Tis he who always tears our books, who leaves
  the door ajar,
Who pulls the buttons from our shirts, and scatters pins afar ;
That squeaking door will always creak, I'm thinking, for, you see,
We leave the oiling to be done by Mr. Nobody.

He puts damp wood upon the fire, that kettles
  cannot boil ;
His are the feet that bring in mud, and all the
  carpets spoil ;
The papers always are mislaid—who had them
  last but he ?
There's no one tosses them about but Mr. Nobody.

The finger-marks upon **the** doors by none of *us*
    are made ;
**We** never leave the blinds unclosed to let the
    curtains fade ;
**The** ink we never spill—the boots, that, lying
    round, you see,
**Are** not *our* boots ! They **all** belong **to Mr.** No-
    body !

ANONYMOUS.

---

## FATHER WILLIAM.

" You are old, **Father** William," the **young** man
    cried ;
  " The few **locks** that are left you are gray :
You are hale, **Father** William, a hearty old man ;
  Now tell me the reason, I **pray**."

" **In the** days **of my** youth," Father William re-
    plied,
  " I remembered that youth would fly fast,
**And abused not** my health **and my** vigor **at first,**
  That I **never** might need them at last."

" **You** are **old,** Father William," the young man
    cried,
  " **And pleasures** with **youth pass** away,
And yet you lament not the **days** that are gone ;
  Now tell me the reason, I **pray**."

" In the days of my youth," Father William re-
    plied,
  " I remembered **that** youth could not last ;
I thought of the future, whatever I did,
  That I never might grieve for the past."

" You **are old,** Father William," the young man
    **cried,**
  " **And life must be** hastening away ;

You are cheerful, and **love to** converse upon
    death ;
  Now tell me **the reason, I pray.**"

" I am cheerful, young **man,**" Father William
    replied—
  " Let the cause thy attention engage—
In the days of my **youth** I remembered **my God,**
  And he hath **not** forgotten my **age.**"
SOUTHEY.

## THE PRIEST AND HIS MARE.

A tale I will tell **of a** priest and **his** mare
**As they merrily** trotted along **to the** fair.
Of **a creature** more docile you never have heard ;
In the height of her speed, she would stop at a
    word ;
And again with a word, when the rider **said**
    " Hey,"
She would put forth her mettle, and gallop **away.**

As along a **smooth lane** he quietly **rode,**
While the sun **of September all** brilliantly
    glowed,
The good man discovered, with eyes of desire,
A mulberry tree in a hedge of wild brier.
High up on the boughs hung the beautiful fruit ;
Its large, glossy charms might have **tempted** a
    brute.

The preacher **was hungry,** and **thirsty** to boot ;
He dreaded **the** thorns, but he longed for the
    fruit.
**With** a word he arrested the courser's keen speed,
**Then** stood up erect **on the** back of his steed.
On the saddle he stood, while the creature kept
    still.
**And he** gathered the fruit till he'd eaten **his fill.**

" Sure, never," said he, " was a creature so rare !
How docile, how true is **this** excellent mare !
See, here I now stand," **and** he gazed all around,
" As safe and as steady as **if** on the ground ;
And yet how she'd fly, if some fellow this way,
Not dreaming of mischief, should chance to **say**
    Hey."

He stood with his head in the mulberry **tree,**
And he spoke out aloud in the height **of his**
    glee ;
At the sound of his " Hey," the mare made a
    push,
And down went the priest in the dense brier-
    bush.
He remembered **to**o late, on his sharp, thorny
    bed,
" Much well may be thought, that should not be
    said."

ANONYMOUS.

---

## THE LITTLE SPEAKER.

You'd scarce expect a boy like me
To get up here where all can see,
And make a speech as *well* as those
Who wear the largest kind **of** clothes.

I think it was in olden time,
That some one said in funny rhyme,
" Tall aches from little toe-corns grow,
Large *screams* from little children flow."

And if that rhymer told the truth,
Though I am now a *little* youth,
Perhaps I'll make as great a *noise,*
As some who are much larger boys.

I will not speak of Greece and Rome,
But tell you what I've learned at home,

And what was taught me when at school,
While sitting on a bench or stool ;

I've learned to talk, and read, and spell,
And don't you think that's pretty well
For such a *little* boy as I ?
But I must leave you—so good-bye.

Anonymous.

## CONTENTED JOHN.

One honest John Tomkins, a hedger and ditcher,
Although he was poor did not want to be richer;
For all such vain wishes in him were prevented
By a fortunate habit of being contented.

Though cold was the weather, or dear was the
    food,
John never was found in a murmuring mood ;
For this he was constantly heard to declare :
What he could not prevent, he would cheerfully
    bear.

" For why should I grumble and murmur ? " he
    said ;
" If I cannot get meat, I can surely get bread ;
And though fretting may make my calamities
    deeper,
It never can cause bread and cheese to be
    cheaper."

If John was afflicted with sickness and pain,
He wished himself better, but did not complain,
Nor lie down to fret in despondence and sorrow,
But said that he hoped to be better to-morrow.

If any one wronged him, or treated him ill,
Why, John was good-natured and sociable still ;
For he said that revenging the injury done
Would be making two rogues, when there need
    be but one.

And thus honest John, though his station was
    **humble,**
Passed through this sad world without ever a
    grumble ;
**And** I wish that some folks who **are** greater and
    richer
**W**ould copy **John** Tomkins, the hedger and
    ditcher.

Emily Taylor.

---

## THE PET LAMB.

**The dew was** falling fast, the stars began to
    blink ;
I heard a voice : it said, " Drink, pretty creature,
    drink ! "
And **looking** o'er the hedge, before me I espied
A snow-white mountain lamb, with a maiden at
    its side.

**No other** sheep was near ; the lamb was all alone,
**And by a** slender cord was tethered to a stone ;
With one knee **on** the grass did the little maiden
    kneel,
While to that mountain lamb she gave its even-
    ing meal.

**"Rest, little** one," she said ; "hast thou forgot
    the day
When my **father** found thee first, in places **far**
    away ?
Many **flocks** were on the hills, but thou wert
    owned by none,
And thy mother from thy side for evermore was
    gone.

**" Thou** know'st that twice a day I have brought
    **thee in** this can
**Fresh water from** the brook, as clear as ever ran ;

And twice, too, in the day, when the ground is
    wet with dew,
I bring thee draughts of milk—warm milk it is,
    and new.

" Thy limbs will shortly be **twice** as stout as they
    are now ;
Then I'll yoke thee to **my** cart, like a **pony in**
    the plow ;
**My** playmate thou shalt be ; and when **the wind**
    is cold,
Our hearth shall **be thy** bed, our **house** shall be
    thy fold.

" See, here thou need'st not fear the raven in the
    sky ;
Both night and day thou'rt safe—our cottage is
    hard by.
Why **bleat so** after me ?  Why pull so at thy
    chain ?
Sleep, and at break of day I'll come to thee
    again."

WORDSWORTH.

---

## WARREN'S ADDRESS BEFORE THE BATTLE OF BUNKER'S HILL.

Stand ! the ground's your own, my braves !
Will ye give it up to slaves ?
Will ye look for greener graves ?
    Hope ye mercy still ?
What's the mercy despots feel ?
Hear it in that battle peal !
Read in **you** bristling steel !
    Ask it—ye who will.

Fear ye foes who kill **for hire ?**
Will ye to your *homes* retire ?
Look behind you ! they're afire !
    And, before you, see

Who have done it !—From the vale
On they come !—and will ye quail ?—
Leaden rain and iron hail
  Let their welcome be !

In the God of battles **trust !**
Die we may—and d**ie** we must :—
But, O, where can dust to dust
  Be consigned so well,
As where heaven its dews shall shed
On the martyr'd patriot's bed,
And the rocks shall raise their head,
  Of his deeds **to** tell ?

PIERPONT.

## THE BEE'S WISDOM.

Said a little wandering maiden to a bee **with**
    honey laden,
" Bee, at all the flowers **you** work, yet in **some**
    does poison **lurk.**"
" That I know, my little maiden," said **the bee**
    with honey laden,
" But the poison I forsake, and the honey only
    take."
" Cunning bee with honey laden, that is right,"
    replied **the** maiden ;
" So will I, from all I meet, only draw the good
    and sweet."

ANONYMOUS.

## THE WOLF AND THE KID.

Cowards most insolent appear
When sure they have naught to fear.

A Kid who felt quite safe, aloof
From harm, high on his master's roof,
Seeing a Wolf beneath him go,

Cried out, " Thief, villain, booby ! Ho !
Come up **here** and I'll put **you** through :
You dare not?   What ! **a** coward too ?
Look here, old fellow, how's your mother ?
Are you as handsome **as** your brother ?
Before you go, unless you'd grieve me,
Be sure a lock of hair to leave me.
You sneaking rascal, base and cruel,
Come here, I'll serve you out your gruel.
You wouldn't like me for your dinner ?
Oh no, you old bloodthirsty sinner !
Only come here, and you shall find
Some grub not suited to your mind.
Of you and twenty like you I
Am not afraid.   Come on and try !"

The Wolf looked up and shook his head,
And to the silly boaster said,
" My dear, rail on, I care not how—
It is the *roof* that speaks, not thou."

ANONYMOUS.

---

### LOVE OF COUNTRY AND HOME.

There is a land, of every land the pride,
Beloved by Heaven o'er all the world beside ;
Where brighter suns dispense serener light,
And milder moons emparadise the night ;—
There is a spot of earth supremely blest,
A dearer, sweeter spot than all the rest,
Where man, creation's tyrant, casts aside
His sword and sceptre, pageantry and pride,
While in his softened looks benignly blend
The sire, the son, the husband, brother, friend;—
" Where shall that *land*, that *spot of earth*, be
      found ? "
Art thou a man ?—a patriot ?—look around !
O, thou shalt find, howe'er thy footsteps roam,
That land thy country, and that spot thy home !

J. MONTGOMERY.

## THE SPIDER AND THE FLY.

"Will you walk into my parlor?" said the
    spider to the fly;
"'Tis the prettiest little parlor that ever you did
    spy;
The way into the parlor is up a winding stair,
And I have many a curious thing to show when
    you are there!"
"Oh no, no!" said the little fly; "to ask me is
    in vain,
For who goes up your winding stair can ne'er
    come down again."

"I'm sure you must be weary, dear, with soaring
    up so high;
Will you rest upon my little bed?" said the
    spider to the fly.
"There are pretty curtains drawn around, the
    sheets are fine and thin,
And if you like to rest a while, I'll snugly tuck
    you in."
"Oh no, no!" said the little fly; "for I've often
    heard it said
They never, never wake again who sleep upon
    your bed."

Said the cunning spider to the fly, "Dear friend,
    what can I do
To prove the warm affection I've always felt for
    you?
I have, within my pantry, good store of all that's
    nice;
I'm sure you're very welcome; will you please
    to take a slice?"
"Oh no, no!" said the little fly; "kind sir, that
    cannot be;
I've heard what's in your pantry, and I do not
    wish to see."

" Sweet creature," said the spider, " you're witty
     and you're wise ;
How handsome are your gaudy wings ! how bril-
     liant are your eyes !
I have a little looking-glass upon my parlor
     shelf :
If you'll step in one moment, dear, you shall be-
     hold yourself."
" I thank you, gentle sir," she said, " for what
     you're pleased to say
And bidding you good-morrow now, I'll call an-
     other day."

The spider turned him round about, and went
     into his den,
For well he knew the silly fly would soon come
     back again.
So he wove a subtle web in a little corner sly,
And set his table ready to dine upon the fly :
Then he came out to his door again, and merrily
     did sing.
" Come hither, hither, pretty fly, with the pearl
     and silver wing ;
Your robes are green and purple, there's a crest
     upon your head ;
Your eyes are like the diamond bright, but mine
     are dull as lead."

Alas ! alas ! how very soon this silly little fly,
Hearing his wily, flattering words, came slowly
     flitting by !
With buzzing wings she hung aloft, then near
     and nearer drew,
Thinking only of her brilliant eyes and green
     and purple hue ;
Thinking only of her crested head, poor foolish
     thing !  At last
Up jumped the cunning spider, and fiercely held
     her fast.

He dragged her up his winding stair into his dismal den.
Within his little parlor, but she ne'er came out
   again!
And now, my dear young pupils who may this
   story read,
To idle, silly, flattering words I pray you give
   **no heed;**
Unto an evil counselor close heart, and ear, and
   eye,
And take a lesson from this tale of the spider
   and the fly.

MARY HOWITT.

---

## THE AUCTION EXTRAORDINARY.

I dreamed a dream in the midst of my slumbers,
And as fast as I dreamed, it was coined into
   numbers.
My thoughts ran along in such beautiful metre,
I am sure I ne'er saw any poetry sweeter.
It seemed that a law had been recently made,
That a tax on old bachelors' pates should be laid;
And, in order to make them all willing to marry,
The tax was as large as a man could well carry.

The bachelors grumbled, and said 't was no use,
'T was cruel injustice and horrid abuse;—
And declared that, to save their own hearts'
   blood from spilling,
Of such a vile tax they would ne'er pay a shil-
   **ling.**
But the rulers determined their scheme to pur-
   sue,
So they set all the bachelors up at vendue.
A crier was sent through the town to and fro,
To rattle his bell and his trumpet to blow,
And to bawl out to all he might meet on his way,
" Ho! forty old bachelors sold here to-day! "

And presently all the old maids of the town,
Each **one in** her **very best bonnet** and gown,
From thirty to sixty, fair, plain, red, and pale,
**Of every** description, all flocked to the sale.
The auctioneer, then, in his labor began ;
And called **out** aloud, as he held up a man,—
" How much for a bachelor ?  Who wants to
      buy ? "
In a twinkling, each maiden responded, " I—I ! "
In short, at a hugely extravagant price,
The bachelors all were sold off in a trice ;
And **forty** old maidens,—some younger, some
      older,—
Each lugged **an** old bachelor **home** on her
      shoulder !

LUCRETIA M. DAVIDSON.

### THE AMERICAN FLAG.

When freedom from her mountain height,
    Unfurled her standard to the air,
She tore the azure robe of night,
    And set the stars of glory there.
She mingled with its gorgeous **dyes**
**The milky** baldric of the skies,
**And** striped its pure celestial white,
**With** streakings of the morning light ;
Then, from his mansion in the sun,
She called her eagle bearer down,
And gave into his mighty hand
The symbol of her chosen land.

Majestic monarch of the cloud,
    Who rear'st **aloft** thy regal form,
**To** hear the tempest trumping loud,
And see the lightning lances driven,
    When stride the warriors of the storm,
And rolls the thunder-drum of Heaven,—
Child of the Sun ! to thee 't is given

To guard the banner of the free;
To hover in the sulphur smoke,
To ward away the battle-stroke ;
And bid its blendings shine afar,
Like rainbows on the cloud of war,
  The harbingers of victory !

**Flag of the brave!** thy folds shall **fly,**
**The sign of** hope and triumph high.
**When** speaks the signal trumpet tone,
And the long line comes gleaming on,—
Ere yet the life blood, warm **and** wet,
Has dimmed **the glistening bayonet,**—
Each soldier's **eye shall brightly** turn
To where **thy** sky-born **glories** burn ;
And, as his springing steps advance,
Catch war **and** vengeance from the glance.
**And, when** the cannon-mouthings loud
**Heave** in wild wreathes the battle shroud,
And gory sabres rise an**d fall**
Like shouts of flame on midnight's pall,
Then shall thy meteor glances glow,
  And cowering foes shall **fall** beneath
Each gallant **arm,** that strikes below
  That lovely messenger of death.

**Flag of the** seas ! on ocean's wave
Thy stars shall glitter o'er the brave,
When Death, careering on **the** gale,
**S**weeps **darkly** round **the bellied sai**l,
And frighted waves rush wildly back,
Before the broadside's reeling rack,
Each dying wanderer of the sea
Shall look at once to Heaven and thee ·
And smile to see thy splendors fly,
In triumph o'er his closing eye.

Flag of the free heart's hope and home !
  By angel hands to Valor given !
**Thy** stars **have** lit **the** welkin dome,

And all thy hues were born in Heaven.
Forever float that standard sheet!
 Where breathes the foe but falls before us,
With Freedom's soil beneath our feet,
 And Freedom's banner streaming o'er us?

J. R. DRAKE.

---

## WHITTLING.

The Yankee boy, before he's sent to school
Well knows the mysteries of that magic tool,
The pocket-knife. To that his wistful eye
Turns, while he hears his mother's lullaby;
His hoarded cents he gladly gives to get it,
Then leaves no stone unturned till he can whet
  it;
And in the education of the lad
No little part that implement hath had.
His pocket-knife to the young whittler brings
A growing knowledge of material things.

Projectiles, music, and the sculptor's art,
His chestnut whistle, and his shingle dart,
His elder pop-gun with its hickory rod,
Its sharp explosion and rebounding wad,
His corn-stalk fiddle, and the deeper tone
That murmurs from his pumpkin-stalk trom-
  bone,
Conspire to teach the boy. To these succeed
His bow, his arrow of a feathered reed,
His windmill, raised the passing breeze to win,
His water-wheel that turns upon a pin;
Or, if his father lives upon the shore,
You'll see his ship, "beam ends upon the floor,"
Full rigged with raking masts, and timbers
  staunch,
And waiting, near the washtub, for a launch.

Thus, by his genius and his jack-knife driven,
Ere long he'll solve you any problem given ;
Make any jim-crack, musical or mute,
A plow, a coach, an organ or a flute ;
Make you a locomotive or a clock,
Cut a canal, or build a floating-dock,—
Or lead forth Beauty from a marble block ;—
Make anything, in short, for sea or shore,
From a child's rattle to a seventy-four.
Make it, said I ?—Ay, when he undertakes it,
He'll make the thing and the machine that
  makes it.

And when the thing is made,—whether it be
To move on earth, in air, or on the sea ;
Whether on water, or the waves to glide,
Or, upon land to roll, revolve, or slide ;
Whether to whirl or jar, to strike or ring,
Whether it be a piston or a spring,
Wheel, pulley, tube sonorous, wood or brass,
The thing designed shall surely come to pass ;
For, when his hand's upon it, you may know
That there's go in it, and he'll make it go.

J. Pierpont.

---

## THE BATTLE OF LIFE.

Now nerve thy spirit to the proof,
  And blench not at thy chosen lot :
The timid good may stand aloof,
  The sage may frown, yet faint thou not.

Nor heed the shaft too surely cast,
  The hissing, stinging bolt of scorn ;
For with thy side shall dwell at last
  The victory of endurance born.

Yea, though thou die upon the dust,
  When those who helped thee flee in fear,

Die full **of hope** and manly trust,
  Like those who fell in battle here.

Another hand thy sword shall wield,
  Another hand the standard wave,
Till from the trumpet's mouth is pealed
  The blast of triumph o'er thy grave.

Truth, crushed to earth, shall rise **again** :
  The eternal years of God are hers;
But Error, wounded, writhes in pain,
  And dies among his worshipers.

BRYANT.

## ROBERT OF LINCOLN.

Merrily swinging on briar and weed,
  Near **to the nest of his** little dame,
Over the mountain-side or mead,
  Robert of Lincoln is telling his name,
    " Bob-o'-link, bob-o'-link,
      Spink, spank, spink ;
Snug and safe is this nest of ours,
Hidden among the summer flowers.
    Chee, chee, chee."

Robert of Lincoln is **gay**ly dressed,
  Wearing a bright, black wedding coat ;
White are his shoulders, and white his crest.
  Hear him call in **his** merry note,
    " Bob-o'-link, bob-o'-link,
      Spink, spank, spink.
Look what **a nice** new coat is mine ;
Sure there was never a bird so fine.
    Chee, chee, chee."

Robert of Lincoln's Quaker wife,
  Pretty and quiet, with plain brown wings,
Passing at home a patient life,
  Broods in the grass while her husband sings,

"Bob-o'-link, bob-o'-link,
Spink, spank, spink;
Brood, kind creature, you need not fear
Thieves and robbers while I am here.
Chee, chee, chee."

Modest and shy as a nun is she,
One weak chirp is her only note;
Braggart and prince of braggarts is he,
Pouring boasts from his little throat:
"Bob-o'-link, bob-o'-link,
Spink, spank, spink;
Never was I afraid of man,
Catch me, cowardly knaves, if you can.
Chee, chee, chee."

WM. C. BRYANT.

## THE RETORT.

One day a rich man, flushed with pride and wine,
Sitting with guests at table, all quite merry,
Conceived it would be vastly fine,
To crack a joke upon his secretary.

"Young man," said he, by what pursuit or trade
Did your good father earn his livelihood?"
"He was a saddler, sir," the young man said,
"And in his line was always reckoned good."

"A saddler, eh! and had you stuffed with Greek,
Instead of teaching you like him to do!
And pray, sir, why did not you father make
A saddler, too, of you?"

At this each flatterer, as in duty bound,
The joke applauded, and the laugh went round,
At length the secretary, bowing low,
Said, (craving pardon if too free he made,)
"Sir, by your leave, I fain would know
Your father's trade?"

"My father's trade!  Why, sir, but that's too
          bad.
  My father's trade!—Why, blockhead, art thou
          mad ?
My father, sir, was never brought so low ;
  He was a gentleman I'd have you know."

"Indeed!  Excuse the liberty I take ;
  But if your story's true,
How happened it your father did not make
  A gentleman of you ? "

ANONYMOUS.

---

### THE BRAVE LITTLE FLOWER.

Daffy-down-dilly came up in the cold
          Through the brown mold,
Although the March breezes blew keen on her
          face,
Although the white snow lay on many a place.
Daffy-down-dilly had heard underground
          The sweet rushing sound
Of the streams as they broke from their white
          winter chains—
Of the whistling spring winds and the pattering
          rains.

"Now, then," thought Daffy, deep down in her
          heart,
          "It's time I should start !"
So she pushed her soft leaves through the hard
          frozen ground
Quite up to the surface, and then she looked
          round.
There was snow all about her—gray clouds over-
          head ;
          The trees all looked dead :
Then how do you think poor Daffy-down felt
When the sun would not shine and the ice would
          not melt ?

"Cold weather," thought Daffy, still working
    away ;
        " The earth's hard to-day !
There's but a half inch of my leaves **to** be seen,
**And** two-thirds of that is more **yellow than**
    green !
**I** can't do much yet, but **I'll do** what I can ;
       **It's** well I began,
**For unless I** can manage to lift up my **head,**
**The people** will think the Spring herself's dead.

**So** little by little she **brought** her leaves out,
      All clustered **about ;**
**And** then her bright flowers began to unfold,
**Till** Daffy **stood** robed in her spring **green**-and-
    gold.
Oh, Daffy-down-dilly, so brave and so true.
      Would all were like **you !**
**So ready** for duty in all sorts **of** weather,
And showing forth courage and beauty together.
                 Miss Warner.

## LOSSES.

    Upon the white sea-sand
    There **sat** a pilgrim band,
**Telling** the **losses** that their lives had known ;
    While evening waned away
    From breezy cliff and bay,
And the strong tides went out **with** weary moan.

    One spake, with quivering lip,
    Of **a** fair freighted **ship,**
With all his household to **the** deep gone down ;
    But one had wilder **woe—**
    For a fair face, long ago
Lost in the darker depths of a great town.

    There **were** who mourned their youth
    With a most loving ruth,
For its brave hopes and memories **ever green ;**

And one upon the west
Turned an eye that **would** not rest,
For **far-off hills** whereon its joy had been.

Some talked of vanished gold,
Some of proud **honors** told,  [more;
**Some** spoke of friends that were their trust no
And one of **a** green grave
Beside a foreign wave,
That made him sit so lonely on the shore.

But when their **tales were** done,
**There spake** among them **one,**
A stranger, seeming from all sorrow free;
" Sad losses **have** ye met,
But mine is **heavier yet;**
For a believing **heart hath** gone from me."

" Alas!" these pilgrims said,
" **For** the living and the dead—
For fortune's cruelty, for love's sure cross,
For the wrecks of **land and** sea!
But, however it came **to** thee,
Thine, stranger, **is life's last and** heaviest loss."

FRANCES BROWN.

---

## THE MOTHER'S JEWELS.

In schools of wisdom all the day was spent;
His steps at eve the rabbi homeward bent,
With homeward thoughts which dwelt upon
 the wife
And two fair children who adorned his life.

She, meeting at the threshold, led him in,
And with these words preventing did begin:
" Ever rejoicing at your wished return,
Yet do I most so now, for since the morn
I have been much perplexed and sorely tried
Upon one point, which *you* shall now decide:

" Some years ago, a friend into my care
Some jewels gave,—rich, precious gems they
    were ;
And, having placed them in my charge, this
    friend
Did after neither come for them **nor send;**
But left **them** in my keeping for so long,
That now **it** almost seems to me a wrong
**That** he should suddenly arrive to-day
And take the jewels that he left away.
What think you?  Shall I freely yield them
    back,
And with **no** murmuring?—**so** henceforth to
    lack
Those gems myself, which I had learned **to** see
Almost as mine for ever,—mine in fee."

" What question *can* be here?  Your own **true**
    heart
Must needs advise you of the *only* part ;
That may be claimed again which was but lent,
And should be yielded with **no** discontent ;
Nor surely, can we find **herein** a wrong
That it was left us to **enjoy so** long."

" **Good is the word !** " she answered, " may we
    now,
And evermore, that it is good allow ! "
And, rising, to an inner chamber led ;
And there she showed him stretched upon one
    bed,
Two children pale,—and **he the** jewels knew,
Which **God** had lent him, **and** resumed anew.
R. C. Trench.

---

## THE TWINS.

In form and feature, face and limb,
  I grew so like my brother,
That folks got taking me for him,
  And each for one another.

It puzzled all our kith and kin,
  It reached a fearful pitch ;
For **one** of us was born **a** twin,
  And not a soul knew which.

One day, to make **the** matter worse,
  Before our names were fixed,
As we were being washed by nurse,
  We got completely mixed ;
And thus you see, by fate's decree,
  Or rather nurse's whim,
My brother John **got** christened me,
  And **I got** christened **him.**

This **fatal likeness ever dogged**
  My footsteps when at school,
And I was always getting flogged,
  When John turned out a fool.
I put this question, fruitlessly,
  To every one I knew,
" What would you do, if you were me,
  To prove that you were you ?"

Our close resemblance turned the tide
  Of my domestic life,
For **somehow,** my intended bride
  Became my brother's wife.
In fact, year after year the same
  Absurd mistakes went on,
And when I died, the neighbors came
  And buried brother John.

HENRY S. LEIGH.

---

## ABOU BEN ADHEM.

Abou Ben Adhem (may his tribe increase !)
Awoke one night from a deep dream of peace,
And saw, within the moonlight in his room
(Making it rich, and like a lily in bloom),
An angel writing in a book of gold.

Exceeding peace had made Ben Adhem **bold,**
And to the presence in the room, he said,
" What writest thou?"  The vision raised its
    head,
And, with **a** look made of all sweet accord,
Answered, " The names of those **who love** the
    Lord,"
" And is mine one?" asked Abou.  " Nay,
    not so,"
Replied the angel.  Abou spake more low,
But cheerily still; and said, " I pray thee,
    then,
Write me as one that loves his fellow-men."
The angel wrote and vanished.  The next
    night
**It** came again, with a great wakening light,
And showed the names whom love of God had
    blest :
And, **lo**! Ben Adhem's name led all the rest!
LEIGH HUNT.

## GRAMMAR IN RHYME.

Three little words you often see
Are articles—A, AN and THE.
**A** Noun **is** the name of anything,
As SCHOOL or GARDEN, HOOP or SWING.
**Adjecti**ves tell the kind of Noun,
As GREAT, SMALL, PRETTY, WHITE or BROWN.
Instead of Nouns the Pronouns stand—
HER head, HIS face, YOUR arm, MY hand.
Verbs tell of something to be done,
To BEAR, COUNT, SING, LAUGH, STUDY, RUN
How things are done the Adverbs tell,
As SLOWLY, QUICKLY, ILL or WELL.
Conjunctions join the words together,
As man AND woman, wind OR weather
The Prepositions stand before
A Noun, **as** OF or THROUGH a door.
**The interjection** shows surprise,

As, AH! how pretty!  OH! how wise!
The whole are called Nine Parts of Speech
Which reading, writing, speaking teach.

ANONYMOUS.

---

## PATRIOTISM.

Breathes there the man with soul so **dead,**
Who never **to himself** hath said,
  " This is my own—my native land !"
Whose heart hath ne'er within him burned,
As home his footsteps he hath turned,
  From wandering on a foreign strand ?
If such there breathe, go. mark him well !
For him no minstrel raptures swell.
High though his titles, proud his name,
Boundless his wealth as wish can claim,—
Despite those titles, power, and pelf,
The wretch, concentred all in self,
Living shall forfeit **fair** renown,
And. doubly dying, shall go **down**
To the **vile** dust from whence he sprung,
Unwept, unhonored, and unsung.

WALTER SCOTT.

---

## THE WAY TO BE HAPPY.

A hermit there was, who lived in a grot,
And the way to be happy they said he had got.
As I wanted to learn it, I went to his cell ;
And this answer he gave, when I asked him
    to tell :
" 'Tis being, and doing, and having, that make
All the pleasures **and** pains of which mortals
    partake :
To *be* what God's pleases, to *do* a man's best
And to *have* a good heart is the way to be
    blest."

ANONYMOUS.

## THE SHIP ON FIRE.

Morning! all speedeth well: the bright **sun**
Lights **up** the deep blue wave, and favoring
    breeze
**Fills** the white sails, while o'er that Southern
    Sea
**T**he ship, **with** all the busy life within,
Holds on her ocean course alone, but glad;
**For all is** yet, as all has been the while
**S**ince the white cliffs were left, without or fear
**O**r danger to those hundreds grouping now
**U**pon the sunny deck.

    Fire!—Fire!—Fire!—**Fire!**
      *      *      *      *

Scorching **smoke** in many a wreath,
    Sulphurous blast of heated air,
Grim presentment of quick death,
    **Cro**uching fear and stern despair,
Hist to what the master saith,—
"Steady, steersman, steady there!"—**Ay! ay!**

  "**To** the mast head!"—it is done;
    "**Look** to **leeward**!"—scores obey;
  "And to windward!"—many a one
    Turns, and never turns away:
Steadfast **is** the word and tone.—
"**Man the boats, and** clear away!"—Ay! ay!

  Hotter! hotter!—heave and strain;
    In the hollow, on the wave:
  "Pump! and flood the deck again;—
    Work! no danger daunts the brave:
Hope and trust are not in vain,—
God looks on, and **he** can save."—Ay! ay!

  "What above?"—nor sail, nor sound;
    "Leeward?"—nothing, far or near;
  "What **to** windward?"—to the bound
    Of the horizon all is clear;—

**Yet** again the words go round,
" **Work**, men, work; we **dare** not fear ! "—
        Ay ! ay !

Hotter ! hotter ! **hotter** still !
    Backward driven every one ;
**All** in vain the **various** skill ;
    All that man may do is done :
" Brave hearts, strive yet with a will !
Never deem that hope is gone ! "—Ay ! **ay** !

Hist !—as if a sudden thought
    Dared not utter what it knew,—
Falls **a trembling** whisper, fraught
    As of hope, to frightened few ;
With **a doubting heart-ache** caught,
And a choking " Is it true ? "—Ay ! ay !

There it comes,—" A sail ! a sail ! "
    Up from prostrate misery,
Up from heart-break, woe, and wail,
    Up to shuddering ecstasy ;—
" Can so strange **a promise** fail ? "—
" Call **the master**; let him see ! "—Ay ! ay !

Silence !   **Silence !**   Silence !—Pray !
        *        *        *        *

Every moment is an hour,
    Minutes long as weary years,
While with concentrated power
    Through the haze that clear eye peers,—
" No "—" Yes "—" No : " the strong men
        cower,
Till he sighs, faith conquering fear,—"Ay! ay!"

Riseth now the throbbing cry,
    Born **of** hope and hopelessness ;
Iron men weep bitterly,
    Unused hands and cheeks caress ;—
Feeling's wild variety—
Strange **and** heartless were it less.—Ay ! ay !

Through the sunlight's glittering gleam,
  On old ocean's rugged breast,
As a fantasy in dream;
  Yet beyond all doubt **confessed,**
Comes the ship—God's gift they deem:
Ah, " He overruleth best!"—Ay! ay!

Coming!—come!—that foremost man
  Shouts as only true heart may,
"Ship on fire!"—" You will"—" You
    can "—
  " Near us, for the rescue, stay ?"
Almost as the words began,
Answering words are on their way,—" Ay!
    ay!"

" Ay! ay!"—words of little worth
  But as imaging the soul.
See, the boats are struggling forth !—
  Marvel! how they pitch and roll
On the dark wave, through the froth!
God can bring them safe and whole.—Ay! ay!

" Have a care, men! have a care !—
  Steady, steady to the stern :
Now, my brave hearts, handy there,—
  See, the deck begins to burn!
Child and woman, soft and fair,
Go—thank God!  Be quick—return."--Ay!
    ay!

All is well! the last man true
  Stands upon the stranger's deck,
And a thrilling pulse runs through
  Those glad hearts, which none may check;
Listen to the wild halloo!
Rainbow joy, in fortune's wreck.—Ay! ay!

Pah!—a rush of smothered light
  Bursts the staggering ship asunder,—
Lightning flashes, fierce and bright,—

  Blasting sounds, as if of thunder,—
  Dread destruction wins the fight,
Round about, above, and under !—Ay ! ay !
       Henry Bateman.

      —

### THE TWO BLACKSMITHS.

A merchant, whose labors a fortune had made,
Resolved at last to retire from trade;
So, looking about a house to find,
He got one at last to please his mind.
The scenery round was lovely and bright,
And nothing was near to offend the sight,
Except two shops, that stood one on each side,
Where two sturdy blacksmiths their hammers
  plied.
"These shops," said he, "shall not stay here
  long;
Such tumble-down sheds can be bought for a
  song."
So he moves to the house all furnished in state,
And goes to his bed while blessing his fate :—
"Away from the town surrounded with joys,
I shall henceforth," he cried, " be free from
  noise."
He slept ; but was roused by the anvil's ring.
And all day long it was ding, ding. ding.
Ding, ding, told the coming of morning light ;
And ding. ding, ding, broke the quiet of night ;
If in conversation he uttered a word,
Ding, ding, was all the answer he heard ;
And whenever his daughter attempted to sing,
The anvils accompanied, ding, ding, ding.
"This ding —dinging," he cried, " I never can
  stand—
I rather would live in a barbarous land."
So he asked the smiths if money or love,
Or anything else could make them remove.
"Oh, yes," said the smiths, " if enough you will
  pay,

We engage to remove any moment you say."
" To each I will give fifty dollars to go."
The smiths shook their heads—" That won't do—
    no, no ! "
" Come, come, my friends, you must not **be**
    tough—
**You'll** surely consider one hundred enough ? "
**They** whispered awhile—" Come, *two* hundred
    **say,**
And we will remove this very day."
" Well, agreed," said he.   The money he paid,
Well pleased with the very **fine** bargain he'd
    made.
" My friends," he said, " I **bid** you farewell—
**I** wish you success wherever you dwell ;
And from the next place to which you may **go,**
May you never remove while the bellows **you**
    blow ;
May your anvils ring as you strike the bar—
But tell me, I pray, do you go very far ? "
" Oh, no," said the smiths, " **that's** not ou**r** de-
    sign—
**I move** to Jack's shop, and **Jack** moves to mine."

Anonymous.

## KATIE'S ANSWER.

Och, Katie's a rogue, **it is thrue,**
But her eyes, like the sky, **are** so blue
    An' her dimples so shwate,
    An' her ankles so nate,
She dazed and she bothered me too.

Till one mornin' we wint for a ride ;
Whin demure as a brid**e, by** my side
    The darlint she **sat,**
    Wid the wickedest hat
'Neath **a** purty girl's chin ever tied.

An' me heart, arrah thin how it bate ;
For my Kate looked so **temptin'** an' shwate
    Wid cheeks like the roses,
    An' **all the** red posies
That grow in her garden **so** nate.

But I sat just as **mute** as the dead
Till she said, wid a toss of her head,
    "If I'd known that to-day
    Ye'd have nothing to say,
I'd **have gone with** my cousin instead."

Thin I felt myself **grow very** bold ;
For I knew she'd **not** scold **if I told**
    Of the love in my heart,
    That would **never** depart,
Though **I** lived to be wrinkled and old.

An' **I** said : " If I dared to do so,
I'd let go of the baste an' I'd throw
    **Both** arms round your waist
    An' be stalin' a taste
Of thim lips **that are** coaxing me so."

Thin she blushed a more illegant red,
As she **said without** raising her head,
    **An' her eyes lookin'** down
    Neath her lashes so brown,
" Would ye like me to drive, Mister Ted ? "
Anonymous.

---

PADDLE YOUR OWN CANOE.

Voyager upon life's sea,
    To yourself be true,
And where'er your lot may be,
    Paddle your own canoe.
Never, though the winds may rave,
    Falter nor look back,
But upon the darkest wave
    Leave **a** shining track.

Nobly dare the wildest storm,
  Stem the hardest gale;
Brave of heart and strong of arm
  You will never fail.
When the world is cold and dark,
  Keep an aim in view,
**And** toward the beacon-mark
  Paddle your own canoe.

Every wave that bears you on
  To **the** silent shore,
From its sunny source has gone,
  To return **no** more.
Then let not an **hour's** delay
  Cheat you of your due;
But, while it is called to-day,
  Paddle your own canoe.

Would you wrest the wreath of fame
  From the hand of Fate;
Would you write a deathless name,
  With the good and great;
Would you bless your fellow-men,
  Heart and soul imbue
With **the** holy task, and then
  Paddle your own canoe.

**Would** you crush the tyrant Wrong,
  **In the world's** free fight,
With a spirit brave and **strong,**
  Battle for the Right;
**And to** break the chains that bind
  The many to the few—
To enfranchise slavish mind,
  Paddle **your** own canoe.

Nothing great is lightly won,
  Nothing won is lost,—
Every good deed, nobly done,
  Will repay the cost.

Leave to Heaven, in humble trust,
 **All** you will to do ;
**But,** if you succeed, you must
 **Paddle** your own canoe.
Mrs. S. T. Bolton.

### THE SOLDIER'S DREAM.

Our bugles sang truce, for the night cloud had
  lowered,
 And the sentinel stars set their watch in the
  sky ;
And thousands had sunk **on** the **ground over-**
  powered,
 **The weary to sleep,** and the wounded to die.

When reposing **that** night on my pallet of straw,
 By the wolf-scaring fagot that guarded **the**
  slain,
At the dead of the night a sweet vision I saw,
 And **thrice** ere the morning I dreamed it again.

Methought from the battle-field's dreadful array
 Far, far I had roamed on a desolate track ;
'Twas autumn, and sunshine arose on the **way**
 To the home of my fathers, that welcomed me
  back.

I flew to the pleasant fields, traversed so oft
 In life's morning march, when my bosom was
  young;
I heard my own mountain-goats bleating aloft,
 And **knew** the sweet strain that the corn-
  reapers sung.

Then pledged **we** the wine-cup, and **fondly I**
  swore
 From my home **and my weeping** friends never
  to part ;
My little ones kissed me a thousand times o'er,
 And my wife sobbed aloud in her fullness of
  heart.

"Stay, stay with us—rest, thou art weary and
    worn ; "
And fain was their war-broken soldier to stay ;
But sorrow returned with the dawning of morn,
    And the voice in my dreaming ear melted
    away.

CAMPBELL.

## THE BIVOUAC OF THE DEAD.

The muffled drum's sad roll has beat
    The soldier's last tattoo !
No more on life's parade shall meet
    That brave and fallen few ;
On Fame's eternal camping-ground
    Their silent tents are spread ;
And Glory guards with silent round
    The bivouac of the dead.

No rumor of the foe's advance
    Now swells upon the wind ;
Nor troubled thought at midnight haunts
    Of loved ones left behind ;
No vision of the warrior's strife
    The warrior's dream alarms ;
No braying horn, no screaming fife
    At dawn shall call to arms.

Their shivered swords are red with rust,
    Their plumed heads are bowed ;
Their haughty banner, trailed in dust,
    Is now their martial shroud ;
And plenteous funeral tears have washed
    The red stains from each brow ;
And the proud forms by battle gashed
    Are free from anguish now.

The neighing troop, the flashing blade
    The bugle's stirring blast,
The charge, the dreadful cannonade,
    The din and shout are passed ;

Nor War's wild notes, nor Glory's peal
　Shall thrill with fierce delight
Those hearts that never more may feel
　The rapture of the fight.

Like the fierce northern hurricane
　That sweeps his great plateau,
Flushed with the triumph yet to gain,
　Came down the serried foe;
Who heard the thunder of the fray
　Break o'er the field beneath,
Knew well the watchword of that day
　Was " Victory or Death!"

Now 'neath their parent turf they rest
　Far from the gory field,
Borne to a Spartan mother's breast
　On many a bloody shield;
The sunshine of their native sky
　Smiles sadly on them here,
And kindred eyes and hearts watch by
　The heroes' sepulchre.

Rest on, embalmed and sainted dead!
　Dear is the blood you gave—
No impious footsteps here shall tread
　The herbage of your grave.
Nor shall your glory be forgot
　While Fame her record keeps,
Or Honor points the hallowed spot
　Where Valor proudly sleeps.
THEODORE O'HARA.

---

## COURTSHIP OF LARRY O'DEE.

Now the Widow McGee
And Larry O'Dee
Had two little cottages, out on the green,
With just enough room for two pig-pens between.
The widow was young, and the widow was fair,

With the brightest of eyes and the brownest of
    hair,
And it frequently chanced, when she came in the
    morn,
With the swill for her pig, Larry came with the
    corn,
And some of the ears that he tossed from his
    hand
In the pen of the widow were certain to land.

One morning said he :
" Och ! Misthress McGee,
Its a washte of good lumber this running two rigs,
Wid a fancy petition betwane our two pigs ! "
" Indade, sure it is ! " answered Widow McGee,
With the sweetest of smiles upon Larry O'Dee.
" And thin it looks kind o' hard-hearted and
    mane
Kapin two frindly pigs so exsaidin'ly near,
That whinever one grunts thin the other can
    hear,
And yit kape a cruel petition betwane ! "

" Shwate Widow McGee,"
Answered Larry O'Dee,
" If ye fale in yer heart we are mane to the pigs,
Ain't we mane to onrsilves to be runnin' two
    rigs ?
Och ! it made me heart ache when I paped
    through the cracks
Of me shanty, last March, at yez shwingin' yer
    ax,
An' a bobbin yer head, an' a shtompin' yer fate,
Wid yer purty white hands jisht as red as a bate,
A sphlittin' yer kindlin'-wood out in the shtorm,
Whin one little shtove it would kape us both
    warm."

" Now, piggy," said she,
" Larry's courtin o' me,

Wid his dilicate, tinder allusion to you;
So now **yez musht** tell me **jusht** what I musht
   do.
For, if I'm **to say** *yes*, shtir **the** shwill wid yer
   shnout;
But if I'm to say *no*, **yez musht** kape yer nose
   out.
**Now**, Larry, **for** shame! to be bribin' a pig
By a-tossin' a handful of corn in its shwig!"
"Me darlint, **the** piggy says *yes!*" answered **he**;
**And** that was the courtship of Larry O'Dee.

W. W. Fink.

---

### THE DESTRUCTION OF SENNACHERIB.

**The Assyrian came down** like the woif on the **fold**,
**And his cohorts were** gleaming in purple and
   gold;
And the **sheen** of their spears was like **stars on**
   the **sea,**
**When** the blue wave rolls nightly on **deep**
   Galilee.

**Like** the leaves **of** the forest when summer is
   green,
**That** host with their banners at sunset were
   seen;
Like the leaves of the forest when autumn hath
   blown,
**That** host on the morrow lay withered and strown.

**For** the angel of death spread his wings on the
   blast,
And breathed in the face of the foe as he passed;
And the eyes of the sleepers waxed deadly and
   chill,
**And** their hearts but once heaved, and forever
   were still!

And there lay the steed with his nostrils all wide,
But through **them there** rolled not the breath of
    his pride;
And the foam of his gasping lay white on **the**
    turf,
**And** cold as the spray on the rock-beating surf.

And there lay the rider, distorted and pale,
**With** the dew on his brow and the rust on **his**
    mail;
And the tents were all silent, the banners alone,
The lances unlifted, the trumpet **un**blown.

And **the** widows of Ashur are loud in their wail,
And the idols **are** broke in the temple of Baal;
And the might **of** the Gentile, unsmote **by the**
    sword,
Hath melted **like snow** in the glance of the Lord.

BYRON.

---

## SONG OF THE MOUNTAIN-BOY.

The mountain shepherd-boy am I!
Castles and lakes beneath me lie!
The sun's first rosy beams are mine;
At eve **his** latest on me shine!
    **I am the mountain**-boy!

**The** flowing torrent here has mirth;
I drink it fresh from out the earth;
It gushes from its rocky bed,
I catch it with my arms outspread!
    I am the mountain-boy!

To me belongs the mountain height;
Around me tempests wing their flight;
From north and south their blasts they call;
My song is heard above them all!
    **I am** the mountain-boy!

Thunder and lightnings under me,
The blue expanse above I see;
I greet the storms with friendly tone:
"Oh leave my father's cot alone!
      I am the mountain-boy!"

And when the tocsin calls to arms,
And mountain bale-fires spread alarms,
Then I descend and join the throng,
And swing my sword, and sing my song:
      I am the mountain-boy!
                  *From the German of* UHLAND.

### RIENZI'S ADDRESS TO THE ROMANS.

  Friends!
I come not here to talk. Ye know too well
The story of our thraldom. We are slaves!
The bright sun rises to his course, and lights
A race of slaves! He sets, and his last beam
Falls on a slave. Not such as, swept along
By the full tide of power, the conqueror leads
To crimson glory and undying fame;—
But base, ignoble slaves!—slaves to a horde
Of petty tyrants, feudal despots; lords,
Rich in some dozen paltry villages;
Strong in some hundred spearmen; only great
In that strange spell—a name! Each hour, dark fraud,
Or open rapine, or protected murder,
Cry out against them. But this very day,
An honest man, my neighbor,—there he stands, —
Was struck—struck like a dog, by one who wore
The badge of Ursini! because, forsooth,
He tossed not high his ready cap in air,
Nor lifted up his voice in servile shouts,
At sight of that great ruffian! Be we men,
And suffer such dishonor? Men, and wash not
The stain away in blood? Such shames are common.

I have known deeper wrongs.  I, that speak **to**
    you,—
I had a brother once, a gracious boy,
**Full** of all gentleness, of calmest ho**pe**,
**Of** sweet and quiet joy; there was **the** look
**Of** Heaven upon his face, which limners give
**To** the beloved disciple.  How I loved
**That** gracious boy!  Younger by fifteen years,
**Brother** at **once** and son!  He left my side,
A summer bloom on his fair cheeks—a smile
Parting his innocent lips.  In one short hour,
The pretty, harmless boy **was** slain!  I saw
The **corse,** the mangled corse, and then I cried
**For** vengeance!  Rouse, **ye** Romans!  Rouse,
    ye slaves!
Have ye brave sons?—Look in the **next fierce**
    brawl
To see them die!  Have ye fair daughters?—
    Look
To see them live, **torn from your** arms, distained,
Dishonored; **and if** ye dare **call for** justice,
Be answered by the lash!  **Yet,** this is Rome,
**That sate on** her seven hills, and from her throne
**Of** beauty ruled the world!  Yet, we are Romans.
**Why,** in that elder day, to be a Roman
**Was** greater than a King!  And once again—
Hear me, ye **walls,** that echoed to the tread
Of **either** Brutus!—once again **I** swear
The Eternal City shall be free!

MARY RUSSELL MITFORD.

---

## BEAUTY, WIT, AND GOLD.

In a bower a widow dwelt;
At her feet three suitors knelt;
Each adored the widow much,
Each essayed her heart to touch;
**One** had wit, and one had gold,
**And one** was **cast** in beauty's mold;

Guess which was it won the prize,
Purse, or tongue, or handsome eyes?

First appeared the handsome man,
Proudly peeping o'er her fan;
Red his lips and white his skin—
Could such beauty fail to win?
Then stepped forth the man of gold;
Cash he counted, coin he told,
Wealth the burden of his tale—
Could such golden projects fail?

Then the man of wit and sense
Wooed her with his eloquence.
Now she blushed, she knew not why;
Now a tear was in her eye;
Then she smiled to hear him speak;
Then the tear was on her cheek;
Beauty, vanish! Gold, depart!
Wit has won the widow's heart.

MOORE.

## THE-BIRD AND THE BABY.

What does little birdie say
In her nest at peep of day?
Let me fly, says little birdie,
Mother, let me fly away.
Birdie, rest a little longer,
Till the little wings are stronger.
So it rests a little longer,
Then it flies away.

What does little baby say,
In her bed at peep of day?
Baby says, like little birdie,
Let me rise and fly away.
Baby, sleep a little longer,
Till the little wings are stronger.
If she sleeps a little longer,
Baby too shall fly away.

ALFRED TENNYSON.

## FROGS AT SCHOOL.

Twenty froggies went to school
Down beside a rushy pool,—
Twenty little coats of green ;
Twenty vests, all white and clean.
" We must be in time," said they :
" First we study then we play :
That **is** how we keep the rule,
When **we** froggies go to school."

Master Bullfrog, grave **and** stern,
Called the classes in their turn ;
Taught them how to nobly **strive**,
Likewise how to leap and dive ;
From **his** seat upon the log,
Showed them how to say " Ker-ch**og !**"
Also how to dodge a blow
From the sticks that bad boys throw.

Twenty froggies grew **up** fast ;
Bullfrogs they became at last ;
Not one dunce among the lot ;
Not one lesson they forgot ;
Polished in a high degree,
As each froggie ought to be.
Now they sit on other logs,
Teaching other little frogs.

Anonymous.

---

## THE JOLLY OLD CROW.

On the limb of an oak sat a jolly old crow,
  And chattered away with glee, with glee,
As he saw the old farmer go out to sow,
  And he cried, **" It's** all for me, for me !

" Look, look, how he scatters his seeds around ;
  **He** is wonderful kind to the poor, the poor ;
**If** he'd empty it **down** in a pile on the ground,
  **I could** find **it** much better, I'm sure, I'm sure !

"I've **learned all** the tricks of this wonderful
        man,
    Who has **such** a regard for the crow, the crow,
That he lays out his grounds in a regular plan,
    And covers his corn in a **row**, a row!

" He must have a very great fancy for **me**;
    He **tries** to entrap me enough, enough;
But I measure his distance as well as he,
    And when he comes near, I'm off, I'm **off**!"
ANONYMOUS.

### THE INQUIRY.

**Tell** me, ye winged winds, that round my  path-
        way **roar**,
Do ye not **know some** spot where mortals weep
        no more?
Some lone and pleasant dell, some valley in **the**
        west,
Where, **free** from toil and  pain, the weary soul
        may rest?
    The loud wind dwindled to a whisper low,
    And sigh'd for pity as it answer'd—" No."

**Tell** me, thou mighty deep, whose billows round
        me play—
**Know'st** thou some favor'd spot, some island far
        away,
**Where** weary man **may** find the bliss for  which
        he sighs—
**Where** sorrow never lives **and** friendship never
        dies?
    The loud waves rolling in perpetual flow
    Stopp'd for awhile, and sigh'd to answer—
        " No."

Then thou, serenest moon, that, with such lovely
        face,
Dost look upon the earth, asleep **in night's** em-
        brace,

Tell me, in all thy round, hast thou not seen
    some spot
Where miserable man might find a happier lot?
    Behind the cloud the moon withdrew in **woe**,
    And a voice, sweet, but sad, responded—"**No**."

Tell me, **my** secret soul—oh, tell me, Hope and
    Faith,
**Is the**re no resting-place from sorrow, sin **and**
    death?—
**Is** there no happy spot where mortals may be
    bless'd,
Where grief may find a balm, and weariness a
    rest?
    Faith, Hope and Love, best boons **to** mortals
    given,
    Waved their bright wings, and whisper'd—
    " Yes, in Heaven !"

Charles Mackay.

---

## THE LADY-BUG AND **THE ANT**.

**The** Lady-bug sat in the rose's heart,
    And smiled with pride and scorn,
As she saw a plain-dressed Ant go by,
    With a heavy grain of corn ;
So she drew the curtains of damask round,
    And **ad**justed her silken vest,
Making her glass of a **drop of** dew,
    That lay in the rose's breast.

Then she laughed so loud, that the Ant looked
    up,
    And seeing her haughty face,
Took no more notice, **but** travelled on
    At the same industrious pace :—
But a sudden blast of autumn came,
    And rudely swept the ground,
And down the rose with the Lady-bug bent,
    And scattered its leaves around.

Then the houseless Lady was much amazed,
  For she knew not where to go,
And hoarse November's early blast
  Had brought with it rain and snow:
Her wings were chilled, and her feet were
    cold,
  And she wished for the Ant's warm cell,
And what she did in the wintry snow
  I'm sure I cannot tell.

But the careful Ant was in her nest,
  With her little ones by her side;
She taught them all like herself to toil,
  Nor mind the sneer of pride;
And I thought, as I sat at the close of the
    day,
  Eating my bread and milk,
It was wiser to work and improve my time,
  Than be idle and dress in silk.

ANONYMOUS.

## THE RIDDLER.

There went a rider on a roan,
By rock and hill, and all alone,
And asked of men these questions three:
" Who may the greatest miller be ?
What baker baked ere Adam's birth ?
What washer washes the most on earth ? "

And still the rider went his way
By cities old and castles gray,
In morning red or moonlight dim,
Unto the sea where ships do swim ;
And yet no man could answer him.

He reined his horse upon the sand :
" There is no lord in any land
Can answer right my questions three :—
Old fisher, sitting by the sea,
Canst tell me where those craftsmen be ? "

Then spoke the fisher of the mere :
" The earth is dark, the water clear,
And where the sea against the land
Is grinding rocks and shells **to** sand,
I see the greatest miller's hand.

" The baker who baked before the morn
**W**hen **A**dam was in Eden born,
**Is** Heat, that God made long before,
**W**hich dries the sand upon the shore,
**A**nd hardens it to rock once more.

" And the water, falling night and day,
**Is** the washer, washing all away ;
All melts in time before the rain,
The mountain sinks into the plain :
So the **great** world comes and goes again."

" Thou, Silver Beard, hast spoken well,
**W**ith wisdom most commendable ;
**So** bind thee with this golden band ! "
**The** light was red upon the strand ;
**The** rider's road lay dark in-land.

CHARLES G. LELAND.

## THE CAPTAIN'S DAUGHTER.

We were crowded in the cabin ;
   Not a soul would dare **to** sleep ;
It was midnight on **t**he wa**ters,**
   And a storm was on the deep.

'Tis a fearful thing in winter
   To be shattered by the blast,
And to hear the rattling trumpet
   Thunder, " Cut away the mast ! "

So we shuddered there in silence :
   For the stoutest held his breath,
While the hungry sea was roaring,
   And the breakers talked with Death.

And as thus we sat in darkness,
    Each one busy in his prayers,
"We are lost!" the captain shouted,
    As he staggered down the stairs.

But his little daughter whispered,
    As she took his icy hand,
"Isn't God upon the ocean,
    Just the same as on the land?"

Then we kissed the little maiden,
    And we spoke in better cheer;
And we anchored safe in harbor,
    When the morn was shining clear.

JAMES T. FIELDS.

## MONTEREY.

We were not many—we who stood
    Before the iron sleet that day;
Yet many a gallant spirit would
Give half his years if he but could
    Have been with us at Monterey.

Now here, now there, the shot it hailed
    In deadly drifts of fiery spray,
Yet not a single soldier quailed
When wounded comrades round them wailed
    Their dying shout at Monterey.

And on—still on our column kept
    Through walls of flame its withering way;
Where fell the dead, the living stepped,
Still charging on the guns that swept
    The slippery streets of Monterey.

The foe himself recoiled aghast,
    When, striking where the strongest lay,
We swooped his flanking batteries past,
And braving full their murderous blast,
    Stormed home the towers of Monterey.

Our banners on those towers wave,
  And there our evening bugles play :
Where orange boughs above their grave,
Keep green the memory of the brave
  Who fought and fell at Monterey.

We were not many—we who pressed
  Beside the brave who fell that day ;
But who of us has not confessed
He'd rather share their warrior rest
  Than not have been at Monterey?

CHARLES F. HOFFMAN.

---

## THE OLD CLOCK ON THE STAIRS.

Somewhat back from the village street
Stands the **old**-fashioned country-seat.
Across **its antique** portico
Tall poplar-trees their shadows throw ;
And from its station in **the** hall
An ancient timepiece says **to** all,—
    " For ever—never !
      Never—for **ever** ! "

Half-way up the stairs **it** stands,
And points and beckons with its hands,
From **its** case of massive oak,
Like a **monk,** who, under his cloak,
Crosses himself, and sighs, alas !
With sorrowful voice **to all** who pass,—
    " For ever—never !
      Never—for ever ! "

By day its voice is low and light ;
But in the silent dead of night,
Distinct as a passing footstep's fall,
It echoes along the vacant hall,
Along the ceiling, along the floor,
And seems to say, at each chamber-door,—
    " For ever—never !
      Never—for ever ! "

Through days of sorrow and of mirth,
Through days of death and days of birth,
Through every swift vicissitude
Of changeful time, unchanged it has stood,
And as if, like God, it all things saw,
It calmly repeats those words of awe,—
      " For ever—never !
      Never—for ever ! "

In that mansion used to be
Free hearted Hospitality ;
His great fires up the chimney soared ;
The stranger feasted at his board ;
But, like the skeleton at the feast,
That warning timepiece never ceased,—
      " For ever—never !
      Never—for ever ! "

There groups of merry children played
There youths and maidens dreaming strayed;
O precious hours !  O golden prime,
And affluence of love and time !
Even as a miser counts his gold,
Those hours the ancient timepiece told,—
      " For ever—never !
      Never—for ever ! "

From that chamber, clothed in white,
The bride came forth on her wedding night ;
There in that silent room below,
The dead lay in his shroud of snow ;
And in the hush that followed the prayer,
Was heard the old clock on the stair,—
      " For ever—never !
      Never—for ever ! "

All are scattered now and fled,
Some are married, some are dead ;
And when I ask, with throbs of pain,
" Ah ! when shall they all meet again ! "

As in the days long since gone by,
The ancient timepiece makes reply,—
    " For ever—never !
      Never—for ever !"

Never here, for ever there,
Where all parting, pain, and care,
And death and time shall disappear,—
For ever there, but never here !
The horologe of Eternity
Sayeth this incessantly,—
    " For ever—never !
      Never—for ever !"

LONGFELLOW.

## ABOUT THE FAIRIES.

Pray, **where are** the little bluebells gone,
  That lately bloomed in the wood?
Why, the little **fairies** have **each** taken one,
  And put it **on for a** hood.

And **where** are the **pretty** grass-stalks gone,
  That waved in the summer breeze?
Oh, the fairies have taken them every one,
  To plant in their gardens, like trees.

And where are the great big bluebottles gone,
  That buzzed in their busy pride?
Oh, the fairies have caught them every one,
  And have broken them in, to ride.

And they've taken the **glowworms** to light
    their halls,
  And the cricket to sing them a song,
And the great red rosé-leaves to paper their
    walls,
  And they're feasting **the** whole night long.

But when spring comes back with its soft, mild
    ray,
  And the ripple of gentle rain,

The fairies bring back what they've taken
		away,
	**And give it** us all again.

ANONYMOUS.

### ADDRESS TO THE OCEAN.

**Roll on,** thou deep and dark blue Ocean—**roll!**
Ten thousand fleets sweep over thee **in vain;**
Man marks **the** earth with ruin—his **control**
Stops with thy shore ;—upon **the watery** plain
**The** wrecks are all thy deed, nor **doth remain**
A shadow **of man's** ravage, **save his** own,
When, for a moment, like a **drop** of rain,
He sinks into thy depths with bubbling groan,
**Without a grave,** unknelled, uncoffined, **and un-**
		**known.**

His steps are not upon thy paths,—thy fields
Are **not** a spoil for him,—thou dost arise
And shake him from thee; **the** vile strength
		he wields
For earth's destruction thou dost all despise,
Spurning him from thy bosom to the skies,
**And** send'st him, shivering, **in** thy playful
		**spray,**
And howling, to his gods, where haply lies
His petty hope in some near port or bay,
**And** dashest him again to earth :—there let him
		lay.

The armaments which thunderstrike the walls
Of rock-built cities, bidding nations quake,
And monarchs tremble in their capitals,
The oak leviathans, whose huge ribs make
Their clay creator the vain title take
Of lord of thee, and arbiter of war ;
These are thy toys, and, as the snowy flake,
They melt into thy yeast of waves, which mar
**Alike the** Armada's pride, or spoils of Trafalgar.

Thy shores are empires, changed in all save
    thee ;—
Assyria, Greece, Rome, Carthage, what are
    they ?
Thy waters wasted them while they were free,
And many a tyrant since ; their shores obey
The stranger, slave, or savage ; their decay
Has dried up realms to deserts : not **so** thou—
**Unchangeable**—save to thy wild waves' play—
Time writes no wrinkles on thine azure brow—
Such as creation's dawn beheld, thou rollest now.

Thou glorious **mirror, where the** Almighty's
    form
Glasses itself **in** tempests ; **in** all **time,**
Calm or convulsed—in breeze, or **gale, or**
    storm,
Icing the pole, or in the torrid clime
Dark-heaving—**bo**undless, endless, and **sub-**
    lime ;
The image of Eternity—the throne
Of **the** Invisible ; even from out thy slime
The monsters **of** the deep are made ; each **zone**
Obeys thee ; thou goest forth, dread, fathomless,
    alone.

BYRON.

## THE LAMB THAT WAS MISSED.

At the shepherd's doorway stands his little son,
Sees the sheep come trooping home, counts them
    one by one ;
But he starts in sorrow when no **trace** is shown
Of the little snow-white lamb, left alone, alone.

Up **the** hill runs Henry, through the drifting
    snow,
Minds not though the icy winds fierce and fiercer
    blow.
He is near the summit ; hark ! he hears a moan—
Yes, he finds the **little** lamb, left alone, alone.

See the **poor** thing panting, struggling on  the
　　ground;
Round the pretty creature's neck Henry's arms
　　**are wound**;
Soon within his bosom, all its bleatings done,
Home he bears the little **lamb**, left alone, alone.

Oh, **the** happy faces by the shepherd's fire!
High without the tempest roars, but the laugh
　　rings higher.
Young and old together make that joy **their** own,
In their midst the little lamb, left alone, alone!
Anonymous.

### CLEON AND I.

Cleon hath a million acres—
　　**Ne'er a one** have I;
**Cleon** dwelleth in a palace—
　　In a cottage, I.
Cleon hath a dozen fortunes—
　　Not a penny, I;
But the poorer of the twain is
　　Cleon, and not **I.**

Cleon, true, possesseth acres,
　　But **the landscape, I** ;
Half the charms to me it yieldeth
　　Money cannot buy;
Cleon harbors sloth and dulness,
　　Freshening vigor, I;
He in velvet, I in fustian,—
　　Richer man am **I.**

Cleon is a slave to grandeur—
　　**Free** as thought am I;
Cleon fees a score of doctors—
　　Need of none have **I**;
Wealth-surrounded, care-environed,
　　Cleon fears to die;
Death may come, he'll find me ready,
　　Happier man am I.

Cleon sees no charms in Nature—
  In a daisy, I ;
Cleon hears no anthem ringing
  In the sea and sky ;
Nature sings to me forever—
  Earnest listener, I ;
**State for** state, with all attendants,
  **Who would** change?—Not I.
CHARLES MACKAY.

## THE OWL AND THE PUSSY-CAT.

The Owl and the Pussy-Cat **went to sea**
  In a beautiful pea-green boat ;
They took some honey and plenty of **money**
  Wrapped up in a five-pound note.
The Owl looked up to the moon above,
  And sang to a small guitar,
"O lovely Pussy!  O Pussy, my love !
  What a beautiful **Pussy you** are,—
                    You **are,**
What **a** beautiful Pussy **you are !**"

Puss said to the Owl, " You elegant fowl !
  How wonderful sweet you sing !
O let us be married,—too long we have tar-
      ried,—
  But what **shall we do for a ring ?**"
They sailed **away for a** year **and a day**
  To the land where the bong-tree grows,
And there in the wood a piggy-wig stood
  With a ring in the end of his nose,—
                    His nose,
**W**ith a ring in the end of his nose.

" Dear Pig, are you willing to sell for one shil-
      ling
  Your ring ?"  Said the piggy, " I will."
So they took it away, and were married next
      day

By the turkey who lives on the hill.
They dined upon mince and slices of quince,
Which they ate with a runcible spoon,
And hand in hand on the edge of the sand
They danced by the **light** of the moon,—
The moon,
They danced by the light of the moon.

ANONYMOUS.

---

### THE BALLAD **OF THE** OYSTERMAN.

It was a tall young oysterman lived **by the river-**
side,
**His** shop was just upon the **bank, his** boat was
**on** the tide ;
The daughter of a fisherman, that was so straight
and **slim,**
Lived **over on the** other bank, right opposite **to**
him.

It was the pensive oysterman that saw a lovely
maid,
Upon **a moonlight** evening, **a** sitting **in the**
shade ;
He saw her wave **her** handkerchief, as **much as**
if to say,
"I'm wide awake, young oysterman, and all the
folks **away."**

Then up arose the oysterman and to himself said
he :
"I guess I'll leave the skiff at home, for fear
that folks should see ;
I read it in the story-book, that, for to kiss his
dear,
Leander swam the Hellespont,—and I will swim
this **here."**

And he has leaped into the waves, and crossed
the shining stream,
And he has clambered up the bank, all in the
moonlight gleam ;

O there were kisses sweet as dew, and  words  as
    soft as rain,—
**But** they have heard her father's step, and in he
    leaps again!

Out spoke the ancient fisherman,—" O what was
    that, my daughter?"
" 'Twas nothing but a  pebble, sir, I  threw  into
    the water.'
" And what is that, pray tell me, love, that pad-
    dles off so fast?"
" It's nothing but a  porpoise, sir, that's  been  a
    swimming past."

**Out** spoke the ancient fisherman,—" Now  bring
    me my harpoon!
I'll get **into my fishing**-boat, and  fix  the  **fellow**
    soon."
Down fell that pretty innocent, as  falls  a  snow-
    white lamb,
Her hair drooped round  her  pallid  cheek, **like**
    seaweed on a clam.

Alas for those **two** loving **ones**! she  waked  **not**
    from her swound,
And he was taken with a cramp, and in the waves
    was drowned;
But fate has  metamorphosed them,  in  pity  of
    their woe,
And now they **keep** an oystershop for  mermaids
    down below.

Oliver Wendell Holmes.

## THE BOY AND THE RING.

**Fair** chance held fast is merit.   Once a king
**Of** Persia had a jewel in a ring.
**He** set it on the dome of Azud high,
And, when they saw it flashing in the sky,
Made proclamation to his royal troop
That who should send an arrow through the hoop
That held the gem should have the ring to wear.

It happened that four hundred archers were
In the king's company about the king.
Each took his aim, and shot, and missed the ring.

A boy at play upon the terraced roof
Of a near building bent his bow aloof
At random, and, behold ! the morning breeze
His little arrow caught and bore with ease
Right through the circlet of the gem. The king,
Well pleased, unto the boy assigned the ring.

Then the boy burnt his arrows and his bow.
The king, astonished, said, " Why dost thou so,
Seeing thy first shot hath had great success ? "
He answered, " Lest my second make that less."
ANONYMOUS.

## THE USE OF FLOWERS.

God might have made the earth bring forth
    enough for great and small—
The oak tree and the cedar tree—without a
    flower at all :
Then wherefore, wherefore were they made, all
    dyed with rainbow light,
All fashioned with supremest grace, upspringing
    day and night—
Springing in valleys green and low, and on the
    mountain high,
And in the silent wilderness where no man
    passes by ?
Our outward life requires them not—then where-
    fore had they birth ?
To minister delight to man ! to beautify the
    earth !
To comfort man—to whisper hope whene'er his
    faith is dim !
For He who careth for the flower will much
    more care for *him.*
MARY HOWITT.

## LORD ULLIN'S DAUGHTER.

A chieftain, to the Highlands bound,
　Cries, " Boatman, do not tarry !
And I'll give thee a silver pound
　To row us o'er the ferry."

" Now, who be ye, would cross Lochgyle,
　This dark and stormy water?"
" O, I'm the chief of Ulva's isle,
　And this Lord Ullin's daughter.

" And fast before her father's men
　Three days we've fled together,
For should he find us in the glen,
　My blood would stain the heather.

" His horsemen hard behind us ride ;
　Should they our steps discover,
Then who would cheer my bonny bride
　When they have slain her lover?"

Out spoke the hardy Highland wight :
　" I'll go, my chief,—I'm ready ;
It is not for your silver bright,
　But for your winsome lady.

" And, by my word ! the bonny bird
　In danger shall not tarry ;
So, though the waves are raging white,
　I'll row you o'er the ferry."

By this the storm grew loud apace,
　The water-wraith was shrieking ;
And in the scowl of heaven each face
　Grew dark as they were speaking.

But still, as wilder grew the wind,
　And as the night grew drearer,
Adown the glen rode armed men,—
　Their trampling sounded nearer.

"O, haste thee, haste!" the lady cries,
  "Though tempests round us gather;
I'll meet the raging of the skies,
  But not an angry father."

The boat has left a stormy land,
  A stormy sea before her,—
When, O, too strong for human hand,
  The tempest gathered o'er her!

And still they rowed amidst the roar
  Of waters fast prevailing:
Lord Ullin reached that fatal shore,
  His wrath was changed to wailing.

For, sore dismayed, through storm and shade,
  His child he did discover;
One lovely hand she stretched for aid,
  And one was round her lover.

"Come back! come back!" he cried in grief,
  "Across this stormy water;
And I'll forgive your Highland chief,
  My daughter! O, my daughter!"

'Twas vain; the loud waves lashed the shore,
  Return or aid preventing;
The waters wild went o'er his child,
  And he was left lamenting.
THOMAS CAMPBELL.

---

## CARVING A NAME.

I wrote my name upon the sand,
  And trusted it would stand for aye;
But soon, alas! the refluent sea
  Had washed my feeble lines away.

I carved my name upon the wood,
  And, after years, returned again;
I missed the shadow of the tree
  That stretched of old upon the plain.

To solid marble next my name
 I gave as a perpetual trust;
An earthquake rent it **to its** base,
 And now it lies o'erlaid **with** dust.

All these have failed.  In wiser mood
 I turn and ask myself, " What then?
If I **would** have my name endure,
 **I'll write it on** the hearts of men,

" In characters of **living** light,
 From kindly words and actions wrought;
And these, beyond the reach of Time,
 Shall live immortal as **my** thought."
HORATIO ALGER.

## BARBARA FRIETCHIE.

Up from the meadows rich with corn,
Clear in the cool September morn,

The clustered spires of Frederick stand
Green-walled by the hills of Maryland.

Round about them orchards sweep,
Apple and peach tree fruited deep,

Fair as a garden of the Lord
To the eyes of the famished rebel horde,

On that pleasant morn of the early fall
When Lee marched over the mountain-wall,

Over the mountains, winding down,
Horse and foot, into Frederick town.

Forty flags with their silver stars,
Forty flags with their crimson bars,

Flapped in the morning wind : the sun
Of noon looked down, and saw not one.

Up rose old Barbara Frietchie then,
Bowed with her fourscore years and ten ;

Bravest of all in Frederick town,
She took up the flag the men hauled down :

In her attic window the staff she set,
To show that one heart was loyal yet.

Up the street came the rebel tread,
Stonewall Jackson riding ahead.

Under his slouched hat left and right
He glanced ; the old flag met his sight.

" Halt ! "—the dust brown ranks stood fast,
" Fire ! "—out blazed the rifleblast.

It shivered the window, pane and sash ;
It rent the banner with seam and gash.

Quick, as it fell, from the broken staff
Dame Barbara snatched the silken scarf ;

She leaned far out on the window-sill,
And shook it forth with a royal will.

" Shoot, if you must, this gray old head,
But spare your country's flag," she said.

A shade of sadness, a blush of shame,
Over the face of the leader came ;

The nobler nature within him stirred
To life at that woman's deed and word :

" Who touches a hair of yon gray head
Dies like a dog ! March on ! " he said.

All day long through Frederick Street
Sounded the tread of marching feet :

All day long that free flag tost
Over the heads of the rebel host.

Ever its torn folds rose and fell
On the loyal winds that loved it well;

And through the hill-gaps sunset light
Shone over it with a warm good-night.

Barbara Frietchie's work is o'er,
And the Rebel rides on his raids no more.

Honor to her! and let a tear
Fall, for her sake, on Stonewall's bier.

Over Barbara Frietchie's grave,
Flag of Freedom and **Union,** wave!

Peace and order and beauty draw
Round thy symbol of light and law;

And ever the stars above look down
On **thy** stars below in Frederick town!

J. G. WHITTIER.

## THE SEMINOLE'S REPLY.

Blaze, with your serried columns!
  I will not bend the knee!
The shackles ne'er again shall bind
  The arm which now is free.
**I've mailed it** with the **thunder,**
  **When** the tempest muttered **low;**
And where it falls, ye well may dread
  The lightning of its blow!

I've scared ye in the city,
  I've scalped ye on the plain;
Go, count your chosen, where they fell
  Beneath my leaden **rain!**
I scorn your proffered treaty!
  The pale-face I **defy!**
Revenge is stamped upon my spear,
  And blood my battle-cry!

Some strike for hope of booty,
　Some to defend their all—
I battle for the joy I have
　To see the white man fall :
I love, among the wounded,
　To hear his dying moan,
And catch while chanting at his side,
　The music of his groan.

Ye've trailed me through the forest,
　Ye've tracked me o'er the stream ;
And struggling through the everglade,
　Your bristling bayonets gleam ;
But I stand as should the warrior,
　With his rifle and his spear ;
The scalp of vengeance still is red,
　And warns ye—Come not here !

I loathe ye in my bosom,
　I scorn ye with mine eye,
And I'll taunt ye with my latest breath,
　And fight ye till I die !
I ne'er will ask ye quarter,
　And I ne'er will be your slave ;
But I'll swim the sea of slaughter,
　Till I sink beneath its wave !

G. W. PATTEN.

---

## PSALM OF MARRIAGE.

Tell me not in idle jingle,
　" Marriage is an empty dream ! "
For the girl is dead that's single,
　And girls are not what they seem.

Life is real !　Life is earnest !
　Single blessedness a fib !
" Man thou art, to man returnest ! "
　Has been spoken of the rib.

Not enjoyment and not sorrow,
  Is our destined end or way ;
But to act that each to-morrow
  Finds us nearer marriage-day.

Life is long, and youth is fleeting,
  And our hearts though light and **gay,**
Still **like** pleasant drums are beating
  **Wedding** marches all the way.

In the world's broad field of battle,
  In the bivouac **of** life,
Be not like dumb-driven cattle !
  Be a heroine—a wife !—

Trust no future, howe'er pleasant,
  Let the dead past bury its dead !
Act —**act to** the living Present !
  Heart within and hope ahead !

Lives of married folks remind us
  We can live our lives **as well,**
And, departing, leave **behind** us
  Such examples as shall " tell."

Such example that another,
  Wasting time in idle sport,
A forlorn, unmarried brother,
  Seeing, **shall** take heart and court.

Let us, **then, be up and doing,**
  With **a** heart on triumph **set,**
Still contriving, still pursuing,
  And each one a husband get.
                    PHŒBE CARY.

E PLURIBUS UNUM.

Though many and bright are the stars that ap-
  pear
  In that flag by our country unfurled,
And the stripes that are swelling in majesty there

Like a rainbow adorning the world—
Their light is unsullied as those in the sky,
    By a deed that are fathers have done,
And they're linked in as true and as holy **a tie**,
    In their motto of " Many in One."


From the hour when those patriots fearlessly
        flung
    That banner **of starlight** abroad,
Ever true to themselves, to that motto they clung
    As they clung to the promise of God ;
By the bayonet traced in the midnight of **war**,
    On the fields where our glory was won—
Oh ! perish the heart or the hand that would mar
    Our motto **of** " Many in One."


'**Mid the** smoke of the conflict, the cannon's deep
        roar,
    How oft it has gathered renown !
While those stars were reflected in rivers of gore,
    Where the **cross** and the lion went down ;
And though few were their lights in the gloom
        of that hour,
    Yet **the** hearts that were striking below
**Had God** for their bulwark, and truth for their
        power,
    And they stopped **not** to number the foe.


From where our green mountain-tops blend with
        the **sky,**
    And the giant St. Lawrence is rolled,
To the waves where the balmy Hesperides **lie,**
    Like the dream of some prophet of old,
They conquered, and, dying, bequeathed **to** our
        care
    Not this boundless dominion alone,
But that banner whose loveliness hallows the air,
    And their motto of " Many in One."

We are many in one, while there glitters a star
  **In** the blue of the heavens above,
And tyrants shall quail, 'mid their dungeons
      afar,
  When they gaze on that motto **of love.**
It shall gleam o'er the sea, 'mid **the bolts of** the
      storm—
  Over tempes**t,** and battle, and wreck—
**And** flame **where** our guns with their thunder
      grow warm,
  'Neath the blood **on** the slippery deck.

The oppressed of the earth to that standard shall
      fly
  Wherever its folds shall be spread,
And the exile **shall** feel 'tis his own native sky,
  Where its stars shall wave over his head;
And those stars shall increase till the fulness of
      time
  Its millions of cycles have run—
Till the world shall have welcomed their mission
      sublime,
  And the nations of earth shall be one.

**Though** the old Allegheny may tower to heaven,
  And the Father of Waters divide,
The links of our destiny cannot be riven
  While the **truth of** those words shall abide.
Then, **oh! let them glow on** each helmet and
      **brand,**
  Though **our** blood like our rivers should run;
Divide as we may in our own native land,
  To the rest of the world **we** are ONE.

Then up with our flag!—let it stream on the air'
  Though our fathers are cold in their graves,
**They** had hands that could strike—they had
      souls that could dare—
  And **their** sons were not born to be slaves.
Up, up **with that** banner!—where'er it may call,
  **Our millions** shall rally around,

And a nation of freemen that moment shall fall,
  When its **stars** shall be trailed on the ground.
G. W. CUTTER.

---

### LOCHINVAR.

O, young Lochinvar is come out of the west,
Through all the **wide** Border his steed was the
    best ;
And save his good broadsword he **weapon** had
    none,
**He rode** all unarmed, and he rode all alone ;
**So faithful in love,** and so dauntless in war,
**There** never was knight like the young Loch-
    invar.

He **stayed not for** brake, and he stopped not for
    **stone,**
**He** swam the Eske river where ford there was
    none,
But, ere he alighted at Netherby gate,
The bride had consented, the gallant came late ;
For a laggard in love, and **a** dastard in war,
Was to wed the fair Ellen of brave Lochinvar.

So boldly he entered the Netherby Hall,
Among bridesmen, and kinsmen, and brothers
    and all ;
Then spoke **the bride's** father, **his** hand **on** his
    sword
(**For** the poor craven bridegroom said never **a**
    word),
" O, come **ye in** peace here, or come ye in war,
Or to dance **at** our bridal, young Lord Loch-
    invar ? "

" I long wooed your daughter, my suit you
    denied ;—
Love swells like the Solway, but ebbs like **its**
    tide,—

And now I am come, with this lost love of mine,
To lead but one measure, drink one cup of wine;
There are maidens in Scotland more lovely by
    far,
That would gladly be bride to the young Loch-
    invar."

The bride **kissed** the goblet; the knight took it
    up,
He quaffed off **the** wine, and he threw down the
    cup.
She looked down to **blush, and she** looked up to
    **sigh,**
**With a** smile on her lips and a tear in **her** eye;
**He took her** soft hand, ere her **mother** could
    **bar,—**
"Now tread we a measure," said young Loch-
    invar.

So stately his form, and so **lovely** her face,
That never a hall such a galliard did grace;
While **her** mother did fret, **and** her father **did**
    fume,
And the bridegroom stood dangling his **bonnet**
    **and** plume;
And the bridemaidens whispered, "'Twere better
    **by** far
**To have** matched our fair cousin with young
    **Lochinvar."**

One touch **to her** hand, and one word in her ear,
When they reached the hall-door, and **the** charger
    stood near;
**So** light to the croupe the fair lady he swung,
**So** light to the saddle before her he sprung;
"She is won! we **are** gone! over bank, bush,
    and scaur;
They'll have fleet steeds that follow," quoth
    young Lochinvar.

There was mounting 'mong Græmes of the
    Netherby clan ;
Forsters, Fenwicks, and Musgraves, they rode
    and they ran ;
There was racing and chasing on Cannobie lea,
But the lost bride of Netherby ne'er did they
    see.
So daring in love, and so dauntless in war,
Have ye e'er heard of gallant like young Loch-
    invar ?

SIR WALTER SCOTT.

## BE CONTENT.

A man in his carriage was riding along,
    His gaily-dressed wife by his side ;
In satins and laces, she looked like a queen,
    And he like a king by her side.

A wood-sawyer stood near the street as they
    passed ;
    The carriage and couple he eyed,
And said, as he worked with his saw on a log,
    " I wish I was rich, and could ride."

The man in the carriage remarked to his wife,
    " One thing I would do, if I could :
I would give all my wealth for the strength
    and the health
    Of the man who is sawing the wood."

A pretty young maid with a bundle of work,
    Whose face like the morning was fair,
Went tripping along with a smile of delight,
    While humming a love-breathing air.

She looked at the carriage ; the lady she saw,
    All dressed in her clothing so fine,
And said, in a whisper, " I wish from my heart
    Those satins and laces were mine."

The lady looked out on the maid with her
    work,
  So fair in her calico dress,
And said, " Ah, how gladly I'd give all my
    wealth,
  Her beauty and youth to possess."

It is thus in this world; whatever our lot,
  Our minds and our time we employ
In longing and sighing for what we have not,
  Ungrateful for what we enjoy.
ANONYMOUS.

---

## THE GLOVE AND THE LIONS.

King Francis was a hearty king, and loved a
  royal sport,
And one day as his lions fought, sat looking on
  the court ;
The nobles filled the benches, with the ladies in
  their pride,
And 'mongst them sat the Count de Lorge, with
  one for whom he sighed :
And truly 'twas a gallant thing to see that crowning show,
Valor and love, and a king above, and the royal
  beasts below.

Ramped and roared the lions, with horrid laughing jaws ;
They bit, they glared, gave blows like beams, a
  wind went with their paws ;
With wallowing might and stifled roar they rolled
  on one another,
Till all the pit with sand and mane was in a
  thunderous smother,
The bloody foam above the bars came whisking
  through the air ;
Said Francis, then, " Faith, gentlemen, we're better here than there ! "

De Lorge's love o'erheard the king, a beauteous
    lively dame,
With smiling lips and sharp bright eyes, which
    always seemed the same;
She thought: " The Count, my lover, is brave,
    as brave can be,
He surely would do wondrous things to show his
    love of me;
King, ladies, lovers, all look on; the occasion is
    divine;
I'll drop my glove, to prove his love; great glory
    will be mine!"

She dropped her glove to prove his love, then
    looked on him and smiled;
He bowed, and in a moment leaped among the
    lions wild;
The leap was quick, return was quick, he has
    regained his place,
Then threw the glove,—but not with love,—right
    in the lady's face.
" By heaven!" said Francis, "rightly done!"
    and he rose from where he sat;
" No love," quoth he, " but vanity, sets love a
    task like that."

Leigh Hunt.

## THE FAIRIES.

Up the airy mountain,
    Down the rushy glen,
We daren't go a-hunting
    For fear of little men;
Wee folk, good folk,
    Trooping all together;
Green jacket, red cap,
    And white owl's feather!

Down along the rocky shore
    Some make their home,—
They live on crispy pancakes
    Of yellow tide-foam;

Some in the reeds
  Of the black mountain-lake,
With frogs for their watch-dogs,
  All night awake.

High on the hill-top
  The old king sits;
He is now so old and gray
  He's nigh lost his wits.
With a bridge of white mist
  Columbkill he crosses,
On his stately journeys,
  From Slieveleague to Rosses;
Or going up with music
  On cold starry nights,
To sup with the queen
  Of the gay Northern Lights.

They stole little Bridget
  For seven years long;
When she came down again
  Her friends were all gone.
They took her lightly back,
  Between the night and morrow;
They thought that she was fast asleep,
  But she was dead with sorrow,
They have kept her ever since
  Deep within the lakes,
On a bed of flag-leaves,
  Watching till she wakes.

By the craggy hillside,
  Through the mosses bare,
They have planted thorn-trees
  For pleasure here and there.
Is any man so daring
  To dig up one in spite,
He shall find the thornies set
  In his bed at night.

Up the airy mountain,
  Down the rushy glen,
We daren't go a-hunting
  For fear of little men;
Wee folk, good folk,
  Trooping all together;
Green jacket, red cap,
  And white owl's feather.

WILLIAM ALLINGHAM.

## THE OLD YEAR AND THE NEW.

Ring out, **wild** bells, to the wild sky,
  The flying cloud, the frosty light;
  The year is dying in the night;
Ring out, wild bells, and let him die.

Ring out the old, ring in the new,
  Ring, happy bells, across the snow;
  The year is going, let him go;
Ring out the false, ring in the true.

Ring out the grief that saps the mind
  For those that here we see no more;
  Ring out the feud of rich and poor,
Ring in redress to all mankind.

Ring out a slowly dying cause,
  And ancient forms of party strife;
  Ring in the nobler modes of life,
With sweeter manners, purer laws.

Ring out false pride in place and blood,
  The civic slander and the spite;
  Ring in the love of truth and right
Ring in the common love of good.

Ring in the valiant man and free,
  The larger heart, the kindlier hand;
  Ring out the darkness of the land;
Ring in the Christ that is to be.

ALFRED TENNYSON.

## ANTONY'S ADDRESS TO THE ROMANS ON THE DEATH OF CÆSAR.

Friends, Romans, countrymen, lend me your
    ears ;
I come to bury Cæsar, not to praise **him.**
The evil that men do lives after them ;
The **good** is oft interred with their bones ;
So **let** it **be with** Cæsar.   The noble Brutus
Hath told you Cæsar was ambitious :
If it were **so, it** was a grievous fault ;
And **grievously hath Cæsar** answered **it.**
Here, under leave of Brutus and the rest,
(For Brutus is an honorable man ;
So are they all, all honorable men),
Come I to speak in Cæsar's funeral.

He was my friend, faithful and just to me :
But Brutus says he was ambitious,
And Brutus is an honorab**le man.**
He hath brought many captives home to Rome,
Whose ransoms did the **general coffers** fill :
**Did** this in Cæsar seem ambitious ?
**When** that that poor **have** cried, Cæsar hath
    wept :
Ambition should be made of sterner stuff :
Yet Brutus says he was ambitious ;
And Brutus is an honorable man.
You all did **see** that on the Lupereal,
I thrice presented him a kingly crown,
Which he **did** thrice refuse : was this ambi-
    tion ?
**Yet** Brutus says he was ambitious,
And, sure, he is an honorable man.
I speak not to disprove what Brutus spoke,
But here I am to speak what I do know.
You all did love him once,—not without
    cause ;—
**What** cause withholds you then to mourn for
    him ?

O judgment ! thou art fled to brutish beasts,
And men have lost their reason !—Bear with
        me ;
My heart is in the coffin there with Cæsar,
And I must pause till it come back to me.

    But yesterday the word of Cæsar might
Have stood against the world : now lies he
        there,
And none so poor to do him reverence.
O masters ! if I were disposed to stir
Your hearts and minds to mutiny and rage,
I should do Brutus wrong, and Cassius wrong,
Who, you all know, are honorable men.
I will not do them wrong ; I rather choose
To wrong the dead, to wrong myself, and you,
Than I will wrong such honorable men.
But here's a parchment, with the seal of
        Cæsar—
I found it in his closet,—'tis his will.
Let but the commons hear this testament,
(Which, pardon me, I do not mean to read),
And they would go and kiss dead Cæsar's
        wounds,
And dip their napkins in his sacred blood ;
Yea, beg a hair of him for memory,
And, dying, mention it within their wills,
Bequeathing it, as a rich legacy,
Unto their issue.

    If you have tears, prepare to shed them now.
You all do know this mantle : I remember
The first time ever Cæsar put it on ;
'Twas on a summer's evening in his tent—
That day he overcame the Nervii.
Look !   In this place ran Cassius' dagger
        through :
See what a rent the envious Casca made :
Through this the well-beloved Brutus stabbed ;
And, as he plucked his cursed steel away,

Mark, how the blood of Cæsar followed it,
As rushing out of doors, to be resolved
If Brutus so unkindly knocked, **or no ;**
For Brutus, as you know, was Cæsar's angel :
Judge, O you gods, how dearly Cæsar loved
     him !
This **was the** most unkindest **cut** of all ;
For **when the** noble Cæsar saw him stab,
Ingratitude, **more** strong than traitors' arms,
Quite vanquished him : then burst his mighty
     heart ;
And, **in his** mantle muffling up his face,
Even **at the** base of Pompey's statue,
Which all the while ran blood, great Cæsar
     fell.
Oh, what a fall was there, **my countrymen !**
Then I, and you, **and** all of **us, fell** down,
Whilst bloody treason flourished over us.
O, **now you** weep ; and, I perceive you feel
The dint of pity :—these **are gracious** drops.
Kind souls, what, weep you when **you** but be-
     hold
Our Cæsar's vesture wounded ? Look ye here !
Here is himself—marred, as you see, by
     traitors.

   **Good friends,** sweet friends, let me not stir
     you **up**
To such **a sud**den flood of mutiny.
They that have done this deed **are** honorable ;
What private griefs they have, alas ! I know
     not,
**That** made them **do** it ;—they are wise and
     honorable,
And will, no doubt, with reasons answer you.
I come not, friends, to steal away your hearts :
I am no orator, as Brutus **is ;**
But as you know me all, a plain, blunt man,

That love my friend ; and that they know full
    well
That gave me public leave to speak of him.
For I have neither wit, nor words, nor worth,
Action, nor-utterance, nor the power of speech,
To stir men's blood : I only speak right on ;
I tell you that which you yourselves do know;
Show you sweet Cæsar's wounds, poor—poor
    dumb mouths,
And bid them speak for me. But were I
    Brutus,
And Brutus Antony, there were an Antony
Would ruffle up your spirits, and put a tongue
In every wound of Cæsar, that should move
The stones of Rome to rise and mutiny.

SHAKESPEARE.

---

## COLD WATER.

The thirsty flowerets droop. The parching grass
Doth crisp beneath the foot, and the wan trees
Perish for lack of moisture.   By the side
Of the dried rills, the herds desparing stand,
With tongue protruded.  Summer's fiery heat
Exhaling, checks the thousand springs of life.
Marked ye yon cloud glide forth on angel wing?
Heard ye the herald-drops, with gentle force
Stir the broad heavens?—And the protracted
    rain
Waking the streams to run their tuneful way ?
Saw ye the flocks rejoice, and did ye fail
To thank the God of fountains ?

                  See the hart
Pant for the water-brooks.  The fevered sun
Of Asia glitters on his leafy lair.
As, fearful of the lion's wrath, he hastes,
With timid footsteps through the whispering
    reeds ;

Quick leaping to the renovating stream,
The copious draught his bounding veins inspires
With joyful vigor.

                        Patient o'er the sands,
The burden-bearer of the desert clime,
The camel, toileth.  Faint with deadly thirst,
His writhing neck of bitter anguish speaks.
Lo! an oasis, and a tree-girt well,—
And moved by powerful instinct, on he speeds,
With agonizing haste to drink or die.
On his swift courser, o'er the burning wild
The Arab cometh.  From his eager eye
Flashes desire.  Seeks he the sparkling wine,
Giving its golden color to the cup?
No! to the gushing spring he flies, and deep
Buries his scorching lip and laves his brow,
And blesses Alla.

                        Christian pilgrim, come!
Thy brother of the Koran's broken creed
Shall teach thee wisdom,—and, with courteous
      hand,
Nature, thy mother, holds the crystal cup,
And bids thee pledge her in the element
Of temperance and health.

                        Drink, and be whole,
And purge the fever-poison from thy veins,
And pass, in purity and peace, to taste
The river flowing from the throne of God!
Lydia H. Sigourney.

## NOT ON THE BATTLE-FIELD.

" To fall on the battle-field fighting for my dear country, that would not be hard."—*The Neighbors.*

        O, no, no—let me lie
Not on a field of battle when I die!
        Let not the iron tread
Of the mad war-horse crush my helmed head ;

Nor let the reeking knife,
That I have drawn against a brother's life,
　Be in my hand when death
Thunders along, and tramples me beneath
　His heavy squadron's heels,
Or gory felloes of his cannon's wheels.

　From such a dying bed,
Though o'er it float the stripes of white and red,
　And the bald eagle brings
The clustered stars upon his wide-spread wings,
　To sparkle in my sight,
O, never let my spirit take her flight!

　I know that beauty's eye
Is all the brighter where the gay penants fly,
　And brazen helmets dance,
And sunshine flashes on the lifted lance:
　I know that bards have sung,
And people shouted till the welkin rung
　In honor of the brave
Who on the battle-field have found a grave:

　I know that o'er their bones
Have grateful hands piled monumental stones.
　Some of these piles I've seen:
The one at Lexington upon the green
　Where the first blood was shed,
And to my country's independence led;
　And others, on our shore,
The "Battle Monument" at Baltimore,
　And that an Bunker's Hill.
Ay, and abroad, a few more famous still;
　Thy "tomb," Themistocles,
That looks out yet upon the Grecian seas,
　And which the waters kiss
That issue from the Gulf of Salamis,
　And thine, too, have I seen,
Thy mound of earth, Patroclus, robed in green,
　That, like a natural knoll,

Sheep climb and nibble over as they stroll,
    Watched by some turbaned boy
**Upon the** margin of the plain **of** Troy.

    Such honors grace the bed,
I know, whereon the warrior lays his head,
    And hears, as life ebbs **out,**
The conquered dying and the conqueror's shout.
    But as his eye grows dim,
**What** is a column or a mound to him?
    What to the parting soul,
The mellow **notes of bugles?** What the roll
    Of drums? **No,** let **me die**
Where the blue heaven bends **o'er me** lovingly,
    And **the** soft summer air,
**As** it goes by **me,** stirs my thin, white hair,
    And **from** my forehead dries
The death damp **as** it gathers, and the skies
    Seem waiting to receive
My **soul** to their **clear** depths! Or let me leave
    The world, when round my bed
Wife, **children,** weeping friends are gathered,
    And **the** calm voice of prayer
**And** holy hymning shall my soul prepare,
    To go and be at rest
With kindred spirits—spirits who have blessed
    The human brotherhood
**By** labors, **cares,** and counsels for their good.

    In **my** dying hour,
When **riches,** fame, and honor have no power
    **To bear** the spirit up,
Or from my lips to turn aside the cup
    That all must drink at last,
O, let me draw refreshment from the past!
    Then let my soul run back,
**With** peace and joy, along my earthly track,
    And see that all the seeds
That I have scattered there, in virtuous deeds,
    Have sprung **up,** and have given
Already, fruits of **which** to taste in heaven!

And though no grassy mound
Or granite pile says 'tis heroic ground
  Where my remains repose,
Still will I hope—vain hope perhaps—that those
  Whom I have striven to bless,
The wanderer reclaimed, the fatherless,
  May stand around my grave,
With the poor prisoner, and the poorest slave,
  And breathe an humble prayer,
That they may die like him whose bones are
  mouldering there.

J. Pierpont.

## THE BELLS.

Hear the sledges with the bells—
  Silver bells !
What a world of merriment their melody foretells!
  How they tinkle, tinkle, tinkle,
    In the icy air of night !
  While the stars that oversprinkle
  All the heavens, seem to twinkle
    With a crystalline delight ;
  Keeping time, time, time,
  In a sort of Runic rhyme,
To the tintinnabulation that so musically wells,
  From the bells, bells, bells, bells,
    Bells, bells, bells—
  From the jingling and the tinkling of the bells

  Hear the mellow wedding bells—
    Golden bells !
What a world of happiness their harmony foretells
  Through the balmy air of night
  How they ring out their delight !
    From the molten-golden notes,
      And all in tune,
    What a liquid ditty floats
To the turtle-dove that listens, while she gloats
      On the moon !
    Oh, from out the sounding cells,

What a gush of euphony voluminously wells!
How it swells!
How it dwells
On the Future! how it tells
Of the rapture that impels
To the swinging and the ringing
Of the bells, bells, bells,
Of the bells, bells, bells, bells,
Bells, bells, bells—
To the rhyming and the chiming of the bells!

Hear the loud alarum bells—
Brazen bells!
What a tale of terror, now, their turbulency tells!
In the startled ear of night
How they scream out their affright!
Too much horrified to speak,
They can only shriek, shriek,
Out of tune,
In a clamorous appealing to the mercy of the fire,
In a mad expostulation with the deaf and frantic
Leaping higher, higher, higher,    [fire
With a desperate desire,
And a resolute endeavor
Now—now to sit or never,
By the side of the pale-faced moon.
Oh, the bells, bells, bells!
What a tale their terror tells
Of Despair!
How they clang, and clash, and roar!
What a horror they outpour
On the bosom of the palpitating air!
Yet the ear it fully knows,
By the twanging,
And the clanging,
How the danger ebbs and flows;
Yet the ear distinctly tells,
In the jangling,
And the wrangling,
How the danger sinks and swells,

By the sinking or the swelling in the anger of
  the bells—
            Of the bells—
        Of the bells, bells, bells, bells,
            Bells, bells, bells—
In the clamor and the clangor of the bells!

        Hear the tolling of the bells—
            Iron bells!
What a world of solemn thought their monody
  compels!
        In the silence of the night,
        How we shiver with affright
    At the melancholy menace of their tone!
        For every sound that floats
        From the rust within their throats
            Is a groan.
    And the people—ah, the people—
    They that dwell up in the steeple,
            All alone,
    And who tolling, tolling, tolling,
        In that muffled monotone,
    Feel a glory in so rolling
        On the human heart a stone—
    They are neither man nor woman—
    They are neither brute nor human—
            They are Ghouls:
    And their king it is who tolls;
    And he rolls, rolls, rolls,
            Rolls,
        A pæan from the bells!
    And his merry bosom swells
        With the pæan of the bells!
    And he dances, and he yells;
    Keeping time, time, time,
    In a sort of Runic rhyme,
        To the pæan of the bells—
            Of the bells:
    Keeping time, time, time,
    In a sort of Runic rhyme,

To the throbbing of the bells—
Of the bells, bells, **bells**—
To the sobbing **of the** bells ;
Keeping time, time, time,
As he knells, knells, knells,
In a happy Runic rhyme,
**To** the rolling of the bells—
**Of the bells**, bells, bells—
To the tolling **of** the bells,
Of the bells, bells, bells, bells—
Bells, bells, bells—

To the moaning and **the groaning of the** bells.

EDGAR A. POE.

---

## THE BIRTH OF IRELAND.

" With due condescension, I'd call your attention
    **to** what I shall mention of Erin so green,
And, without hesitation, I'll show how **that** nation
    became, of creation, the gem an**d the** queen.

" 'Twas early one morning, without any warning,
    that Vanus was born in the beautiful Say ;
And, by the same token, and sure 'twas provok-
    ing, her pinions were soaking, and wouldn't
    give **play**.

" Old **Neptune, who** knew her, began **to** pursue
    her, **in order** to woo her—the **wicked** old
    Jew—
And **almost** had caught her atop of the **water**—
    great Jupiter's daughter!—which never
    would do.

" But Jove, the great janius, looked down and
    saw Vanus and Neptune so heinous pursuing
    her wild,
And he spoke out in thunder he'd rend him
    asunder—and sure 'twas no wonder—for
**tazing his** child.

" A star that was flying hard by him espying. he
  caught with small trying and down let it
  snap ;
It fell quick as winking on Neptune a-sinking,
  and gave him, I'm thinking, a bit of a rap.

" *That star it was dryland, both lowland and
  highland, and formed a sweet island, the
  land of my birth :*
Thus plain is the story that, sent down from
  glory, old Erin *asthore* is the gem of the
  earth !

" Upon Erin nately jumped Vanus so stately,
  but fainted *kase* lately so hard she was
  pressed ;
Which much did bewilder. but, ere it had killed
  her, her father distilled her a drop of the
  best.

" That sup was victorious; it made her feel
  glorious—a little uproarious, I fear it might
  prove—
So how can ye blame us that Ireland's so famous
  for drinking and beauty, for fighting and
  love ?"

Anonymous.

---

### PETER'S RIDE TO THE WEDDING.

Peter would ride to the wedding—he would,
  So he mounted his ass—and his wife
She was to ride behind, if she could,
  " For," says Peter, " the woman, she should
  Follow, not lead through life."

" He's mighty convenient, the ass, my dear,
  And proper and safe—and now
You hold by the tail, while I hold by the ear,
And we'll ride to the kirk in time, never fear,
  If the wind and the weather allow."

The wind and the weather were not to **be**
   blamed,
  But the ass had adopted the whim
That two at a time was a load never framed
For the back of one ass, and he **seemed** quite
   ashamed
  **That two should** stick fast upon **him.**

" Come, Dobbin," says Peter, " I'm thinking
   we'll trot."
  " I'm thinking **we won't," says** the ass,
In language of conduct, and stuck to the spot
As if he had shown he would sooner be shot
  Than lift up a toe from the grass.

Says Peter, says he, " I'll whip him **a** little,"—
  " Try it, my **dear**," says she,—
But he might just as well have whipped a
   brass kettle ;
The ass was made of such obstinate mettle
  That never **a step moved** he.

**" I'll** prick **him,** my dear, with a needle," **said**
   she,
  " I'm thinking he'll alter his mind,"—
The ass felt the needle, and up went his heels ;
" I'm thinking," says she, " he's beginning to
   feel
  Some notion of moving—behind."

" Now lend me the needle and I'll prick his
   ear,
  And set t'other end, **too,** agoing."
The ass felt the needle, and upward he reared ;
But kicking and rearing was all, it appeared,
  He had any intention of doing.

Says Peter, says he, " We get on rather slow ;
  While one end is up t'other sticks to the
   **ground** ;

But I'm thinking a method to move him I
    know,
Let's prick head and tail together, and so
    Give the creature a start all around."

So said, so done ; all hands were at work,
    And the ass he did alter his mind,
For he started away with so sudden a jerk,
That in less than a trice he arrived at the kirk,
    But he left all his lading behind.

ANONYMOUS.

## LITTLE GOLDENHAIR.

Goldenhair climbed up on grandpapa's knee ;
Dear little Goldenhair, tired was she,
All the day busy as busy could be.

Up in the morning as soon as 'twas light,
Out with the birds and butterflies bright,
Skipping about till the coming of night.

Grandpapa toyed with the curls on her head.
" What has my darling been doing," he said,
" Since she arose with the sun from her bed ? "

" Pitty much," answered the sweet little one.
" I cannot tell so much things I have done,
Played with my dolly and feeded my bun.

" And then I jumped with my little jump-rope,
And I made out of some water and soap
Bootiful worlds, mamma's castles of hope.

" Then I have readed in my picture-book,
And Bella and I we went to look
For the smooth little stones by the side of the
    brook.

" And then I comed home and eated my tea,
And I climbed up on grandpapa's knee,
And I jes as tired as tired can be."

Lower and lower the little head pressed,
Until **it** had dropped upon grandpapa's breast;
**Dear** little Goldenhair, sweet **be** thy rest !

**We** are but children ; things that **we do**
**Are** as sports **of a** babe to the Infinite view,
**That marks all** our weakness, and pities it too.

God grant that when night overshadows our **way,**
And we shall be called to account for our day,
He shall find us as guileless as Goldenhair's lay.

And O, when aweary, may we be so blest,
And sink like the innocent child to our rest,
And feel ourselves clasped to the Infinite breast!

ANONYMOUS.

## MRS. LOFTY AND I.

Mrs. Lofty keeps a carriage,
    So do I ;
She has dapple grays to draw it ;
    None have I ;
She's no prouder with her coachman
    Than am I
**With my** blue-eyed laughing baby,
    Trundling by ;
**I hide his** face lest she should see
The cherub boy, and envy me.

**Her fine** husband has **white** fingers,
    Mine has not ;
He could give his bride a palace,—
    Mine a cot ;
Hers comes home beneath the starlight,
    Ne'er cares she ;
Mine comes in the purple twilight,
    Kisses me,
And prays that He who turns life's sands
Will hold His loved ones in His hands.

Mrs. Lofty has her jewels,
　　So have I;
She wears hers upon her bosom,—
　　Inside I;
She will leave hers at Death's portal,
　　By-and-by;
I shall bear my treasure with me
　　When I die;
For I have love, and she has gold;
She counts her wealth;—mine can't be told.

She has those who love her station,
　　None have I;
But I've one true heart beside me—
　　Glad am I;
I'd not change it for a kingdom,
　　No, not I;
God will weigh it in his balance,
　　By-and-by;
And the difference define
'Twixt Mrs. Lofty's wealth and mine.

ANONYMOUS.

## LITTLE AND GREAT.

A little spring had lost its way
　Amid the grass and fern;
A passing stranger scooped a well,
　Where weary men might turn.

He walled it in and hung with care
　A ladle at the brink:
He thought not of the deed he did,
　But judged that toil might drink.

He passed again—and lo! the well,
　By summers never dried,
Had cooled ten thousand parching tongues,
　And saved a life beside.

ANONYMOUS.

## THE HUNTERS.

In the bright October morning
  Savoy's Duke had left his bride;
From the Castle, past the drawbridge,
  Flowed the hunters' merry tide.

Steeds are neighing, gallants glittering.
  Gay, her smiling lord to greet,
From her mullioned chamber casement
  Smiles the Duchess Marguerite.

From Vienna by the Danube
  Here she came, a bride, in spring.
Now the autumn crisps the forest;
  Hunters gather, bugles ring.

Hark! the game's on foot, they scatter:
  Down the forest riding lone,
Furious, single horsemen gallop.
  Hark! a shout—a crash—a groan!

Pale and breathless, came the hunters;
  On the turf, dead lies the boar,
But the Duke lies stretched beside him,
  Senseless, weltering in his gore.

In the dull October evening,
  Down the leaf-strewn forest road,
To the Castle, past the drawbridge,
  Came the hunters with their load.

In the hall, with sconces blazing,
  Ladies waiting round her seat,
Clothed in smiles, beneath the dais
  Sat the Duchess Marguerite.

Hark! below the gates unbarring!
  Tramp of men and quick commands!—
" 'Tis my lord come back from hunting."
  And the Duchess claps her hands.

Slow and tired came the hunters ;
  Stopped in darkness in the court.—
" Ho, this way, ye laggard hunters !
  To the hall ! What sport, what sport ? "

Slow they entered with their Master ;
  In the hall they laid him down.
On his coat were leaves and blood-stains,
  On his brow an angry frown.

Dead her princely youthful husband,
  Lay before his youthful wife ;
Bloody 'neath the flaring sconces :
  And the sight froze all her life.

In Vienna by the Danube
  Kings hold revel, gallants meet.
Gay of old amid the gayest
  Was the Duchess Marguerite.

In Vienna by the Danube
  Feast and dance her youth beguiled.
Till that hour she never sorrowed ;
  But from then she never smiled.
MATTHEW ARNOLD.

## BETTER THINGS.

Better to smell the violet cool, than sip the glowing wine ;
Better to hark a hidden brook, than watch a diamond shine.

Better the love of a gentle heart, than beauty's
  favor proud ;
Better the rose's living seed, than roses in a
  crowd.

Better to love in loneliness, than to bask in love
  all day ;
Better the fountain in the heart, than the fountain by the way.

Better be fed by a mother's hand, than eat alone
    at will ;
Better **to** trust in God, than say : "My goods
    my storehouse fill."
Better to be **a little** wise, **than in knowledge to**
    abound ;
Better to teach a **child**, than toil to **fill** perfec-
    tion's round.

Better to sit **at** a master's feet, than thrill a list-
    ening State ;
Better suspect that thou art proud, than be sure
    that thou art great.
Better to walk the real unseen, than watch the
    hour's event ;
Better **the** " Well done ! " at the last, **than the**
    air **with** shouting rent.

Better to have **a quiet** grief, than a hurrying de-
    light ;
Better the twilight of the dawn, than the **noon-**
    day burn**ing** bright.

**Better** a death when work is done, than **earth's**
    most favored **birth** ;
Better a child in God's great house, than the king
    of all **the** earth.

GEORGE MacDONALD.

---

## AN **ELEGY ON** THE DEATH **OF A MAD** DOG.

    Good people all **of** every sort,
      Give ear unto my song ;
    And if you find it wondrous short,
      It cannot hold you long.

    In Islington there lived a man,
      **Of** whom the world might say,
    That still **a** goodly race he ran
      Whene'er he went to pray.

A kind and gentle heart had he,
  To comfort friends and foes;
The naked every day he clad
  When he put on his clothes.

And in that **town a dog was found,**
  As many dogs there be,
**Both** mongrel, puppy, whelp, and hound,
  And **curs of** low degree.

This dog **and man at first were friends;**
  But when a pique began,
The **dog to gain** his private ends,
  **Went mad, and** bit **the** man.

Around **from all** the neighboring streets
  The wondering neighbors ran,
And swore the dog had lost his wits,
  **To** bite so good a man.

The wound it seemed both sore and sad
  To every Christian eye;
And while **they sw**ore the dog was mad,
  They swore the **man** would **die.**

But soon a wonder came to light,
  That showed the rogues **they** lied:
The man recovered of the **bite,**
  The dog it was that died.
OLIVER GOLDSMITH.

---

## OLD TUBAL CAIN.

Old **Tu**bal Cain was a man o**f might**
  In the days when the earth was young;
By the fierce red light of his furnace bright
  **The strokes of** his hammer rung;
And he lifted high his brawny hand
  On the iron glowing clear,
Till the sparks rushed out in scarlet showers
  As he fashioned the sword and **spear:**

And he sang, " Hurrah for my handiwork !
   Hurrah for the spear and sword !
Hurrah for the hand that wields them well,
   For he shall be king and lord !"

To Tubal Cain came many a one,
   As he wrought by his roaring fire ;
And each one prayed for a strong steel blade,
   As the crown of his heart's desire.
And he made them weapons sharp and strong,
   Till they shouted loud for glee,
And gave him gifts of pearl and gold,
   And spoils of the forest-tree ;
And they sang, " Hurrah for Tubal Cain,
   Who has given us strength anew !
Hurrah for the smith, and hurrah for the
    fire,
   And hurrah for the metal true !"

But a sudden change came o'er his heart
   Ere the setting of the sun :
And Tubal Cain was filled with pain
   For the evil he had done.
He saw that men, with rage and hate,
   Made war upon their kind—
That the land was fed with the blood they
    shed,
   And their lust for carnage blind ;
And he said, " Alas ! that ever I made,
   Or that skill of mine should plan,
The spear and sword for man, whose joy
   Is to slay his fellow-man."

And for many a day old Tubal Cain
   Sat brooding o'er his woe ;
And his hand forebore to smite the ore,
   And his furnace smouldered low ;
But he rose at last with a cheerful face,
   And a bright courageous eye,
And he bared his strong arm for the work,

While the quick flames mounted high;
And he said, " Hurrah for my handiwork!"
   And the fire-sparks lit the air;
" Not alone for the blade was the bright
     steel made!"
   And he fashioned the first ploughshare!

And men, taught wisdom from the past,
   In friendship joined their hands;
Hung the sword in the hall, and the spear
     on the wall,
   And ploughed the willing lands;
And sang, " Hurrah for Tubal Cain!
   Our staunch good friend is he;
And for the ploughshare and the plough
   To him our prize shall be!
But when oppression lifts its hand,
   Or a tyrant would be lord,
Though we may thank him for the plough,
   We'll not forget the sword!"

CHARLES MACKAY.

### ARNOLD WINKELRIED.

In the battle of Sempach, in the fourteenth century, this
martyr-patriot, perceiving that there was no other means
of breaking the heavy-armed lines of the Austrians than
by gathering as many of the spears as he could grasp together, opened, by this means, a passage for his fellow-
combatants, who, with hammers and hatchets, hewed
down the mailed men-at-arms, and won the victory.

" Make way for liberty!" he cried—
Made way for liberty, and died!

In arms the Austrian phalanx stood,
A living wall, a human wood;
Impregnable their front appears,
All horrent with projected spears.
Opposed to these, a hovering band
Contended for their fatherland,

Peasants, whose new-found strength **had**
   broke
From manly necks the ignoble yoke;
Marshalled once more at Freedom's call,
They came to conquer or **to fall.**

And **now the** work of life and death
Hung **on the** passing of a breath;
The fire **of** conflict burned within;
The battle trembled **to** begin;
**Yet,** while the **Austrians** held their ground,
**Point for assault was nowhere** found;
Where'er the impatient Switzers gazed,
The **unbro**ken line of **lances** blazed;
That line 'twere suicide to meet,
**A**nd perish at their tyrants' feet.
How could they **rest** within **their** graves,
To leave their homes the haunts of slaves?
Would they not **feel their child**ren tread,
With clanking chains, above their head?

It must not be; this day, this hour,
**A**nnihilates the invader's power!
**All** Switzerland is in the field—
**She** will not fly; she cannot yield;
**She** must not fall; her better fate
Here gives her an immortal date.
**Few** were **the** numbers she could boast,
But every freeman was a host,
And felt as 'twere a secret known
That **one** should turn the scale alone,
**Whi!e** each unto himself **was** he
**On** whose sole arm hung victory.

**It** did depend **on** one, indeed;
Behold him—Arnold Winkelried!
There sounds not to **the** trump of Fame
The echo **of** a nobler name.
**Unmarked,** he stood amid the throng,
**In** rumination deep and long,

Till you might see, with sudden grace,
The very thought come o'er his face;
And, by the motion of his form,
Anticipate the bursting storm;
And, by the uplifting of his brow,
Tell where the bolt would strike, and how.

But 'twas no sooner thought than done—
The field was in a moment won!
"Make way for liberty!" he cried,
Then ran, with arms extended wide,
As if his dearest friend to clasp;
Ten spears he swept within his grasp.
"Make way for liberty!" he cried;
Their keen points crossed from side to side;
He bowed among them, like a tree,
And thus made way for liberty.

Swift to the breach his comrades fly—
"Make way for liberty!" they cry,
And through the Austrian phalanx dart,
As rushed the spears through Arnold's heart,
While, instantaneous as his fall,
Rout, ruin, panic seized them all.
An earthquake could not overthrow
A city with a surer blow.

Thus Switzerland again was free—
Thus death made way for liberty!

JAMES MONTGOMERY.

## CHARGE OF THE LIGHT BRIGADE AT BALAKLAVA.

Half a league, half a league,
 Half a league onward,
All in the valley of Death
 Rode the six hundred.
"Forward, the Light Brigade!"
"Charge for the guns!" he said:
Into the valley of Death
 Rode the six hundred.

" Forward, **the** Light Brigade ! "
Was there a man dismayed ?
Not though the soldier knew
  Some one had blundered :
Theirs not to make reply,
Theirs not to reason why,
**Theirs but** to do and die,
**Into the** valley of Death
  Rode the six hundred.

Cannon to right **of** them,
Cannon to left **of** them,
Cannon in front **of them,**
  Volleyed and thundered ;
Stormed at with shot and shell,
Boldly they rode and well,
Into the jaws of Death,
Into the mouth of Hell
  Rode the **six** hundred :

Flashed all **their sabres bare,**
Flashed as they **turned in air,**
Sabring the gunners there,
Charging an army, while
  All the world wondered :
Plunged in the battery-smoke,
Right through the line they broke ;
  Cossack and Russian
Reeled from the sabre-stroke
  Shattered and sundered.
Then they rode back, but not—
  **N**ot the six hundred.

Cannon to **right** of them,
Cannon to **left** of them,
Cannon behind them
  Volleyed and thundered ;
Stormed at with shot and shell,
**While** horse and hero fell,
**They** that had fought so well

Came through the jaws of Death
Back from the mouth of Hell,
All that was left of them,
    Left of six hundred.

When can their glory fade!
  O, the wild charge they made!
    All the world wondered.
Honor the charge they made!
Honor the Light Brigade,
    Noble six hundred!

ALFRED TENNYSON.

## BEAUTIFUL SNOW.

Oh! the snow, the beautiful snow,
Filling the sky and the earth below;
Over the house-tops, over the street,
Over the heads of the people you meet;
        Dancing,
            Flirting,
                Skimming along.
Beautiful snow! it can do nothing wrong.
Flying to kiss a fair lady's cheek;
Clinging to lips in a frolicsome freak.
Beautiful snow, from the heavens above
Pure as an agel and fickle as love!

Oh! the snow, the beautiful snow!
How the flakes gather and laugh as they go!
Whirling about in its maddening fun,
It plays in its glee with every one.
        Chasing,
            Laughing,
                Hurrying by
It lights up the face and it sparkles the eye;
And even the dogs, with a bark and a bound,
Snap at the crystals that eddy around.
The town is alive, and its heart in a glow.
To welcome the coming of beautiful snow.

How the wild crowd goes swaying along,
Hailing each other with **humor and song**!
How the gay sledges like meteors flash by—
Bright for a moment, then lost to the eye,
    Ringing,
        Swinging,
            Dashing they go
Over the crest of the beautiful snow :
Snow so pure when it falls from the sky,
To be trampled in mud by the crowd rush-
    ing by :
To be trampled **and** tracked by the thou-
    sands of feet
Till it blends with the filth in the horrible
**street.**

Once I was pure as the snow—but **I** fell :
Fell, like the snow-flakes, from heaven—to
    hell :
Fell, to be tramped as the filth of the street :
Fell, to be scoffed, to be spit on, and beat.
    Pleading,
        Cursing,
            Dreading to die,
Selling **my soul** to whoever would buy,
Dealing in shame **for a morsel** of bread,
**Hating the living** and fearing the dead.
**Merciful God !** have I fallen **so low ?**
And **yet I** was once like this beautiful snow !

Once I was fair as the beautiful snow,
With an eye like its crystals, a heart like its
    glow :
Once I was loved for my innocent grace—
Flattered and sought for the charm of my
    face.
    Father,
        Mother,
            Sisters all,
God, and myself, I have lost by my fall.

The veriest wretch that **goes** shivering by
Will take **a** wide sweep, lest I wander too
    nigh ;
For all that is on or about me, I know
There **is** nothing **that's** pure but the beauti-
    ful snow.

How strange it should be that this beautifu.
    snow
Should fall on a sinner with nowhere **to go** !
How strange it would be, when the night
    comes again,
**If the snow and** the ice struck my desperate
    **brain** !
        **Fainting,**
            Freezing,
                Dying alone !
**Too** wicked for prayer, too weak for **my**
    moan
To be heard in the crash of the crazy town,
Gone mad in their **joy** at the **snow's** coming
    down ;
To lie and to die in my **terrible** woe,
With a bed and **a** shroud **of the** beautiful
    snow !

John **W. Watson**.

---

## BINGEN **ON** THE RHINE.

**A** soldier **of** the Legion lay dying in Algiers,
There was lack of woman's nursing, there was
    dearth of woman's tears ;
But a comrade stood beside him, while his life-
    blood ebbed away,
And bent, with pitying glances, to hear what he
    might say.
The dying soldier faltered, as he took that com-
    rade's hand,
And he said, " I never more shall **see my own,**
    my native land :

Take a message, and a token, to some distant
    friends of mine,
For I was born at Bingen—at Bingen on the
    Rhine !

" Tell my brothers and companions, when they
    meet and crowd around
To hear my mournful story in the pleasant vine-
    yard ground,
That we fought the battle bravely, and when the
    day was done,
Full many a corpse lay ghastly pale, beneath the
    setting sun.
And midst the dead and dying were some grown
    old in wars,
The death-wound on their gallant breasts, the
    last of many scars :
But some were young—and suddenly beheld
    life's morn decline ;
And one had come from Bingen—fair Bingen on
    the Rhine !

" Tell my mother that her other sons shall com-
    fort her old age,
And I was aye a truant bird, that thought his
    home a cage :
For my father was a soldier, and even as a child
My heart leaped forth to hear him tell of strug-
    gles fierce and wild :
And when he died and left us to divide his
    scanty hoard,
I let them take whate'er they would, but kept
    my father's sword ;
And with boyish love I hung it where the bright
    light used to shine,
On the cottage-wall at Bingen—calm Bingen on
    the Rhine !

" Tell my sister not to weep for me, and sob with
    drooping head,

When the troops are marching home again, with
    glad and gallant tread;
But to look upon them proudly, with a calm and
    steadfast eye,
For her brother was a soldier too, and not afraid
    to die.
And if a comrade seek her love, I ask her in my
    name
To listen to him kindly, without regret or shame;
And to hang the old sword in its place (my
    father's sword and mine)
For the honor of old Bingen—dear Bingen on
    the Rhine!

"There's another—not a sister: in the happy
    days gone by,
You'd have known her by the merriment that
    sparkled in her eye;
Too innocent for coquetry—too fond for idle
    scorning—
Oh! friend, I fear the lightest heart makes
    sometimes heaviest mourning;
Tell her the last night of my life (for ere the
    moon be risen
My body will be out of pain—my soul be out of
    prison).
I dreamed I stood with her, and saw the yellow
    sunlight shine
On the vine-clad hills of Bingen—fair Bingen on
    the Rhine!

"I saw the blue Rhine sweep along—I heard, or
    seemed to hear,
The German songs we used to sing, in chorus
    sweet and clear;
And down the pleasant river, and up the slant-
    ing hill,
The echoing chorus sounded, through the even-
    ing calm and still;

And her glad blue eyes were on me as we passed
    with friendly talk
Down many a path beloved of yore, and well-
    remembered walk.
And her little hand lay lightly, confidingly **in**
    mine :
**But** we'll meet no more at Bingen—loved Bing-
    en on the Rhine!"

His voice grow faint and hoarser—his grasp **was**
    **childish** weak—
His eyes put on a dying look—he sigh'd and
    ceased to speak :
**His** comrade bent to lift him, **but** the spark of
    life had fled—
The soldier of the Leigon, in a foreign land—
    was dead !
And the soft moon rose up slowly, and calmly
    she looked down
On the red sand of the battle-field, with bloody
    corpses stro**wn** ;
**Yea,** calmly on that dreadful scene her pale light
    seemed to shine,
**As it** shone on distant Bingen—fair Bingen on
    the Rhine !

Mrs. Caroline Norton.

---

## THE BOBOLINK.

Once **on** a golden afternoon,
With radiant faces and hearts in tune,
Two fond lovers, in dreaming mood,
Threaded a rural solitude.
Wholly happy, they only knew
That the earth was bright and the sky was blue,
**That** light and beauty and joy and song
Charmed the way as they passed along :
The air was fragrant with woodland scents ;
**The** squirrel frisked on the roadside fence ;
**And hovering near** them, " Chee, chee, chink ?"
Queried the **curious bobo**link,

Pausing and peering with sidelong head,
As saucily questioning all they said ;
While the ox-eye danced on its slender stem,
And all glad nature rejoiced with them.
Over the odorous fields were strewn
Wilting windrows of grass new mown,
And rosy billows of clover bloom
Surged in the sunshine and breathed perfume.
Swinging low on a slender limb,
The sparrow warbled his wedding hymn,
And balancing on a blackberry briar
The bobolink sang with his heart on fire,—
" Chink ?   If you wish to kiss her, do !
Do it, do it !   You coward, you !
Kiss her ! kiss, kiss her !   Who will see?
Only we three ! we three ! we three !"

Tender garlands of drooping vines,
Through dim vistas of sweet-breathed pines,
Past wide meadow-fields, lately mowed,
Wandered the indolent country road.
The lovers followed it, listening still,
And loitering slowly, as lovers will,
Entered a gray-roofed bridge that lay
Dusk and cool, in their pleasant way.

Fluttering lightly from brink to brink,
Followed the garrulous bobolink,
Rallying loudly with mirthful din
The pair who lingered unseen within.
And when from the friendly bridge at last
Into the road beyond they passed,
Again beside them the tempter went,
Keeping the thread of his argument,—
" Kiss her ! kiss her !   Chink-a-chee-chee !
I'll not mention it !   Don't mind me !"
But ah ! they noted—nor deemed it strange—
In his rollicking chorus a trifling change,—
" Do it ! do it !"—with might and main
Warbled the tell-tale—" Do it again !"

ANONYMOUS.

## THROUGH DEATH TO LIFE.

Have you heard the tale of the Aloe plant,
   Away in the sunny clime?
By humble growth of a hundred years
   It reaches its blooming time;
And then a wondrous bud at its crown
   Breaks into a thousand flowers;
This floral queen, in its blooming seen,
   Is the pride of the tropical bowers.
But the plant to the flower is a sacrifice,
For it blooms but once, and in blooming dies.

Have you further heard of this Aloe plant
   That grows in the sunny clime,
How every one of its thousand flowers,
   As they drop in the blooming time,
Is an infant plant that fastens its roots
   In the place where it falls on the ground;
And, fast as they drop from the dying stem,
   Grow lively and lovely around?
By dying it liveth a thousandfold
In the young that spring from the death of the
    old.

Have you heard the tale of the Pelican,
   The Arab's Gimel el Bahr,
That lives in the African solitudes,
   Where the birds that live lonely are?
Have you heard how it loves its tender young,
   And cares and toils for their good?
It brings them water from fountains afar,
   And fishes the seas for their food.
In famine it feeds them—what love can de-
    vise!—
The blood of its bosom, and feeding them dies.

Have you heard the tale they tell of the Swan,
   The snow-white bird of the lake?
It noiselessly floats on the silvery wave,
   It silently sits in the brake;

For **it saves** its song till the end of life,
   And then, in the soft **still** even,
'Mid the golden light of **the** setting sun,
   It sings as **it** soars into heaven!
And the blessed notes **fall** back from the skies;
'Tis **its** only song, for **in** singing it dies.

You have heard these tales; shall I tell you
   one
   A greater and better than all?
Have you heard **of Him whom the** heavens
   adore,
   Before whom **the** hosts of **them fall?**
**How** He left **the** choirs and anthems above,
   For earth in **its** wailings **and** woes,
To suffer the shame and pain of the cross,
   And die for the life of his foes?
O prince of the noble! O sufferer **divine!**
What sorrow and sacrifice equal to Thine!
HENRY HARBAUGH.

---

### AFTER THE BATTLE.

The drums are all muffled, the bugles are still;
**There's a pause** in the valley, a halt on the hill;
**And** bearers of standards swerve back with a
   thrill
   Where sheaves of the dead bar the way;
**For** a great field is reaped, Heaven's garners to
   fill,
   And stern Death holds his harvest to-day.

There's a voice in **the** wind like a spirit's low
   cry;
'Tis the muster-roll sounding—and who shall
   reply
**For** those whose wan faces glare white to the
   sky,
   **With** eyes **fixed** so steadfast and dimly,

As they wait the last trump, which they may not
        defy !
    Whose hands **clutch** the sword-hilt so grimly.

The brave heads late lifted are solemnly  bowed,
As the riderless chargers stand quivering and
        **cowed—**
**As the burial** requiem is chanted aloud,
    **T**he groans of the death-stricken drowning**,**
While Victory looks **on** like a queen pal**e** and
        proud
    Who waits till the morn**ing her** crowning.

There is no mocking blazon, as clay sinks to clay;
The vain pomps of peace-time are all **s**wept away
In the terrible face of the dread battle-day ;
    Nor coffins nor shroudings are  here ;
Only relics that lay where thickest the fray—
    A rent casque and a headless spear.

Far away, **tramp on tramp,** sounds the march **of**
        **the foe,**
**Like** a storm-wave retreating, spent, fitful **and**
        slow ;
With sound like their spirits that faint as they
    .     go
    By the red-glowing river, whose waters
Shall darken with sorrow the land where they
        flow
    To the eyes of her desolate daughters.

They are fled—they are gone ; but oh ! not as
        they came ;
In the pride of those numbers they staked on the
        game,
Never more shall they stand in the vanguard  of
        fame,
    Never lift the stained sword which they drew ;
Never more shall they boast of a glorious name,
    **Never march with the** leal and the true.

Where the wreck of our legions lay stranded and
     torn,
They stole on our ranks in the mist of the morn ;
Like the giant of Gaza, their strength it was
     shorn
  Ere those mists have rolled up to the sky ;
From the flash of the steel a new day-break
     seemed born,
  As we sprang up to conquer or die.

The tumult is silenced ; the death-lots are cast,
And the heroes of battle are slumbering their
     last :
Do you dream of yon pale form that rode on the
     blast ?
  Would ye see it once more, oh ye brave !
Yes—the broad road to honor is red where ye
     passed,
  And of glory ye asked—but a grave !

ANONYMOUS.

---

## CATO'S SOLILOQUY ON IMMORTALITY.

It must be so.—Plato, thou reasonest well ;
Else whence this pleasing hope, this fond desire,
This longing after immortality ?
Or whence this secret dread, and inward horror,
Of falling into nought ?  Why shrinks the soul
Back on herself, and startles at destruction ?
'Tis the divinity that stirs within us,
'Tis Heaven itself, that points out an hereafter,
And intimates eternity to man.

Eternity !—thou pleasing, dreadful thought !
Through what variety of untried being,
Through what new scenes and changes must we
     pass ?
The wide, the unbounded prospect lies before
    me !
But shadows, clouds, and darkness rest upon it.

Here will I hold.   If there's a Power above us—
And that there is, **all** Nature cries aloud
Through all her works—He must delight in  vir-
      tue ;
**And** that which he delights in must **be happy.**
**But when** ? or where ?  This world was made for
      Cæsar.
I'm weary of conjectures—this must end 'em.

    Thus am **I** doubly armed.   My death and life,
My bane and antidote, are both before me.
This* in a moment brings me to my end ;
But this† informs **me** I shall never die.
The soul, secure in her existence, **smiles**
At the drawn dagger, and defies **its** point.
The stars shall fade away, the sun himself
Grow dim with age, and Nature sink in years,
But thou shalt flourish in immortal youth,
Unhurt amid the war of elements,
The wreck of matter, and the crush of worlds.
JOSEPH ADDISON.

## ANNIE AND WILLIE'S PRAYER.

'Twas the **eve** before Christmas ; " Good **night,**"
      had been said,
And  Annie **and** Willie had crept into bed ;
There were tears on their  pillows, and  tears  in
      **their eyes,**
And each little bosom was heaving **with** sighs,
For to-night  their  stern  father's command had
      been given
That they should retire precisely at seven
Instead of at eight ; for they troubled him more
With questions unheard of than ever **before** ;
He had told them he thought this delusion a sin,
No such being as " Santa Claus " ever had been,
And he hoped after this he  should  never  more
      hear,

---

*The dagger.            †Plato's Treatise.

How he scrambled down **chimneys** with pres-
    ents, **each** year.
And this **was** the reason that two little heads
So restlessly tossed on their soft downy beds.
Eight, nine, **and** the clock **on** the steeple tolled
    ten—
Not **a word** had been spoken by either till then;
When **Willie's** sad face from the blanket did
    peep,
And whispered, "Dear Annie, is **you fast**
    asleep?"
"**Why,** no, brother Willie," a sweet voice re-
    plies,
"I've tried **it** in vain, but I can't shut my eyes;
For somehow, it makes me so sorry because
Dear papa has said there is no 'Santa Claus';
Now we know there is, and it can't be denied,
For he came every year before mamma died;
But then, I've been thinking that she used to
    pray,
And God would hear everything mamma would
    say,
And perhaps she asked him to send Santa Claus
    here
With the **sacks full** of presents he brought every
    year."
" Well, why tant we pay dest as mamma did
    then,—
And ask Him to send him with presents aden?"
" I've been thinking so, too," and, without a
    word more
Four **little bare** feet bounded out on the floor,
And four little knees the soft carpet pressed,
And two tiny hands were clasped close to each
    breast.
"Now, Willie, you know we must firmly believe
That the presents we **ask** for we're sure to re-
    ceive;
You must **wait** just as still till I say the '**Amen**,'

And by that you will know that your turn has
    come then.
Dear Jesus, look down on my brother and me,
And grant us the favor we are asking of Thee,
I want a wax dolly, a tea-set and ring,
And an ebony work-box that shuts with a spring:
Bless papa—dear Jesus, and cause him to see
That Santa Claus loves us far better than he;
Don't let him get fretful and angry again,
At dear brother Willie, and Annie.   Amen!"
" Peas Desus, 'et Santa Taus tum down to-night,
And bing us some pesents before it is 'ight;
I want he should div me a nice 'ittle sed,
With bight, shiny 'unners, and all painted yed;
A box full of tandy, a book and a toy,
Amen,—and then, Desus, I'll be a dood boy."

Their prayers being ended, they raised up their
    heads,
And with hearts light and cheerful again sought
    their beds;
And were soon lost in slumber both peaceful
    and deep,
And with fairies in dreamland were roaming in
    sleep.

Eight, nine, and the little French clock had
    struck ten,
Ere the father had thought of his children again;
He seems now to hear Annie's half-suppressed
    sighs,
And to see the big tears stand in Willie's blue
    eyes;
" I was harsh with my darlings," he mentally
    said,
" And should not have sent them so early to bed;
But then I was troubled—my feelings found
    vent,
For bank-stock to-day has gone down ten per
    cent.

But of course they've forgotten their troubles ere
    this,
And that I denied them the thrice-asked-for
    kiss;
But just to make sure I'll steal up to their door,
For I never spoke harsh to my darlings before."
So saying, he softly ascended the stairs
And arrived at the door to hear both of their
    prayers.
His Annie's "bless papa" draws forth the big
    tears,
And Willie's grave promise falls sweet on his
    ears.
"Strange, strange I'd forgotten," said he with a
    sigh,
"How I longed when a child to have Christmas
    draw nigh.
I'll atone for my harshness," he inwardly said,
" By answering their prayers, ere I sleep in my
    bed."

Then he turned to the stairs, and softly went
    down,
Threw off velvet slippers and silk dressing-gown;
Donned hat, coat, and boots, and was out in the
    street,
A millionaire facing the cold, driving sleet;
Nor stopped he until he had bought everything,
From the box full of candy to the tiny gold ring.
Indeed, he kept adding so much to his store,
That the various presents outnumbered a score;
Then homeward he turned with his holiday load,
And with Aunt Mary's aid in the nursery 'twas
    stowed.
Miss Dolly was seated beneath a pine-tree,
By the side of a table spread out for a tea;
A work-box well filled in the center was laid,
And on it the ring for which Annie had prayed;
A soldier in uniform stood by a sled

With bright, shining runners, and all painted
    red ;
There were balls, dogs, and horses, books pleas-
    ing to see,
And birds of all colors were perched in the tree,
While Santa Claus laughing stood up in the top,
As if getting ready more presents to drop.
And as the fond father the picture surveyed,
He thought, for his trouble he had amply been
    paid ;
And he said to himself as he brushed off a tear,
" I'm happier to-night than I've been for a year,
I've enjoyed more true pleasure than ever be-
    fore—
What care I if bank-stocks fall ten per cent.
    more ?
Hereafter I'll make it a rule, I believe,
To have Santa Claus visit us each Christmas
    eve."
So thinking he gently extinguished the light,
And tripped down the stairs to retire for the
    night.

As soon as the beams of the bright morning sun
Put the darkness to flight, and the stars, one by
    one ;
Four little blue eyes out of sleep opened wide,
And at the same moment the presents espied ;
Then out of their beds they sprang with a bound,
And the very gifts prayed for were all of them
    found ;
They laughed and they cried in their innocent
    glee,
And shouted for " papa " to come quick and see
What presents old Santa Claus brought in the
    night,
(Just the things that they wanted) and left before
    light ;
" And now," added Annie, in a voice soft and
    low,

"You'll believe there's a Santa Claus, papa, I
      know ";
While dear little Willie climbed up on his knee,
Determined no secret between them should be,
And told in soft whispers how Annie had said,
That their blessed mamma so long ago dead,
Used to kneel down and pray by the side of her
      chair,
And that God, up in Heaven, had answered her
      prayer !
" Then we dot up, and payed dust as well as we
      tould,
And Dod answered our payers ; now wasn't he
      dood ? "
"I should say that he was if he sent you all these,
And knew just what presents my children would
      please.—
Well, well. let him think so, the dear little elf,
'Twould be cruel to tell him I did it myself."

Blind father ! who caused your proud heart to
      relent,
And the hasty word spoken so soon to repent ?
'Twas the Being who made you steal softly up-
      stairs,
And made you his agent to answer their prayers.
                              SOPHIA P. SNOW.

_______

### SHERIDAN'S RIDE.

Up from the south, at break of day,
Bringing to Winchester fresh dismay,
The affrighted air with a shudder bore,
Like a herald in haste to the chieftain's door,
The terrible grumble, and rumble. and roar,
Telling the battle was on once more,
    And Sheridan twenty miles away.

And wider still those billows of war
Thundered along the horizon's bar ;
And louder yet into Winchester rolled

The roar of that red sea uncontrolled,
Making the blood of the listener cold,
As he thought of the stake in that fiery fray,
  **And** Sheridan twenty miles awa**y.**

But there is a road from Winchest**er town,**
A good, **broad** highway leading down;
**And there,** through the flush of the morning
    **light,**
A **steed as black** as the steeds of night
Was **seen** to pass, as **with** eagle flight,
As if he knew the terrible need;
He stretched away with his utmost speed;
**H**ills rose and fell; but **his** heart was gay,
  With Sheridan fifteen miles away.

Still **sprang** from those swift hoofs, **thundering**
    south,
The dust, like smoke from the cannon's mouth;
Or **the trail of a** comet, sweeping faster and
    faster,
Foreboding to traitors the doom of disaster.
The heart of the steed and the heart of the mas-
    **ter**
**W**ere beating **like** prisoners assaulting their
    walls,
Impatient to be where the battle-field calls;
**E**very **nerve of the** charger **was st**rained to full
    play,
  W**ith** Sheridan only ten miles **away.**

**U**nder **his** spurning feet, **the** road
Like an arrowy Alpine riv**er** flowed,
**A**nd the landscape sped away behind
Like an ocean **fl**ying before the wind;
And the steed, like a bark **fed** with furnace ire,
Swept on, with his wild eye full of fire.
**B**ut, lo! he is nearing his heart's desire;
**H**e is snuffing the smoke of the roaring **fray,**
  **With** Sheridan only five miles away.

The first that the General saw were the groups
Of stragglers, and then the retreating troops;
What was done? what to do? a glance told him
　　both.
Then striking his spurs with a terrible oath,
He dashed down the line 'mid a storm of huzzas,
And the wave of retreat checked its course there,
　　because
The sight of the master compelled it to pause.
With foam and with dust the black charger was
　　gray;
By the flash of his eye, and the red nostril's play
He seemed to the whole great army to say,
" I have brought you Sheridan all the way
From Winchester down, to save the day."

Hurrah! hurrah for Sheridan!
Hurrah! hurrah for horse and man!
And when their statues are placed on high,
Under the dome of the Union sky,
The American soldier's Temple of Fame,
There with the glorious General's name
Be it said, in letters both bold and bright:
　" Here is the steed that saved the day
By carrying Sheridan into the fight,
　From Winchester—twenty miles away!"
　　　　　　　　　T. BUCHANAN READ.

## BRIDGE OF SIGHS.

*Drowned, drowned.—Hamlet.*

One more Unfortunate,
　Weary of breath,
Rashly importunate,
　Gone to her death!

Take her up tenderly,
　Lift her with care,—
Fashioned so slenderly,
　Young and so fair!

Look at her garments
Clinging like cerements;
  Whilst the wave constantly
Drips from her clothing;
  Take her up instantly,
Loving, not loathing.—

Touch her not scornfully;
Think of her mournfully,
  Gently and humanly;
Not of the stains of her,
All that remains of her
  Now is pure womanly.

Make no deep scrutiny
Into her mutiny
  Rash and undutiful:
Past all dishonor,
  Death has left on her
Only the beautiful.

Still, for all slips of hers,
  One of Eve's family—
Wipe those poor lips of hers,
  Oozing so clammily.
Loop up her tresses
  Escaped from the comb,
Her fair auburn tresses;
Whilst wonderment guesses
  Where was her home?

Who was her father?
Who was her mother?
Had she a sister?
Had she a brother?
  Or was there a dearer one
  Still, and a nearer one
Yet, than all other?

Alas! for the rarity
  Of Christian charity
Under the sun!

Oh! it was pitiful!
  Near a whole city full,
**Home** she had none.

Sisterly, brotherly,
Fatherly, motherly
  Feelings had changed:
**Love**, by harsh evidence,
**Thrown** from its eminence;
Even God's providence
  Seeming estranged.

Where the lamps **quiver**
So far in the river,
**With** many **a light**
  From window and casement,
  From garret to basement,
  She stood, with amazement,
**Houseless** by night.

The bleak winds of March
  Made her tremble and shiver:
But not the dark arch,
  Or **the** black flowing river;
Mad from life's history,
Glad to death's mystery,
  Swift to be hurled—
Anywh**ere, any**where
  Out **of the world!**

**In** she plunged boldly,
**No** matter how coldly
  The rough river ran,—
Over **the** brink of it,
Picture it—think of it,
  Dissolute man!
**La**ve in it, drink of it
  Then, if **you** can!

Take her up tenderly,
  Lift her with care;
Fashioned **so** slenderly,

Young, and so fair!
Ere her limbs frigidly
Stiffen too rigidly,
Decently,—kindly,—
Smooth and compose them;
And her eyes, close them,
Staring so blindly!

Dreadfully staring
Through muddy impurity,
As when with the daring
Last look of despairing
Fixed on futurity.

Perishing gloomily,
Spurred by contumely,
Cold inhumanity,
Burning insanity,
Into her rest.—
Cross her hands humbly,
As if praying dumbly,
Over her breast!

Owning her weakness,
Her evil behavior,
And leaving, with meekness,
Her sins to her Saviour!

THOMAS HOOD.

## BUGLE SONG.

The splendor falls on castle walls
And snowy summits old in story;
The long light shakes across the lakes,
And the wild cataract leaps in glory.
Blow, bugle, blow, set the wild echoes flying:
Blow, bugle; answer, echoes, dying, dying, dying.

O hark, O hear! how thin and clear,
And thinner, clearer, further going;
O sweet and far, from cliff and scar,

The horns of Elfland faintly blowing!
Blow, let us hear the purple glens replying:
Blow, bugle; answer, echoes, dying, dying, dying.

O love, they die in yon rich sky,
　They faint on hill or field or river:
Our echoes roll from soul to soul,
　And grow **for ever** and for ever.
Blow, bugle, blow, set the wild echoes flying,
And answer echoes, answer, dying, dying, dying.

ALFRED TENNYSON.

---

## THE MADDENING BOWL.

Oh! take the maddening bowl away,
　Remove the poisonous cup!
My soul is sick—its burning ray
　Hath drunk my spirit up:
Take—take it from my loathing lip,
　Ere madness fires my brain;
Take—take it hence, nor let **me** sip
　Its liquid death again!

Oh! dash it on the thirsty earth,
　**For** I will drink no more;
It cannot cheer the heart with mirth
　That grief hath wounded sore;
For serpents wreath its sparkling brim,
　**And adders lurk** below;
**It** hath no soothing charm for him
　**Who** sinks oppressed with woe.

Then, hence! away, thou deadly foe,—
　I scorn thy base control.
Away, *away!* I fear thy blow,
　　Thou palsy of the soul!
Henceforth I drink no more of thee,
　Thou bane of Adam's race;
But to a heavenly fountain **flee,**
　And drink the dews of grace.

ANONYMOUS.

## KATIE LEE AND WILLIE GRAY.

Two brown heads with tossing curls,
Red lips shutting over pearls,
Bare feet, white and wet with dew,
Two eyes black and two eyes blue—
Little boy and girl were they,
Katie Lee and Willie Gray.

They were standing where a brook,
Bending like a shepherd's crook,
Flashed its silver, and thick ranks
Of willow fringed its mossy banks—
Half in thought and half in play,
Katie Lee and Willie Gray.

They had cheeks like cherry red,—
He was taller, 'most a head;
She with arms like wreaths of snow
Swung a basket to and fro,
As they loitered, half in play,
Katie Lee and Willie Gray.

" Pretty Katie," Willie said,
And there came a dash of red
Through the brownness of the cheek,
" Boys are strong and girls are weak,
And I'll carry, so I will,
Katie's basket up the hill."

Katie answered with a laugh,
" You shall only carry half ;"
Then said, tossing back her curls,
" Boys are weak as well as girls."
Do you think that Katie guessed
Half the wisdom she expressed?

Men are only boys grown tall;
Hearts don't change much, after all;
And when, long years from that day,
Katie Lee and Willie Gray
Stood again beside the brook
Bending like a shepherd's crook—

Is it strange that Willie said,
While again a dash of red
Crowned the brownness of his cheek,
" I am strong and **you** are weak ;
Life is but a slippery steep,
Hung with shadows cold and deep.

" **Will** you trust me, Katie dear ?
Walk beside me without fear ?
May I carry, **if I will,**
All your burdens **up the hill ?** "
And she answered, **with a laugh,**
" **No,** but you may carry half."

**Close** beside **the little brook,**
Bending like a **shepherd's crook,**
Working **with its** silver hands
Late and early at the sands,
**Stands a** cottage, where, to-day,
Katie lives with Willie Gray.

In the **porch** she sits, and **lo !**
Swings a basket **to and** fro,
Vastly different **from the** one
That she swung **in years** agone ;
This is long, and deep, and wide,
**And has** rockers **at** the side.

Anonymous.

---

## "ROCK OF AGES."

" Rock of ages, **cleft for** me,"
　Thoughtlessly the maiden **sung,**
Fell the words unconsciously
　From her girlish, gleeful tongue,
Sung as little **children** sing,
　Sung as sing the birds in June ;
Fell the words like light leaves sown
　On the current of the tune—
" Rock of Ages, cleft for me,
Let me hide myself in Thee."

Felt her soul no need to hide—
  Sweet the song as song could be,
And she had no thought beside;
  All the words unheedingly
Fell from lips untouched by care,
  Dreaming not that each might be
On some other lips a prayer—
  " Rock of Ages, cleft for me,
  Let me hide myself in Thee."

" Rock of Ages, cleft for me—"
  'Twas a woman sung them now,
Pleadingly and prayerfully;
  Every word her heart did know;
Rose the song as storm-tossed bird
  Beats with weary wing the air,
Every note with sorrow stirred,
  Every syllable a prayer—
" Rock of Ages, cleft for me,
Let me hide myself in Thee."

" Rock of Ages, cleft for me—" -
  Lips grown aged sung the hymn
Trustingly and tenderly,
  Voice grown weak and eyes grown dim—
" Let me hide myself in Thee."
  Trembling though the voice, and low,
Rose the sweet strain peacefully
  As a river in its flow;
Sung as only they can sing,
  Who life's thorny paths have pressed;
Sung as only they can sing,
  Who behold the promised rest.

" Rock of Ages, cleft for me,"
  Sung above a coffin-lid;
Underneath, all restfully
  All life's cares and sorrows hid.
Never more, O storm-tossed soul,
  Never more from wind or tide,

Never more from billow's roll
　Wilt thou need thyself to hide.
Could the sightless, sunken eyes,
　Closed beneath the soft gray hair,
Could the mute and stiffened lips,
　Move again in pleading prayer,
Still, aye still  the words would be,
" Let me hide myself in Thee."

Anonymous.

## A LEGEND OF THE NORTHLAND.

Away, away in the Northland,
　Where the hours of the day are few,
And the nights are so long in winter,
　They cannot sleep them through;

Where they harness the swift reindeer
　To the sledges when it snows;
And the children look like bears' cubs,
　In their funny, furry clothes;

They tell them a curious story,—
　I don't believe 'tis true;
And yet you may learn a lesson,
　If I tell the tale to you.

Once, when the good St. Peter
　Lived in the world below,
And walked about it, preaching,
　Just as he did, you know;

He came to the door of a cottage,
　In traveling around the earth,
Where a little woman was making cakes
　In the ashes on the hearth.

So she made a very little cake,
　But, as it baking lay,
She looked at it, and thought it seemed
　Too large to give away.

Therefore she kneaded another,
  And still a smaller one;
**But** it looked, when she turned it over,
  As large as the first had done.

Then she took a tiny scrap of dough,
  And **rolled** and rolled it flat;
**And baked** it thin as a wafer,—
  But **she** couldn't part with that.

For she **said,** " **My** cakes that seem so **small**
  When I eat them myself,
Are yet too large **to** give away,"
  So she put them on a shelf.

Then good Saint Peter grew angry,
  For he was hungry and faint;
And **surely** such **a** woman
  Was enough to provoke a saint.

And he said, " **You are** far too selfish
  To dwell in a **human form,**
To have both food **and shelter,**
  And fire to keep **you warm.**

" Now you **shall** build **as** the birds **do,**
  And **shall** get your scanty food
By **boring** and boring and boring
  **All day** in the hard dry wood."

Then she **went** up through the chimney,
  **Never** speaking a word;
**And** out of the top flew **a** woodpecker,
  For she was changed to a bird.

She had a scarlet cap on her head,
  And that was left the same,
But all the rest of her clothes were burned
  Black as a coal in the flame.

And every country school-boy
  Has seen her **in** the wood,

Where she lives in the trees to this very day,
    Boring and boring for food.

And this is the lesson she teaches:
    Live not for yourselves alone,
Lest the needs you will not pity
    Shall one day be your own.

Give plenty of what is given you,
    Listen to pity's call;
Don't think the little you give is great,
    And the much you get is small.

Now, my little boy, remember that,
    And try to be kind and good,
When you see the woodpecker's sooty dress,
    And see her scarlet hood.

You mayn't be changed to a bird, though
        you live
As selfishly as you can;
But you will be changed to a smaller thing—
    A mean and selfish man.

                          PHŒBE CARY.


### BRUCE'S ADDRESS.

Scots, wha hae wi' Wallace bled,
Scots, whom Bruce has often led,
Welcome to your gory bed,
Or to glorious victory.

Now's the day, and now's the hour;
See the front o' battle lower,
See approach proud Edward's power—
Edward! chains and slavery!

Wha will be a traitor knave?
Wha can fill a coward's grave?
Wha sae base as be a slave?
Traitor! coward! turn and flee!

Wha for Scotland's king and law
Freedom's sword will strongly **draw,**
Freeman stand, or freeman fa',
Caledonian! **on** wi' me.

By oppression's woes and pains!
By your sons in servile chains!
**We will** drain our dearest veins,
**But they** shall be—shall be free!

Lay the proud usurpers low!
Tyrants fall in every foe!
Liberty's in every blow!
Forward! let us do, or die!

ROBERT BURNS.

## CLARIBEL'S PRAYER.

The day, with cold, gray feet, clung shivering to
    the hills,
    While o'er the valley still night's rain-fring'd
      curtains fell;
But waking Blue Eyes **smiled:** "'Tis ever **as**
    God wills;
    **He knoweth best;** and **be it** rain or shine, 'tis
      well;
    Praise God!" cried always little Claribel.

Then **sunk** she **on** her knees; with eager, lifted
    hands,
    Her rosy lips made haste some dear request to
      tell:
"O Father, smile, and save this fairest of all
    lands,
    And make her free, whatever hearts rebel.
    Amen! Praise God!" cried little Claribel.

"And, Father,"—still arose another pleading
    prayer,—
    "O, save my brother in the rain of shot and
      shell!

**Let** not the death-bolt, with its horrid, streaming
　　　hair,
　　Dash light from those sweet eyes I love **so**
　　　well!
　　Amen!　Praise God!" wept little Claribel.


" **But,** Father, grant that when the glorious **fight**
　　　is done,
　　And up the crimson sky the shouts **of freed-**
　　　men swell,
Grant that there **be no nobler victor 'neath the**
　　sun
　　Than he whose golden hair I love so **well;**
　　**Amen!**　Praise God!" cried little Claribel.


**When the** gray and dreary day shook hands **with**
　　　graver night,
　The heavy air was thrilled with clangor of **a**
　　　bell.
**"O,** shout!" the herald cried, his worn **eyes**
　　　brimmed with light;
　　"'Tis victory! O, what glorious news to tell!"
　　" Praise God!　He heard my prayer," cried
　　Claribel.


" **But, pray you,** soldier, was my brother in the
　　　fight
　　**And** in the fiery rain?　O, fought **he** brave
　　　and well?"
" Dear child," the herald cried, " there was no
　　　braver sight
　　Than his young form, so grand 'mid shot and
　　　shell."
　　" Praise God!" cried trembling little Claribel,


" And rides **he** now with victor's plumes of red.
　While trumpets' golden throats his coming
　　　steps foretell?"
The herald dropped a tear.　" Dear child," he
　　softly said,

" Thy brother evermore with conquerors shall
  dwell."
" Praise God!  He heard my prayer," cried
  Claribel.

" With victors, wearing crowns and bearing
  palms," he said.
  And snow of sudden fear upon the rose lips
  fell ;
" O, sweetest herald, say my brother lives !" she
  plead.
  " **Dear** child, he walks **with** angels, who in
  strength excel ;
  Praise God, who gave **this** glory, **Claribel.**"

**The** cold, gray day died sobbing on the weary
  hills,
  While bitter mourning on the night-wind **rose**
  and fell.
" O **child**,"—the herald **wept,—**" 'tis as the dear
  Lord wills ;
  He knoweth best, and, be **it life** or death, **'tis**
  well."
  " Amen !  Praise God !" sobbed little Claribel.
M. L. Parmelee.

---

## THE RAVEN.

Once upon **a mi**dnight dreary, **while** I pondered,
  weak and weary,
  Over many a quaint and curious volume of
  forgotten lore !
While I nodded, nearly napping, suddenly there
  came a tapping,
  As of some one gently rapping, rapping at my
  chamber door,
  " 'Tis some visitor," I muttered, " tapping at
  my chamber door ;
    Only this—and nothing more."

Ah, distinctly I remember it was in the bleak
    December,
  And each separate dying ember wrought its
    ghost upon the floor.
Eagerly I wished the morrow ;—vainly I had
    tried to borrow
  From my books surcease of sorrow—sorrow
    for the lost Lenore —
  For the rare and radiant maiden whom the
    angels name Lenore—
    Nameless here forevermore.

And the silken sad uncertain rustling of each
    purple curtain
  Thrilled me—filled me with fantastic terrors
    'never felt before,
So that now, to still the beating of my heart, I
    stood repeating,
  "'Tis some visitor entreating entrance at my
    chamber door—
  Some late visitor entreating entrance at my
    chamber door ;
    This it is and nothing more."

Presently my soul grew stronger ; hesitating
    then no longer,
  "Sir," said I, "or Madam, truly your forgive-
    ness I implore ;
But the fact is I was napping, and so gently you
    came rapping,
  And so faintly you came tapping, tapping at
    my chamber door, .
  That I scarce was sure I heard you."—Here I
    opened wide the door ;—
    Darkness there and nothing more.

Deep into that darkness peering, long I stood
    there wondering, fearing,
  Doubting, dreaming dreams no mortal ever
    dared to dream before ;
But the silence was unbroken, and the stillness
    gave no token,

And the only word there spoken was the whispered word, " Lenore ! "
This I whispered, and an echo murmured back
the word, " Lenore ! "
Merely this and nothing more.

Back into the chamber turning, all my soul within me burning,
Soon I heard again a tapping, somewhat
louder than before.
" Surely," said I, " surely that is something at
my window lattice ;
Let me see, then, what thereat is—and this
mystery explore—
Let my heart be still a moment—and this
mystery explore ;—
'Tis the wind, and nothing more ! "

Open here I flung the shutter, when, with many
a flirt and flutter,
In there stepped a stately Raven of the saintly
days of yore.
Not the least obeisance made he ; not an instant
stopped or stayed he,
But with mien of lord or lady, perched above
my chamber-door—
Perched upon a bust of Pallas just above my
chamber-door—
Perched, and sat, and nothing more.

Then this ebon bird beguiling my sad fancy into
smiling,
By the grave and stern decorum of the coun-
tenance it wore,
" Though thy crest be shorn and shaven, thou,"
I said, " art sure no craven,
Ghastly, grim, and ancient Raven, wandering
from the Nightly shore—
Tell me what thy lordly name is on the Night's
Plutonian shore ! "
Quoth the Raven, " Nevermore."

Much I marvelled this ungainly fowl to hear dis-
    course so plainly,
  Though its answer little meaning—little rele-
    **vancy** bore ;
**For we** cannot help agreeing that no living
    human being
  Ever yet was blest with seeing bird above his
    chamber-door—
  Bird or beast upon the sculptured bust above
    his chamber-door,
      With such name as " Nevermore."

**But the Raven,** sitting lonely on the placid bust,
    **spoke only**
  That one **word**. as if his soul in that one word
    **he did** outpour.
**Nothing** farther then he uttered ; not a feather
    then **he fluttered**—
  **Till** I scarcely more than muttered, " Other
    friends have flown before—
  **On** the morrow *he* will leave me, as my **Hopes**
    have **flown before."**
      Then **the bird** said, " Nevermore."

Startled at **the** stillness broken by reply so aptly
    spoken,
  " Doubtless," said **I,** " what it utters is its only
    stock **and store**
Caught from some unhappy master whom un-
    merciful Disaster
  **Followed** fast and followed faster till his song
    one **burden** bore—
  Till the dirges of his Hope **the** melancholy
    burden bore—
      Of ' Never '—of ' Nevermore.' "

But the Raven still beguiling all my sad soul
    into smiling,
  Straight I wheeled a cushioned seat in front
    of **bird, and bust,** and door ;

Then, upon the velvet sinking, I betook myself
    **to linking**
  Fancy unto fancy, thinking what this ominous
    bird of yore—
  What this grim, ungainly, ghastly, gaunt, and
    ominous bird of yore
      Meant in croaking " Nevermore."

This I sat engaged in guessing, but no syllable
    expressing
  To the fowl whose fiery eyes now burned into
    my bosom's core ;
**This** and more I sat divining, with my head at
    ease reclining
  On the cushion's velvet lining that the **lamp-**
    light gloat**ed** o'er,
  But whose velvet **v**iolet lining with the lamp-
    light gloating o'er—
      *She* shall press, ah, nevermore !

Then, methought, the **air grew** denser, perfumed
    from an unseen censer
  Swung by seraphim whose faint footfal**ls**
    tinkled **on** the tufted floor.
" Wretch," I cried, " thy God hath lent thee—
    by these angels he hath sent thee
  Respite—respite and nepenthe from thy mem-
    **ories of Lenore !**
  Quaff, **oh q**uaff this kind nepenthe and forget
    this **lost** Lenore ! "
      Quoth the Raven, **" Ne**vermore."

" Prophet ! " said I, " thing of evil ! prophet
    still, if bird **or** devil !—
  Whether Tempter sen**t, or** whether tempest
    tossed thee here asho**re,**
Desolate yet all undaunted, **on** this desert land
    enchanted—
  **On** this home by Horror haunted—tell me
    truly, I implore—

Is there—*is* there balm in Gilead?—tell me,
    **tell me. I** implore!"
      Quoth the Raven, " Nevermore."


"Prophet!" said I, "thing of evil,—prophet
    **still, if** bird or devil!
By that Heaven that bends above us—by that
    **God we** both adore—
Tell this soul with sorrow laden if, within **the**
    distant **Aiden,**
    It shall clasp a sainted maiden **whom the angels**
    name Lenore—
Clasp **a rare** and radiant maiden whom the
    angels **name Lenore."**
      Quoth the Raven, " Nevermore."


"Be that word our sign of parting, bird **or**
    **fiend!"** I shrieked, upstarting—
    "**Get** thee back into the tempest and **the**
    Night's Plutonian shore!
Leave no black plume as a token of that lie thy
    soul hath spoken!
    Leave my loneliness unbroken! quit the bust
    above my door!
Take thy beak from out my heart, and take
    thy form from off my door!".
      Quoth the Raven, " Nevermore."


And the Raven, never flitting, still is sitting, still
    is sitting
    On the pallid bust **of Pallas** just above **my**
    chamber-door;
And his eyes have all the seeming **of** a demon's
    that is dreaming,
    And the lamplight o'er him streaming throws
    his shadow on the floor;
And my soul from out that shadow that lies
    floating on the floor
    Shall be lifted—nevermore!
             EDGAR A. **POE.**

## WE ARE SEVEN.

I met a little cottage girl,
  She was eight years old, she said;
Her hair was thick with many a **curl**
  That clustered round her head.

She had a rustic, woodland air,
  And she was wildly clad;
Her eyes were fair, and very fair—
  Her **beauty** made me glad.

" Sisters and **brothers, little** maid,
  How many may **you be ?** "
" How many? seven **in all,**" she said,
  And wondering looked **at** me.

" **And** where are they, I pray you tell ? "
  She answered, " Seven are we;
**And** two of us **at** Conway dwell,
  And two are **gone to** sea;

" **T**wo of us in the churchyard lie,
  My sister and my brother:
And in the churchyard cottage I
  Dwell **near** t**hem** with my mother."

" You **say** that two at Conway dwell,
  **And** t**wo** are gone to sea,
**Y**et ye are seven; I pray you tell,
  **Sweet** maid, how this **may** be ? "

**Then** did the little maid reply:
  " Seven boys and girls are we;
Two of us in the churchyard lie,
  Beneath **the** churchyard tree."

" You run about, my little maid,
  Your limbs they are alive;
If two are in the churchyard laid,
  **Then ye are only** five."

" Their graves are green, they may be **seen,**"
　　The little maid replied,
" Twelve steps or more from my mother's
　　　door,
　　And they are side **by** side.

" **My** stockings there I often knit,
　　My 'kerchief there I hem ;
And there upon **the ground I sit—**
　　I sit and sing **to them.**

" And often **after sunset, sir,**
　　When **it is light** and fair,
I take **my little porringer**
　　And **eat my supper** there.

" The **first** that **died** was little Jane :
　　In bed she moaning lay,
**Till** God released her of her pain,
　　And then she went away.

" So in the churchyard she was laid ;
　　And, when **the grass** was dry,
Together round her grave we played,
　　My brother **John** and I.

"And when the ground was **white** with snow,
　　And I could run and slide,
**My** brother John was forced to go,
　　And **he** lies by her side."

" How many are **you, then,**" said I,
　　" If they two **are in heaven ? "**
The little maiden did reply,
　　" **O** master ! we are seven."

" But **they are dead—**those two are dead ;
　　Their spirits are in heaven " :
'Twas throwing words away ; for still
The little maid would have her will,
　　And **said,** " Nay, we are seven."
WILLIAM WORDSWORTH.

## THE VILLAGE BLACKSMITH.

Under a spreading chestnut tree
  The village smithy stands;
The smith, a mighty man is he,
  With large and sinewy hands;
And the muscles of his brawny arms
  Are strong as iron bands.

His hair is crisp, and black, and long,
  His face is like the tan;
His brow is wet with honest sweat,
  He earns whate'er he can,
And looks the whole world in the face,
  For he owes not any man.

Week in, week out, from morn till night,
  You can hear his bellows blow;
You can hear him swing his heavy sledge,
  With measured beat and slow,
Like a sexton ringing the village bell,
  When the evening sun is low.

And children coming home from school
  Look in at the open door;
They love to see the flaming forge,
  And hear the bellows roar,
And catch the burning sparks that fly
  Like chaff from a threshing-floor.

He goes on Sunday to the church,
  And sits among his boys;
He hears the parson pray and preach,
  He hears his daughter's voice,
Singing in the village choir,
  And it makes his heart rejoice.

It sounds to him like her mother's voice,
  Singing in Paradise!
He needs must think of her once more,
  How in the grave she lies;
And with his hard, rough hand he wipes
  A tear out of his eyes.

Toiling—rejoicing—sorrowing,
  Onward through life he goes;
Each morning sees some task begin,
  Each evening sees it close;
Something attempted, something done,
  Has earned a night's repose.

Thanks, thanks to thee, my worthy friend,
  For the lesson thou hast taught!
Thus at the flaming forge of life
  Our fortunes must be wrought;
Thus on its sounding anvil shaped
  Each burning deed and thought.

HENRY W. LONGFELLOW.

---

## A WOMAN'S ANSWER ON BEING ACCUSED OF BEING A MANIAC ON THE SUBJECT OF TEMPERANCE.

Go, feel what I have felt;
  Go, bear what I have borne—
Sink 'neath a blow a father dealt,
  And the cold world's proud scorn,
Then suffer on from year to year—
Thy sole relief the scorching tear.

Go, kneel as I have knelt;
  Implore, beseech, and pray—
Strive the besotted heart to melt,
  The downward course to stay;
Be dashed, with bitter curse, aside;
Your prayers burlesqued, your tears defied.

Go, weep as I have wept,
  O'er a loved father's fall—
See every promised blessing swept,
  Youth's sweetness turned to gall;
Life's fading flowers strewed all the way,
That brought me up to woman's day.

Go, see what I have seen,
  Behold the strong man bow,
With gnashing teeth, lips bathed in blood,
  And cold and livid brow;
Go catch his withering glance, and see
There mirrored his soul's misery.

Go to thy mother's side,
  And her crushed bosom cheer;
Thy own deep anguish hide;
  Wipe from her cheek the bitter tear;
Mark her worn frame and withered brow,
The gray that streaks her dark hair now;
With fading frame and trembling limb,
And trace the ruin back to him
Whose plighted faith, in early youth,
Promised eternal love and truth;

But who, forsworn, hath yielded up
That promise to the cursed cup,
And led her down through love and light,
And all that made her promise bright,
And chained her there, 'mid want and strife,
That lowly thing—a drunkard's wife!
And stamped on childhood's brow so mild
That withering blight—the drunkard's child

Go, hear, and feel, and see, and know
  All that *my soul* hath felt and known,
Then look upon the wine-cup's glow,
  See if its beauty can atone;
Think if its flavor you will try,
  When all proclaim, " 'Tis drink and die."

Tell me I hate the bowl—
  Hate is a feeble word:
I loathe—abhor—my very soul
  With strong disgust is stirred,
Whene'er I see, or hear, or tell
Of the dark beverage of hell.

Anonymous.

### IVRY.—A SONG OF THE HUGUENOTS.

Now glory to the Lord of Hosts, from whom all
    glories are !
And glory to our Sovereign Liege, King Henry
    of Navarre !
Now let there be the merry sound of music and
    of dance,
Through thy cornfields green, and sunny vines,
    oh pleasant land of France !
And thou, Rochelle, our own Rochelle, proud
    city of the waters,
Again let rapture light the eyes of all thy mourn-
    ing daughters ;
As thou wert constant in our ills, be joyous in
    our joy,
For cold, and stiff, and still are they who wrought
    thy walls annoy.
Hurrah ! Hurrah ! a single field hath turned the
    chance of war,
Hurrah ! Hurrah ! for Ivry, and Henry of Na-
    varre.

Oh ! how our hearts were beating, when at the
    dawn of day,
We saw the army of the League drawn out in
    long array ;
With all its priest-led citizens, and all its rebel
    peers,
And Appenzel's stout infantry, and Egmont's
    Flemish spears.
There rode the brood of false Lorraine, the curses
    of our land ;
And dark Mayenne was in the midst, a truncheon
    in his hand :
And as we looked on them, we thought of Seine's
    empurpled flood,
And good Coligni's hoary hair all dabbled with
    his blood ;

And we cried unto the living God who rules the
    fate of war,
To fight for his own holy name, and Henry **of**
    Navarre.

The King is come to marshal **us, all in** his armor
    **drest,**
And **he has** bound a snow-white plume upon his
    **gallant crest,**
He looked upon his people, and a tear was in **his**
    eye ;
He looked upon the traitors, and his glance was
    stern and high.
Right graciously he smiled on us, as rolled from
    wing **to** wing,
Down all our line, in deafening shout, **" God**
    save our Lord, the King."
" And if my standard-bearer fall, as fall full well
    he may,
For never saw I promise yet of such a bloody
    fray,
Press where ye see my white plume shine, amidst
    the ranks of war,
And be your oriflamme to-day the **helmet of**
    Navarre."

Hurrah ! the foes are moving. Hark to the
    **mingled din,**
Of fife, and steed, and trump, and drum, and
    **roaring culverin.**
The **fiery** Duke is pricking fast across Saint
    **Andre's** plain,
With all the hireling chivalry of Guelders and
    Almayne.
Now by the lips of those ye love, fair gentlemen
    of France,
Charge for the golden lilies ! upon them with
    the lance !
A thousand spurs are striking deep, a thousand
    spears in rest,

A thousand knights are **pressing close behind the**
    snow-white crest;
And in they burst, and on they rushed, while,
    like **a** guiding star,
Amidst the thickest carnage blazed the helmet
    of Navarre.

Now, God be praised, the day is ours. Mayenne
    hath turned his rein,
D'Aumale hath cried for quarter. The Flemish
    count is slain.
Their ranks are breaking like thin clouds before
    a Biscay gale;
**The** field is heaped with bleeding steeds, and
    flags, **and** cloven mail.
And then we thought on vengeance, and, **all**
    along our van,
" Remember St. Bartholomew," was passed from
    **man** to man.
But out spake gentle Henry, " No Frenchman is
    my foe:
Down, down, with every foreigner, but let your
    brethren go."
Oh! was there ever such a knight, in friendship
    **or in** war,
As **our** Sovereign Lord, King Henry, the soldier
    of Navarre?

Right well fought all the Frenchmen who fought
    for France to-day;
And many a lordly banner God gave them for a
    prey.
But we of the religion have borne us best in
    fight;
And the good Lord of Rosny hath ta'en the cor-
    net white.
Our own true Maximilian the cornet white hath
    ta'en,
The cornet white with crosses black, the flag of
    false Lorraine.

Up with it high; unfurl **it** wide; that all the
   host may know
How God hath humbled the proud house which
   wrought his church such woe.
Then on the ground, while trumpets **sound their**
   loudest point of war,
Fling the red shreds, a footcloth meet for Henry
   of Navarre.

Ho! maidens of Vienna; ho! matrons of Lu-
   cerne;
Weep, weep, and rend your hair for those who
   never shall return.
Ho! Philip, send for **charity,** thy Mexican pis-
   toles,
That Antwerp monks may sing a mass **for** thy
   poor spearmen's souls.
Ho! gallant nobles of the League, look that **your**
   arms be bright;
Ho! burghers of Saint Genevieve, keep watch
   and ward to-night.
For our God hath crushed the tyrant, our **God**
   hath raised the slave,
And mocked the counsel of the wise, and the
   valor of the brave.
Then glory to His holy name, from whom **all**
   glories are ;
**A**nd glory **to our** Sovereign Lord, King Henry
   of Navarre.

T. B. Macaulay.

---

## CATILINE'S DEFIANCE.

Conscript fathers!
I do not rise to waste the night in words;
Let that plebeian talk; 'tis not my trade;
But here I stand for right—let him show proofs—
For Roman right; though none, it seems, dare
   stand

To take their share with me.   Ay, cluster there!
Cling to your master, judges, Romans, slaves!
His charge is false ;—I dare him to his proofs.
You have my answer.   Let my actions speak !

But this I will avow, that I have scorned,
And still do scorn, to hide my sense of wrong!
Who brands me on the forehead, breaks my
   sword,
Or lays the bloody scourge upon my back,
Wrongs me not half so much as he who shuts
The gates of honor on me—turning out
The Roman from his birthright ; and, for what ?
                   [*Looking round him.*
To fling your offices to every slave !
Vipers, that creep where man disdains to climb,
And, having wound their loathsome track to the
   top
Of this huge, mouldering monument of Rome,
Hang hissing at the nobler man below !

Come, consecrated lictors, from your thrones ;
                  [*To the Senate.*
Fling down your sceptres ; take the rod and axe,
And make the murder as you make the law !

Banished from Rome !   What's banished, but
   set free
From daily contact of the things I loathe ?
" Tried and convicted traitor ! "   Who says this ?
Who'll prove it, at his peril, on my head ?
Banished !   I thank you for 't.   It breaks my
   chain !
I held some slack allegiance till this hour ;
But now my sword's my own.   Smile on, my
   lords !
I scorn to count what feelings, withered hopes,
Strong provocations, bitter, burning wrongs,
I have within my heart's hot cells shut up,
To leave you in your lazy dignities.

But here I stand and scoff you! here, I fling
Hatred and full defiance in your face!
Your consul's merciful.   For this, all thanks.
He dares not touch a hair of Catiline!

 "Traitor!"  I go; but I return. This—trial!
Here I devote your Senate!   I've had wrongs
To stir a fever in the blood of age,
Or make the infant's sinews strong as steel.
This day's the birth of sorrow!  This hour's
    work
Will breed proscriptions!   Look to your hearths,
    my lords!
For there, henceforth, shall sit, for household
    gods,
Shapes hot from Tartarus!—all shames and
    crimes:
Wan treachery, with his thirsty dagger drawn;
Suspicion, poisoning his brother's cup;
Naked rebellion, with the torch and axe,
Making his wild sport of your blazing thrones;
Till anarchy comes down on you like night,
And massacre seals Rome's eternal grave.

 I go; but not to leap the gulf alone.
I go; but, when I come, 'twill be the burst
Of ocean in the earthquake—rolling back
In swift and mountainous ruin.  Fare you well;
You build my funeral pile; but your best blood
Shall quench its flame!   Back, slaves!
                    [*To the lictors.*
 I will return.

                    GEORGE CROLY.

---

## WHEN MARY WAS A LASSIE.

The maple trees are tinged with red,
    The birch with golden yellow,
And high above the orchard wall
    Hang apples, rich and mellow;

And that's the way through yonder lane
　That looks so still and grassy,—
The way I took one Sunday eve,
　When Mary was a lassie.

You'd hardly think that patient face,
　That looks so thin and faded,
Was once the very sweetest one
　That ever bonnet shaded;
But when **I** went through yonder lane,
　That looks so still and grassy,
Those eyes were bright, those cheeks **were**
　　　fair,
　**When Mary was a** lassie.

But many a tender sorrow since,
　**And** many a patient care,
Have made those furrows on the face
　That used to be so fair.
Four times to yonder churchyard,
　Through the lane so still and grassy
We've borne and laid away our dead,—
　Since Mary was a lassie.

**And so** you see I've grown to love
　**The** *wrinkles* more than *roses;*
Earth's winter flowers are sweeter far
　Than all spring's dewy posies;
They'll carry *us* through yonder lane
　That looks so still and grassy,—
Adown the lane I used **to** go,
　When Mary **was a** lassie.

Anonymous.

———

## CUDDLE **DOON.**

The bairnies cuddle doon at nicht,
　Wi' mickle faucht an' din;
" Oh, try and sleep, ye waukrife rogues,
　Your faither's comin' in."

They never heed a word I speak ;
  I try to gie a froon,
But aye I hap them up, an' cry,
  " Oh, bairnies, cuddle doon."

Wee Jamie wi' the curly head,
  He aye sleeps next the wa',
Bangs up an' cries, " I want a piece "—
  The rascal starts them **a'**.
**I rin' an'** fetch them pieces, drinks ;
  They stop awee the soun',
Then draw the blankets up an' cry,
  " Noo, weanies, cuddle doon."

But ere five minutes gang, wee Rab
  Cries out frae' neath the claes,
" Mither, mak' Tam gie ower at ance,
  He's kittlin wi' his taes."
The mischief's in that Tam for tricks,
  He'd bother half the toon,
But aye I hap them up **an'** cry,
  " Oh, bairnies, cuddle **doon**."

At length they hear their faither's fit,
  An' as he steeks the door
They turn their faces to the wa',
  While Tam pretends to snore.
" Hae a' the weans been gude ? " he asks
  As he pits off his shoon :
" The bairnies, John, are **in** their beds,
  An' lang since cuddle **doon**."

An' just afore we bed oursel's,
  We look at oor wee lambs ;
Tam has his airm roun' wee Rab's neck,
  An' Rab **his** airm roun' Tam's.
I lift wee Jamie up the bed,
  An' as I straik each croon
I whisper, till my heart fills up,
  " Oh, bairnies, cuddle doon."

The bairnies cuddle doon at nicht
  Wi' mirth that's dear to me;
But sune the big warl's cark an' care
  Will quaten doon their glee.
Yet come what will to ilka ane,
  May He who sits aboon,
Aye whisper, though their pows be bauld,
  "Oh, bairnies, cuddle doon."

Alexander Anderson.

## SMALL BEGINNINGS.

A traveller through a dusty road strewed acorns
  on the lea;
And one took root and sprouted up, and grew
  into a tree.
Love sought its shade at evening time, to breathe
  its early vows;
And age was pleased, in heats of noon, to bask
  beneath its boughs;
The dormouse loved its dangling twigs, the birds
  sweet music bore;
It stood a glory in its place, a blessing evermore.

A little spring had lost its way amid the grass
  and fern,
A passing stranger scooped a well, where weary
  men might turn;
He walled it in, and hung with care a ladle at
  the brink;
He thought not of the deed he did, but judged
  that toil might drink.
He passed again, and lo! the well, by summers
  never dried,
Had cooled ten thousand parching tongues, and
  saved a life beside.

A dreamer dropped a random thought; 'twas old,
  and yet 'twas new;
A simple fancy of the brain, but strong in being
  true.

It shone upon a genial mind, and lo! its light
    became
A lamp of life, a beacon ray, a monitory flame.
The thought was small, its issue great; a watch-
    fire on the hill,
**It** sheds its radiance far adown, and cheers **the**
    valley still!

A nameless man, amid a crowd that thronged the
    **daily** mart,
Let **fall** a word of hope and love, unstudied, from
    the heart;
A **whisper** on the tumult thrown,—a transitory
    breath,—
**It** raised a brother from the dust; it sa**ved a soul
from death.**
O germ! **O fount!** O word of love! **O thought**
    at random cast!
Ye were but little at the first, but mighty at the
    **last.**

CHARLES **MACKAY.**

## A NAME IN THE SAND.

Alone I walked the ocean strand;
A pearly shell was in my hand;
I stooped and wrote upon the sand
   **My** name—the year—the day.
**As onward** from the spot I passed,
**One** lingering look behind I cast—
A wave came rolling, high and fast,
   And washed my lines **away.**

And **so,** methought, **'twill** shortly **be**
With every mark on earth from me;
A wave of **dark oblivion's** sea
   Will sweep across the place
Where I have trod the sandy shore
Of time,—and been, to be no more ;—
Of me, my name, the name I bore,
   To leave no track nor trace.

And yet, with Him who counts the sands,
And holds the waters in His hands,
I know a lasting record stands
　Inscribed against my name,
Of all this mortal part has wrought,
Of all this thinking soul has thought,—
And from these fleeting moments caught,—
　For glory or **for** shame.

GEORGE D. PRENTICE.

---

## THE PAUPER'S DEATH-BED.

Tread softly! bow the head—
　In **reverent silence** bow!
No passing bell doth toll;
Yet an immortal soul
　Is passing now.

Stranger, however great,
　With holy reverence bow!
There's one in that poor shed—
One by that paltry bed—
　Greater than thou.

Beneath that beggar's roof,
　Lo! Death doth keep his state:
Enter!—no crowds attend;
Enter!—no guards defend
　This palace gate.

That pavement damp and cold
　No smiling courtiers **tread**;
One silent woman stands,
Lifting with meagre hands
　A dying head.

No mingling voices sound—
　An infant wail alone;
A sob suppressed—again
That short deep gasp—and then
　The parting groan!

Oh, change!—oh! wondrous change!
  Burst are the prison bars!
This moment, there, so low,
So agonized, and now
  Beyond the stars!

Oh, change!—stupendous change!
  There lies **the** soulless clod!
**The sun** eternal breaks;
**The** new immortal wakes—
  Wakes with his God!

CAROLINE BOWLES SOUTHEY.

---

## **THE** SEVEN AGES **OF** MAN.

All **the** world's **a** stage,
And all the men and women merely players;
They have their exits and their entrances,
And one man in his time plays many parts,
His acts being seven ages. At first, the infant,
Mewling and puking in his nurse's arms:
**And** then the whining school-boy, with **his** satchel
And shining **morning** face, creeping like snail
Unwillingly to school. And then, the lover,
Sighing like furnace, with **a** woeful ballad
Made to his mistress' eyebrow. Then, the soldier,
Full of strange oaths, and bearded like the pard,
Jealous in honor, sudden, and quick in quarrel,
**Seeking** the bubble reputation
Even in the cannon's mouth. And then the justice,
In fair round belly **with** good capon lined,
With eyes severe and beard of formal cut,
Full of wise saws and modern instances;
And so he plays his part. The sixth age shifts
Into the lean and slippered pantaloon,
With spectacles on nose and pouch on side;
His youthful **hose,** well saved, a world too wide

For his shrunk shank ; and his big manly voice,
Turning again towards childish treble, pipes
And whistles in his sound.   Last scene of all,
That ends this strange, eventful history,
Is second childishness, and mere oblivion :
Sans teeth, sans eyes, sans taste, sans everything.
WILLIAM SHAKESPEARE.

## THE FISHERMEN.

Three fishers went sailing out into the west—
 Out into the west as the sun went down :
Each thought of the woman who loved him the
  best,
 And the children stood watching them out of
  the town ;
For men must work, and women must weep,
And there's little to earn, and many to keep,
 Though the harbor bar be moaning.

Three wives sat up in the lighthouse tower,
 And trimmed the lamps as the sun went down ;
And they looked at the squall, and they looked
  at the shower,
 And the rack it came rolling up, ragged and
  brown ;
But men must work, and women must weep,
Though storms be sudden, and waters deep,
 And the harbor bar be moaning.

Three corpses lay out on the shining sands
 In the morning gleam as the tide went down,
And the women are weeping and wringing their
  hands,
 For those who will never come back to the
  town ;
For men must work, and women must weep,—
And the sooner it 's over, the sooner to sleep,—
 And good-by to the bar and its moaning.
CHARLES KINGSLEY.

# LINES ON A SKELETON.

Behold this ruin! 'Twas a skull
Once of ethereal spirit full;
This narrow cell was life's retreat;
This space was thought's mysterious seat.
What beauteous visions filled this spot;
What dreams of pleasure long forgot!
Nor hope, nor love, nor joy, nor fear,
Has left one trace of record here.

Beneath this mouldering canopy
Once shone the bright and busy eye.
But start not at the dismal void,
Nor sigh for greatness thus destroyed.
If with no lawless fire it gleamed,
But through the dews of kindness beamed,
That eye shall be for ever bright,
When stars and suns are sunk in night.

Within this hollow cavern hung
The ready, swift, and tuneful tongue.
If falsehood's honey it disdained,
And where it could not praise was chained;
If bold in virtue's cause it spoke,
Yet gentle concord never broke;
This silent tongue shall plead for thee
When time unveils eternity.

Say, did these fingers delve the mine,
Or with its envied rubies shine?
To hew the rock or wear the gem,
Can little now avail to them:
But if the page of truth they sought,
Or comfort to the mourner brought,
These hands a richer meed shall claim
Than all that wait on wealth or fame.

Avails it whether bare or shod
These feet the paths of duty trod?
If from the bowers of ease they fled,
To seek affliction's humble shed;

If grandeur's guilty bribe **they** spurned,
And home to virtue's cot returned;
These feet with angels' wings shall vie,
And tread **the** palace of the sky.

ANONYMOUS.

---

## THE FISHERMAN'S SONG.

[This spirited **lyric** appeared anonymously in an old Irish
magazine.]

Away—away o'er the feathery crest
  Of the beautiful blue are we:
For our toil-lot lies on its boiling **breast**,
  And our wealth's in the glorious sea:
And we've hymned in the grasp of the fiercest
    night,
  To the God of the sons of toil,
As we cleft the wave by its own white light,
  And away with its scaly spoil.
    Then oh for the long and the strong oar-
      sweep
     We have given, and will again ;
    For when children's weal lies in the **deep**,
    Oh ! their **fathers** *must* be men.

And **we'll** think, as the blast grows **loud** and
    long,
  That we hear our offspring's **cries**—
And we'll think, **as the** surge grows tall **and**
    strong,
  Of the tears in their **mothers'** eyes :
And we'll reel through **the clutch** of the shiver-
    ing green,
  For the warm, warm clasp at home—
For the soothing smile of each heart's own queen,
  And her arms, like **the flying** foam.
    Then oh for the long and strong oar-sweep
     We have given, and will again ;
    For when children's weal **lies** in the deep,
    Oh ! their fathers *must* **be** men.

Do we yearn for the land when tossed on this?
    Let it ring to the proud one's tread:
Far worse than the waters and winds may hiss
    Where the poor man gleans his bread.
**If** the adder-tongue of the upstart knave
    Can bleed what it may not bend,
'Twere better to battle the wildest wave,
    That the spirit of storms could send,
        Than **be singing** farewell to the bold oar-
            sweep
        We have given, and will again;
    If our souls should **bow to** the mighty deep
    Oh! they'll never **to** savage men.

And if death, at times, through a foamy cloud,
    On the brown-browed boatman glares,
He can pay him his glance with a soul as **proud**
    As the form of a mortal bears;
And oh 'twere glorious, sure, to die,
    In **our** toils for *some* on shore,
With a hopeful eye fixed calm on the sky,
    And a hand on the broken **oar**.
        Then oh, for a long, strong, steady sweep;
            Hold to it—hurrah—dash on:
        If our babes must fast till we rob the deep,
            'Tis time that we had begun.

---

## THE BATTLE OF WATERLOO.

**There was a** sound of revelry by night,
    And Belgium's capital had gathered then
Her Beauty and her Chivalry, and bright
    The lamps shone o'er fair **women** and brave
        men;
    A thousand hearts beat happily; and when
Music arose with its voluptuous swell,
    Soft eyes looked love to eyes which spake
        again,
And all went merry as a marriage bell;
But hush! hark! a deep sound strikes like a ris-
    ing knell!

Did ye not hear it?—No; 'twas but the wind,
  Or the car rattling o'er the stony street;
On with the dance! let joy be unconfined;
  No sleep till morn, when Youth and Pleas-
      ure meet
  **To** chase the glowing Hours with flying
      feet—
But, hark!—that heavy sound breaks in once
      more
  As **if the clouds its echo would repeat;**
And nearer, clearer, **deadlier than before!**
Arm! arm! it is—it is—the **cannon's** opening
      **roar!**

Ah! then and there was hurrying to and fro,
  **And** gathering tears and tremblings of **dis-**
      tress,
**And cheeks** all pale, which but an hour ago
  Blushed at the praise of their own loveli-
      ness;
  And there **were** sudden partings, such as
      press
The life from out young hearts, and **choking**
      sighs
  **Which** ne'er might be repeated; who **shall**
      guess
If evermore should meet those mutual **eyes,**
Since upon night so sweet such awful morn could
      rise?

And there **was** mounting in **hot** haste: the
      steed,
  The mustering squadron, **and the** clattering
      car,
Went pouring forward with impetuous speed,
  And **swiftly** forming in the ranks of war;
  And the deep thunder peal on peal afar;
And near, the beat **of the** alarming drum
  Roused up the **soldier ere the** morning star;

While thronged the citizens with terror dumb,
Or whispering, with white **lips**—" The foe ! they
    come ! they come !"

And wild and high the " Cameron's **gather-**
    ing " rose !
  The **war-note of** Lochiel, which **Albyn's**
  hills
**Have heard, and** heard, too, have her **Saxon**
    **foes :—**
  How **in the noon of night** that pibroch
  thrills,
  Savage and **shrill !** **But** with the breath
  which fills
Their mountain-pipe, so **fill** the mountaineers
  With the fierce native daring, which instils
The stirring memory of a thousand years,
And Evan's, Donald's fame rings in each clans-
    man's ears !

And Ardennes waves above them her green
    leaves,
  Dewy with nature's tear-drops, as they pass,
**Grie**ving. if aught inanimate e'er grieves,
  Over the unreturning brave,—alas !
  Ere evening **to** be trodden like the grass
Which **now** beneath them, but above shall
    grow
**In its next** verdure, when this fiery mass
Of **living** valor, rolling on the **foe**
And **burning** with high hope, shall moulder cold
    **and** low.

Last noon beheld them full **of** lusty life,
  Last eve in Beauty's circle proudly gay,
The midnight brought **the** signal-sound of
    strife,
  The morn, the marshalling in arms—the
  day,
Battle's magnificently-stern array !

The thunder-clouds close o'er it, which when
rent
The earth is covered thick with other clay,
Which her own clay shall cover, heaped and
pent,
Rider and horse,—friend, foe,—in one red burial
blent!

LORD BYRON.

---

## PLATONIC.

I had sworn to be a bachelor, she had sworn to
be a maid,
For we quite agreed in doubting whether matri-
mony paid;
Besides, we had our higher love—fair Science
ruled my heart,
And she said her young affections were all bound
up in Art.

So we laughed at those wise men who say that
friendship can not live
'Twixt man and woman, unless each has something more to give;
We would be friends, and friends as true as e'er
were man and man,
I'd be a second David, and she Miss Jonathan.

We scorned all sentimental trash—vows, kisses,
tears, and sighs;
High friendship, such as ours, might well such
childish arts despise.
We liked each other, that was all, quite all there
was to say,
So we just shook hands upon it in a business sort
of way.

We shared our secrets and our joys, together
hoped and feared,
With common purpose sought the goal that
young ambition reared;

We dreamed together of the days, those dream-
    bright days to come;
We were strictly confidential, and we called each
    other " chum."

And many a day we wandered together o'er the
    hills,
I seeking bugs and butterflies, and she the
    ruined mills,
And rustic bridges, and the like, that picture-
    makers prize,
To run in with their waterfalls and groves and
    summer skies.

And many a quiet evening, in hours of full re-
    lease,
We floated down the river or loafed beneath the
    trees,
And talked in long gradation from the poets to
    the weather,
While the western skies and my cigar burned
    slowly out together.

Yet through it all no whispered word, no tell-tale
    glance or sigh
Told aught of warmer sentiment than friendly
    sympathy.
We talked of love as coolly as we talked of
    nebulæ.
And thought no more of being one than we did
    of being three.

    *    *    *    *    *    *

" Well, good-by, chum!" I took her hand for
    the time had come to go—
My going meant our parting, when to meet we
    did not know.
I had lingered long and said farewell with a very
    heavy heart,
For although we were but friends, 'tis hard for
    honest friends to part.

" Good-by, old-fellow! don't forget your friends
    beyond the sea,
And some day, when you have lots of time, drop
    a line or two to me."
The words came lightly, gayly, but a great sob
    just behind
Welled upward with a story of quite a different
    kind.

And then she raised her eyes to mine, great
    liquid eyes of blue,
Filled to the brim and running o'er, like violet
    cups of dew.
One long, long glance and then I did what I
    never did before—
Perhaps the tears meant friendship, but I'm sure
    the kiss meant more!

ANONYMOUS.

---

## WHICH SHALL IT BE ?

Which shall it be ? which shall it be ?
I looked at John—John looked at me.
(Dear patient John, who loves me yet
As well as though my locks were jet.)
And when I found that I must speak,
My voice seemed strangely low and weak,
" Tell me again what Robert said ? "
And then I list'ning, bent my head.
This is the letter :

    " I will give
A house and land while you shall live,
If, in return for, out of seven,
One child to me for aye is given."

I looked at John's old garments worn,
I thought of all that John had borne
Of poverty, and work, and care,
Which I, though willing, could not share ;

I thought of seven months to feed,
Of seven little children's need,
**And** then of this.

"Come, John," said I.
" We'll choose among them as the lie
Asleep;" so, walking hand in hand,
**Dear John** and I surveyed our band.

First to the **cradle** lightly stepped,
Where Lillian, the baby, slept ;
**Her** damp curls lay like gold alight,
A glory 'gainst the pillow white.
Soft her father stooped to lay
His rough hand down in loving way ;
When dream or whisper made her stir,
And huskily, John : " Not her—not her."

We stooped beside the trundle-bed,
And one long ray of lamp-light shed
Athwart the boyish faces there,
In sleep so beautiful and fair ;
I saw on Jamie's rough, **red** cheek
**A tear** undried.   Ere John could speak,
" **He**'s but a baby, too," said **I**,
**And** kissed him as we hurried by.

Pale, **patient Ro**bbie's angel face
Still in his **sleep** bore suffering's trace.
" No, for a **tho**usand crowns not him,"
We **whispered,** while our eyes were dim.

Poor Dick ! bad Dick ! our wayward son,
**Tur**bulent, reckless, idle one—
Could he be spared ?  Nay, He who gave,
Bids us befriend him to the grave.
Only **a** mother's heart can be
Patient enough for such as he ;
" **And** so," said John, " I would not dare
**To** send him from our bedside prayer."

Then stole we softly up above,
And knelt by Mary, child of love ;
" Perhaps for her 'twould better be,"
I said to John quite silently.
He lifted up a curl that lay
Across her cheek in willful way,
And shook his head.  " Nay, love, not **thee !** "
The while my heart beat audibly.

Only **one** more, our oldest lad,
**Trusty** and truthful, good and glad—
**So like** his father.  " No, John, **no,**
I cannot, will not, let him go."

**And** so we wrote in courteous way,
We could not give one child away ;
And afterward toil lighter seemed,
**Thinking** of that of which we had dreamed.
**Happy**, in truth, that not one face
**We** missed from its accustomed place ;
Thankful to work for all the seven,
Trusting the rest **to** One in heaven.

ANONYMOUS.

## SATURDAY NIGHT.

Placing the little hats all in a row,
Ready for church on the morrow, you know ;
Washing wee faces and little black fists,
**Getting** them ready **and fit** to be kissed ;
Putting them into clean garments and white—
That is what mothers are doing to-night.

Spying out holes in the little worn hose,
**Laying** by shoes that **are** worn through the toes,
Looking o'er garments so faded and thin—
Who but a mother knows where to begin ?
Changing a button to make it look right—
**That** is what mothers are doing to-night.

Calling her little ones all round her chair,
Hearing them lisp forth their evening prayer,
Telling them stories of Jesus of old,
Who loved to gather the lambs to his fold ;
Watching, they listen with weary delight—
That is what mothers are doing to-night.

Creeping so **soft**ly to take a last peep,
After the little ones all are asleep ;
Anxious to know if **the children are** warm,
Tucking the blanket round **each little** form ;
Kissing each little face **rosy and** bright—
**That is** what mothers are **doing** to-night.

Kneeling **down** gently beside **the** white bed,
Lowly and meekly she bows down her head.
Praying as only a mother can **pray,**
" God guide and keep them from going astray."

ANONYMOUS.

---

## THE SILENT WARRIORS.

The sun shone in at the **window,**
  **On the** printer's **case** and type,
**And the** heaps of mystic letters
  **Were** bathed in its golden light ;
**And I** thought of the truths there hidden,
  Of the mighty power there laid,
In those piles of dusky metal,
  **When** in marshaled ranks arrayed.

For by them our souls find voices
  For truths the ages have taught ;
In volumes the dead have treasured,
  In words in immortal thought ;
And they have tongues for our sorrows,
  And songs for our joys or woe,
And in them life's records are written,
  Of all that we mortals know.

As the knights who, clad in their armor,
  Went forth in the olden days
To war 'mid the downtrod nations,
  With wrongs that stood in their ways;
Thus our thoughts in this dusky metal
  Are clad in their coats of mail,
To conquer the wrongs that oppress us,
  **Or evils** our follies entail.

The sun in its golden glory,
  Went down 'neath the rim of night,
And each leaden **shape** was gleaming
  In flames of its dying light;
Then stars in their hosts came marching,
  As their silver lances fell
And flashed on the dull, cold metal,
  Where truths we know not dwell.

A child in his feeble wisdom,
  Might place them with tiny hand,
But a **king with** his steel-armed legions
  In vain would their force withstand;
For they are the silent warriors,
  **Whose tents** are folded away,
**Whose footprints** go down through the ages
  **Whose** mandates the world shall obey.

And a thought in my soul seemed striving,
  As our own good angel strives,
To warn the clay that infolds us
  And wake from **our** sluggish lives;
That we, too, are symbols waiting
  The touch of the Master's hand,
When the truths that sleep within us
  May light up each darkened land;
And each soul in its earthly journey
  May toil with hope sublime,
To leave for the unborn nations
  Great thoughts on the scroll of time.

ANONYMOUS.

## LANDING OF **THE** PILGRIM FATHERS.

·The breaking waves dashed high
　　On the stern and rock-bound coast,
And the woods against a stormy sky
　　Their giant branches tossed ;

**And** the heavy night hung dark
　　The hills and waters o'er,
**When a** band of exiles moored their bark
　　**On the** wild New England shore.

Not as **the conqueror comes,**
　　They, the true-hearted, came ;
**N**ot **with** the roll of the stirring **drums,**
　　And the trumpet that sings of fame :

Not **as** the flying come,
　　In silence and in fear ;
**T**hey shook the depth of the desert's gloom
　　With their hymns of lofty cheer.

**Amid** the storm they sang,
　　And the stars heard, and the sea ;
And the sounding aisles of the dim **woods**
　　　　rang
　　**To the** anthem of the free.

**The ocean** eagle soared
　　**From his** nest by **the white** wave's foam,
And the rocking pines of the forest roared :
　　This was their welcome home.

There were men with hoary hair
　　Amid that pilgrim band,
Why have they come to wither there,
　　Away from their childhood's land ?

There was woman's fearless eye,
　　Lit **by** her deep love's truth ;
There was manhood's brow, serenely high,
　　**A**nd the fiery heart of youth.

What sought they thus, afar?
  Bright jewels of the mine?
The wealth of seas, the spoils of war?
  They sought a faith's pure shrine!

Ay, call it holy ground,
  The soil where first they trod!
They have left unstained what **there they
        found—**
  **Freedom to** worship God!

Felicia Hemans.

## KEEP IT BEFORE THE PEOPLE.

Keep it before the people!
  That Earth was made for Man!
    That flowers were strown,
    And fruits were grown,
  To bless, and never to ban—
    That sun and rain,
    And corn and grain,
  Are yours and mine, my brother!
    Free gifts from heaven,
    And freely given
  To one as well as another!

Keep it before the people!
  That man is the image of God!
    His limbs or soul
    Ye may not control
  With shackle or shame or rod!
    We may not be sold
    For silver or gold,
  Neither you nor I, my brother!
    For freedom was given
    By God, from heaven,
  To one as well as another!

Keep it before the people !
  That famine and crime and woe
    For ever abide,
    Still side by side
  With luxury's dazzling show !
    That Lazarus crawls
    From Dives' halls,
**And** starves at his gate, my brother !
    **Yet life** was given
    **By** God, from heaven,
**To one as well as** another !

Keep **it** before **the** people !
  That the poor man claims his meed—
    The right of soil,
    **A**nd the right of toil,
**From** spur and bridle freed !
    The right to bear,
    And the right to share,
With you and **me**, my brother !
    Whatever is given
    By God, from heaven,
To one **as** well as another !
A. J. H. DUGANNE.

---

### YE MAY DRINK, IF YE LIST.

**Ye** may drink, if ye list,
  **The** red sparkling wine,
From beakers that gleam
  With the gems of the vine ;
Ye may quaff, if ye **will**,
  When the **foam** bends the brim,
From a flagon **or** goblet,
  Till your eye **shall** grow dim ;
But I've sworn on the altar,
  And my soul is **now** free,
Nor beaker, nor flagon,
  Nor goblet **for** me.

Ye may light the avenger
　On ruin's wild path,
Like a raging volcano,
　In the blaze of its wrath;
But your fire-crested waves,
　All gory with blood,
Shall be hissing like serpents,
　And quenched in the flood;
For I've sworn on the altar,
　And my soul is now free,
This hand shall ne'er falter
　In its warfare with thee.

But Nature's pure nectar
　Is the draught that I sip,—
What God has appointed
　To moisten the lip;
And the gleam of its glory,
　Through the cycles of years,
Shall dry the rivers of shame,
　And the fountains of tears;
For I've sworn on the altar,
　In youth's radiant glow,
Not to lay down my arms
　Till I've *conquered* the foe.

Then come to the altar,
　And come to the shrine,
Dash down your red goblets,
　And your flagons of wine;
Young heroes are thronging
　Where the battle's begun,
And the sheen of their banners
　Flashes bright in the sun.
When the shock of the onset,
　As a rock meets the flood,
Shall roll back the fountains
　And rivers of blood.

PEASE.

## LABOR IS WORSHIP.

Pause not to dream of the future before us;
Pause not to weep the wild cares that come o'er
    us;
Hark, how Creation's deep, musical chorus,
  Unintermitting, goes up into heaven!
Never the ocean wave falters in flowing;
Never the little seed stops in its growing;
More and more richly the rose-heart keeps glow-
    ing,
  Till from its nourishing stem it is riven.

" Labor is worship!"—the robin is singing;
" Labor is worship!"—the wild bee is ringing:
Listen! that eloquent whisper upspringing
  Speaks to thy soul from out Nature's great
    heart.
From the dark cloud flows the life-giving
    shower;
From the rough sod blows the soft-breathing
    flower;
From the small insect, the rich coral bower;
  Only man, in the plan, shrinks from his part.

Labor is life! 'Tis the still water faileth;
Idleness ever despaireth, bewaileth;
Keep the watch wound, for the dark rust as-
    saileth;
  Flowers droop and die in the stillness of noon.
Labor is glory!—the flying cloud lightens;
Only the waving wing changes and brightens;
Idle hearts only the dark future frightens;
  Play the sweet keys, wouldst thou keep them
    in tune!

Labor is rest from the sorrows that greet us,
Rest from all petty vexations that meet us,
Rest from sin-promptings that ever entreat us,
  Rest from world-sirens that lure us to ill.

Work—and pure slumbers shall wait **on thy** pil-
    low ;
Work—thou shalt ride over Care's **coming** bil-
    low ;
Lie not down wearied 'neath Woe's weeping-
    willow ;
    Work with a stout heart and resolute will !

Labor is health !  **Lo** ! the husbandman **reaping,**
How through his **veins** goes the life **current** leap-
    ing,
How his **strong** arm, in its stalwart pride sweep-
    ing,
    True **as a** sunbeam, the swift sickle guides !
Labor is wealth—in the sea the pearl groweth ;
Rich the queen's robe from the frail **cocoon**
    floweth ;
From the fine acorn the strong forest bloweth ;
    Temple and statue the marble block hides.

Droop not, though shame, sin, and anguish are
    around thee !
Bravely fling off the cold chain that hath **bound**
    thee !
Look to you pure heaven smiling beyond thee !
    Rest not content in thy darkness—a clod!
Work—for some good, be it ever so slowly ;
Cherish some flower, be it ever so lowly ;
Labor !—all labor is noble and holy ;
    Let thy great deeds be thy prayer to thy God !
FRANCES S. OSGOOD.

---

## "LOOK NOT UPON THE WINE WHEN IT IS RED."

    Look **not** upon the wine when it
      Is red within **the** cup ;
    Stay not for pleasure when **she** fills
      Her tempting beaker up ;
    Though clear its **depths,** and rich its glow,
    A spell of madness lurks below.

They say 'tis pleasant on the lip,
  And merry on the brain;
They say it stirs the sluggish blood,
  And dulls the tooth of pain:
Ay, but within its gloomy deeps
A stinging serpent unseen sleeps.

Its rosy lights will turn to fire,
  Its coolness change to thirst;
And by its mirth within the brim
  A sleepless worm is nursed.
There's not a bubble at the brim
That does not carry food to him.

Then dash the burning cup aside
  And spill its purple wine:
Take not its madness to thy lips—
  Let not its curse be thine.
'Tis red and rich, but grief and woe
Are hid those rosy depths below.

Nathaniel P. Willis.

## THE VILLAGE SCHOOLMASTER.

Beside yon straggling fence that skirts the
    way,
With blossomed furze unprofitably gay,
There, in his noisy mansion skilled to rule,
The village master taught his little school.
A man severe he was, and stern to view;
I knew him well, and every truant knew:
Well had the boding tremblers learned to
    trace
The day's disasters in his morning face;
Full well they laughed with counterfeited
    glee,
At all his jokes, for many a joke had he;
Full well the busy whisper, circling round,
Conveyed the dismal tidings when he frowned.
Yet he was kind, or if severe in aught,

The love he bore to learning was his fault.
The village all declared how much he knew ;
'Twas certain he could write and cipher too ;
Lands he could measure, terms and tides  pre-
    sage,
And e'en the story **ran**—that he could gauge :
In arguing, **too,** the parson owned his skill,
For e'en **though** vanquished he could **argue**
    still ;
While words of learned length, **and**  thunder-
    ing sound,
Amazed the grazing rusties ranged around ;
And still they gazed, and still the wonder
    grew,
That one small head could carry all he knew.
But past is all his fame.   The very spot
Where many a time he triumphed is forgot.

OLIVER GOLDSMITH.

---

## NOTHING BUT LEAVES.

Nothing but leaves ; the spirit grieves
    Over a wasted life ;
Sin committed while conscience slept,
Promises made but never kept,
    Hatred, battle, and strife ;
        *Nothing but leaves !*

Nothing but leaves ; no garnered sheaves
    Of life's fair, ripened grain ;
Words, idle words, for earnest deeds ;
We sow our seeds—lo ! tares and weeds ;
    We reap with toil and pain
        *Nothing but leaves !*

Nothing but leaves ; memory weaves
    No vail to screen the past :
As we retrace our weary way,
Counting each lost and misspent day—
    We find, sadly, at last,
        *Nothing but leaves !*

And shall we meet the Master so,
  Bearing our withered leaves?
The Saviour looks for perfect fruit,—
We stand before him, humbled, mute;
  Waiting the words he breathes,—
  " *Nothing but leaves?* "

ANONYMOUS.

## THE CREEDS OF THE BELLS.

How sweet the chime of Sabbath bells!
Each one its creed in music tells,
In tones that float upon the air,
As soft as song, as pure as prayer.
And I will put in simple rhyme
The language of the golden chime:
My happy heart with rapture swells
Responsive to the bells, sweet bells.

"In deeds of love excel! excel!"
Chimed out from ivied towers a bell;
" This is the church not built on sands,
Emblem of one not built with hands;
Its forms and sacred rites revere,
Come worship here! come worship here!
In rituals and faith excel!"
Chimed out the Episcopalian bell.

" O heed the ancient landmarks well!"
In solemn tones exclaimed a bell;
" No progress made by mortal man
Can change the just, eternal plan;
With God there can be nothing new;
Ignore the false, embrace the true,
While all is well! is well! is well!"
Pealed out the good old Dutch church bell.

"O swell! ye purifying waters, swell!"
In mellow tones rang out a bell,
" Though faith alone in Christ can save,
Man must be plunged beneath the wave,

To show the world unfaltering faith
In what the Sacred Scriptures saith:
O swell! ye rising waters, swell!"
Pealed out the clear-toned Baptist bell.

"Not faith alone, but works as well,
Must test the soul!" said a soft bell;
"Come here and cast aside your load,
And work your way along the road,
With faith in God, and faith in man,
And hope in Christ, where hope began;
Do well! do well! do well! do well!"
Rang out the Unitarian bell.

"Farewell! farewell! base world, farewell!"
In touching tones exclaimed a bell;
"Life is a boon, to mortals given
To fit the soul for bliss in Heaven;
Do not invoke the avenging rod,
Come here and learn the way to God;
Say to the world, Farewell! farewell!"
Pealed forth the Presbyterian bell.

"To all the truth we tell! we tell!"
Shouted in ecstasies a bell;
"Come, all ye weary wanderers, see!
Our Lord has made salvation free!
Repent, believe, have faith, and then
Be saved, and praise the Lord, Amen!
Salvation's free, we tell! we tell!"
Shouted the Methodistic bell.

George W. Bungay.

---

## JOAN OF ARC'S FAREWELL TO HOME.

Farewell, ye mountains, ye beloved glades,
Ye lone and peaceful valleys, fare ye well!
Through yon Johanna never more may stray!
For aye Johanna bids yon now farewell.
Ye meads which I have watered, and ye trees

Which I have planted, still in beauty bloom!
Farewell, ye grottos, and ye crystal springs!
Sweet echo, vocal spirit of the vale,
Who sang'st responsive to my simple strain,
Johanna goes, and ne'er returns again.

Ye scenes where all my tranquil joys **I knew,**
Forever **now** I leave you far behind!
Poor foldless lambs, no shepherd now have
      you!
**O'er the wide** heath **stray** henceforth uncon-
      fined!
**For I to** danger's field **of** crimson line
Am summoned hence, another flock **to** find.
Such is to me the Spirit's high behest;
No earthly vain ambition fires my breast.

For who in **glory** did on **Horeb's** height
Descend to Moses in the bush of flame,
And bade him stand in royal Pharaoh's sight—
Who once to Israel's pious shepherd came,
And sent him forth his champion in the fight—
Who aye hath loved the lowly shepherd train—
He from these leafy boughs thus spake to me;
"Go forth! **Thou** shalt **on** earth my witness
      be.

"Thou in rude armor must thy limbs invest,
A plate of steel upon thy bosom wear;
Vain earthly love may never stir thy breast,
Nor passion's sinful glow be kindled there.
Ne'er with the bride-wreath shall thy locks be
      dressed,
Nor on thy bosom bloom an infant fair.
But war's triumphant glory shall be thine;
Thy martial fame all women shall outshine.

"For, when in fight the stoutest hearts de-
      spair,
When direful ruin threatens France, forlorn,

Then **thou aloft** my oriflamme shall bear
And swiftly as the reaper mows the corn
Thou shalt lay low the haughty conqueror;
His fortune's wheel thou rapidly shalt turn,
To Gaul's heroic sons deliv'rance bring,
Relieve beleaguered Rheims, and crown thy
　　king!"

The heavenly spirit promised me a sign;
He sends the helmet, it hath **come** from him.
Its iron filleth me with strength **divine**—
I feel the courage of the **cherubim**;
As with the rushing of a mighty wind,
It drives me forth to join the battle's din;
The clanging trumpets sound, the chargers
　　rear,
**And** the loud war-cry thunders in mine **car.**

SCHILLER.

---

### HOW HE SAVED ST. MICHAEL'S.

'Twas long ago—ere the signal gun
That blazed above Fort Sumter had wakened
　　the north as **one**;
Long ere the wondrous pillar of battle-cloud and
　　fire
Had marked where the unchained millions
　　marched on **to their heart's** desire.

On roofs and glittering turrets, that night as
　　the sun went down,
The mellow glow of the twilight shone like **a**
　　jewelled **crown,**
And, bathed in the living glory, **as the people**
　　lifted their eyes,
They saw the pride of the city, the spire of St.
　　Michael's, rise

High over the lesser steeples, tipped with a
　　golden ball,
That hung like a radiant planet caught in its
　　earthward fall;

First glimpse of home to the sailor who made
    the harbor round,
And last slow-fading vision dear to the outward
    bound.

The gently-gathering shadows shut out the wan-
    ing light;
The children prayed at their bedsides, as they
    **were wont** each night:
The noise **of** buyer and seller from the busy mart
    was **gone,**
And in dreams **of** a peaceful morrow the city
    slumbered on.

But another light than sunrise aroused the sleep-
    ing street,
For a cry was heard at midnight, and the rush **of**
    trampling feet;
Men stared in each other's faces, thro' mingled
    fire and smoke,
While the frantic bells went clashing clamorous,
    stroke on stroke.

By the glare of her blazing roof-tree the house-
    less mother fled,
With the babe she pressed to her bosom shriek-
    ing in nameless dread,
While the fire-king's wild battalions scaled wall
    and capstone high,
And planted their glaring banners against an
    inky sky.

From the death that raged behind them, and the
    crush of ruin loud,
To the great square of the city, were driven the
    surging crowd,
Where yet firm in all the tumult, unscathed by
    the fiery flood,
With its heavenward pointing finger the church
    of St. Michael's stood.

But e'en as they gazed upon it, there rose a sud-
　　den wail,
A cry of horror blended with the roaring of the
　　gale,
On whose scorching wings updriven, a single
　　flaming brand,
Aloft on the towering steeple clung like a bloody
　　hand.

"Will it fade?" the whisper trembled from a
　　thousand whitening lips;
Far out on the lurid harbor they watched it from
　　the ships,
A baleful gleam, that brighter and ever brighter
　　shone,
Like a flickering, trembling will-o'-the-wisp to a
　　steady beacon grown.

"Uncounted gold shall be given to the man
　　whose brave right hand,
For the love of the perilled city, plucks down
　　yon burning brand!"
So cried the Mayor of Charleston, that all the
　　people heard,
But they looked each one at his fellow, and no
　　man spoke a word.

Who is it leans from the belfry, with face up-
　　turned to the sky—
Clings to a column and measures the dizzy spire
　　with his eye?
Will he dare it, the hero undaunted, that terrible
　　sickening height,
Or will the hot blood of his courage freeze in his
　　veins at the sight?

But, see! he has stepped on the railing, he climbs
　　with his feet and his hands,
And firm on a narrow projection, with the belfry
　　beneath him he stands!

Now, once, and once only, they cheer him—a
    single tempestuous breath,
**And** there falls on the multitude gazing a hush
    like the stillness of death.

Slowly, steadily mounting, unheeding aught save
    the goal of the fire,
Still **higher** and higher, an atom, he moves on
    the face of the spire;
He stops! Will **he** fall? **Lo!** for answer, **a**
    **gleam like a meteor's track,**
**And, hurled on** the stones of the pavement, the
    **red brand** lies shattered and black!

**O**nce more **the** shouts of the people have rent the
    quivering air;
At the **church** door, mayor and council wait with
    their feet on the stair,
And the eager throng behind them press for **a**
    touch of his hand,
The unknown saviour whose daring could com-
    pass a deed so grand.

But why does a sudden tremor seize on them as
    they gaze?
And what meaneth that stifled murmur of won-
    der **and** amaze?
He **stood in** the gate of the temple he had
    **perilled his** life to save,
And **the** face of the unknown hero was the sable
    **face of** a slave!

With folded arms he **was** speaking in tones that
    were clear, not loud,
And his eyes, ablaze **in** their sockets, burnt into
    the eyes of the crowd.
"Ye may keep your gold, I scorn it! but answer
    me, ye who can,
If the deed I have done before you be not the
    **deed of a *man*?** "

He stepped but a short space backward, and from
  all the women and men
There were only sobs for answer, and the mayor
  called for a pen,
And **the** great seal of **the** city, **that he** might
  read who ran,
And the slave who saved St. Michael's went **out**
  **from** its door a man.

MARY A. P. STANSBURY.

----

### THE CHILDREN.

When the lessons and tasks are all ended,
  And the school for the day is dismissed,
And the little ones gather around me,
  To bid me good night and be kissed:
Oh, the little white arms that encircle
  My neck in a tender embrace!
Oh, the smiles that are halos of heaven,
  Shedding sunshine of love on my face!

And when they **are gone I** sit dreaming
  Of my childhood, **too** lovely to last:
**Of** love **that** my heart will remember
  **When it** wakes to the pulse **of the** past,
Ere the world and its wickedness made me
  A partner of sorrow and sin;
When the glory of God was about me,
  And **the** glory of gladness within.

Oh! my heart grows as weak as a woman's,
  And the fountains of feeling will flow,
When I think of paths steep and stony,
  Where the feet of the dear ones must go;
Of the mountains of sin hanging o'er them,
  **Of** the tempest of fate blowing wild;
Oh! there is nothing on earth half so holy
  **As the** innocent **heart of** a child.

They are idols of hearts and of households:
  They are angels of God in disguise;
His sunlight still sleeps in their tresses,
  His glory still beams in their eyes.
Oh! those truants from home and from heaven,
  **They have** made me more manly and mild,
And **I know** how Jesus could liken
  **The** kingdom of God to a child.

I ask not **a** life for the dear ones,
  All radiant, as others have done,
But that life may have just enough shadow
  To temper the glare of the sun:
I would pray God to guard them from evil,
  But my prayer would bound back to myself;
Ah! a seraph may pray for a sinner,
  But a sinner must pray for himself.

The twig is so **easily bended,**
  I have banished **the rule** and the rod;
I have taught them the goodness of knowledge,
  They have taught **me the** goodness of God;
My heart is a dungeon of darkness,
  Where I **shut** them from breaking a **rule;**
My frown **is** sufficient correction;
  My love **is the** law **of the** school.

I shall **leave** the old home **in the** autumn,
  To **traverse** its threshold **no more;**
Ah! how shall I sigh for the dear ones
  **That** meet me each morn at the door!
I shall miss the " good-nights " and the kisses,
  And the gush of their innocent glee,
The group on **the** green, and the flowers
  That are brought every morning to me.

I shall miss them at morn and at eve,
  Their song in the school and the street;
I shall miss the low hum of their voices,
  **A**nd the tramp of their delicate feet.

When the lessons and tasks are all ended,
  And death says, " The school is dismissed ! "
May the little ones gather around me,
  To bid me good-night, and be kissed !
Charles S. Dickinson.

---

## THE LOVE-KNOT.

Tying her bonnet under her **chin**,
She tied her raven ringlets in ;
But not alone in the silken snare,
**Did** she **catch** her lovely floating **hair** ;
**But** tying her bonnet under her chin,
She tied a young man's heart within.

They were strolling together up the hill,
**Where** the wind comes blowing merry  and
    chill,
And it blew the curls, a frolicsome race,
All over the happy peach-colored face ;
Till, scolding and laughing, she tied them **in**,
Under her beautiful, dimpled chin.

And it blew a **color** as bright as the bloom
**Of the** pinkest fuchsia's tossing plume,
**All** over the cheeks **of the** prettiest girl
**T**hat ever imprisoned a romping curl, .
Or, in tying her bonnet under her chin,
Tied a young man's heart within.

Steeper **and steeper** grew the hill ;
Madder, merrier, chillier still
The western wind blew down **and** played
The wildest tricks with the little maid,
**As,** tying her bonnet under her chin,
**She tied** a young man's heart within.

O, western wind ! do you think **it** was fair
To play such tricks with her floating hair ?
**To** gladly, gleefully **do** your best

To blow her against the young man's breast,
Where he as gladly folded her in,
And kissed her mouth and dimpled chin?

ANONYMOUS.

## THE CHURNING.

No graceful shape like a Grecian urn,
But upright, downright, stands the churn.
Broad at the base and tapering small,
Above it the dasher straight and tall—
Windowless tower with flagstaff bare,
Warrior or warden, nobody there!
Fashioned of cedar, queen of the wood,
Cedar as sweet as a girl in a hood
Hiding her face like a blush-rose bud.

The dasher waits knee-deep in the cream,
As cattle wade in the shady stream,
And flat in the foot as a four-leafed clover
Just waits the touch to trample it over.
Beside the churn a maiden stands,
Nimble and naked her arms and hands—
Another Ruth when the reapers reap.
Her dress, as limp as a flag asleep,
Is faced in front with a puzzling check ;
Her feet are bare as her sun-browned neck ;
Her hair rays out like a lady fern.
With a single hand she starts the churn ;
The play at the first is free and swift,
Then she gives both hands to the plunge and
    lift.

A short quick splash in the Milky Way—
One-two, one-two, in Iambic play—
A one-legg'd dance in a wooden clog,
Dancing a jig in a watery bog—
A soberer gait at an all-day jog—
Up-down, up-down like a pony's feet,

A steady trot in a sloppy street,
The spattering dash and the tinkling wash
Deaden and dull to a creamy swash—
Color of daffodil shows in the churn!
Glimpses of gold!  Beginning to turn!
Slower—and lower—deader and dumb—
Daisies and Buttercups!  Butter has come!

What thinks the maiden all the while?
Whatever she thinks, it makes her smile,
Whatever she does is only seeming,
Spinning and weaving, wedding and dreaming,
Ah, charms are hid in the ingot's gold,
And more come out than the churn can hold!
Not butter at all, but bonnets sown
With gardens of flowers and all full blown;
A clouded comb of the tortoise-shell,
Ah, it is a beauty and she a belle!
A grape-leaf breast-pin's restless shine
Is twinkling up from the fairy mine.
The dasher clinks on a bright gold ring,
Morocco shoes, like a martin's wing,
Come up with a gown of flounces silk—
Some fairy lost in the buttermilk!
Ribbons of blue for love-knot ties
To match the tint of her longing eyes;—
Ribbons of pink and a belt of gray
Rippling along in a watery way.

She looks at herself in Fancy's glass,
And she sees her own lithe figure pass—
She closes her eyes and looks again,
And sees, as she dreams, the prince of men—
She closes her eyes and, side by side,
He is the bridegroom and she the bride!
Ah, never, my girl, will visions burn
As bright as those in the cedar churn;
Ah, what have we won if this be lost;
THE BLESSING FREE AND THE BLISS AT COST?

B. F. TAYLOR.

## FALL OF WARSAW, 1794.

O! sacred Truth! thy triumph ceased a while,
And Hope, thy sister, ceased with thee to smile,
When leagued Oppression poured **to** Northern
    wars
**Her** whiskered pandours and her fierce hussars;
**Waved** her **dread** standard to the breeze of morn,
Pealed **her lou**d drum, and twanged her trum**pet**
    horn:
Tumultuous horror brooded o'er her van,
Presaging wrath to Poland—and to man!
  Warsaw's last champion from her heights sur-
    veyed
**Wi**de o'er the fields a waste of ruin laid—
O Heaven! he cried, my bleeding country save!
Is there no hand on high to shield the brave?
Yet, though destruction sweep these lovely
    plains,
Rise, fellow-men! our country yet remains!
By that dread name, we wave the sword on high,
And swear for her to live!—with her to die!
  **He** said; and on the rampart heights arrayed
**His** trusty warriors, few, but undismayed;
**Firm** paced and slow, a horrid front they form,
**Still** as the breeze, but dreadful as the storm;
**Low,** murmuring sounds along their banners
    fly,—
" Revenge, or death! "—the watchword and **re-**
    **ply:**
Then pealed the notes, omnipotent to **charm,**
And the loud tocsin tolled their last alarm!
  In vain, alas! in vain, ye gallant few!
From rank to rank your volleyed thunder flew;—
**O!** bloodiest picture in the book of Time,
Sarmatia fell, unwept, without a crime;
**Found** not a generous friend, a pitying foe,
Strength in her arms, nor mercy in her woe!
Dropped from her nerveless grasp the shattered
    **spear,**

Closed her bright eye, and **curbed her** high
    career,
Hope, for a season, bade the world farewell,
And freedom shrieked, as Kosciusko fell!
  O righteous Heaven! ere Freedom found a
    grave,
Why **slept the sword,** omnipotent to save?
Where was thine arm, O vengeance! where **thy**
    rod,
That smote **the foes of Sion and of God?**
  Departed spirits of the mighty dead!
**Ye that** at Marathon and Leuctra bled!
**Friends** of the **world!** restore your swords to
    man,
Fight in his sacred cause, and lead the van!
Yet for Sarmatia's tears of blood **atone,**
And make her arm puissant as your own!
O! once again to Freedom's cause return
The patriot Tell,—the **Bruce** of Bannockburn!
  Yes, thy proud lords, unpitied land! shall see
That man hath yet a soul,—and dare be free!
A little while, along thy saddening plains,
The starless night of Desolation reigns;
Truth shall **restore** the light by Nature given,
And, like Prometheus, bring the fire of Heaven!
Prone to the dust Oppression shall be hurled.
**Her** name, her nature, withered from the world!
Thomas Campbell.

---

### THE STUDENT.

"Poor fool!" the base and soulless worldling
    cries,
"To waste his strength for nought,—to blanch
    his cheek,
And bring pale Death upon him in his prime.
Why did he not to pleasure give his days,—
His nights to rest,—and live while live he
    might?"
What is't **to live?** To **breathe the** vital air,

Consume the fruits **of** earth, and doze away
Existence?  Never! this **is** living death,—
'Tis brutish life,—base grovelling.  E'en the
        brutes
**Of** nobler nature, live not lives like this.
Shall man, then, formed to be creation's lord,
Stamped with the impress of Divinity, and sealed
**With God**'s own signet, sink below the brute?
**Forbid it,** Heaven! it cannot, must not be!

Oh! **when the** mighty God from nothing
        brought
This universe,—when at **His word** the light
Burst forth,—the sun was set in heaven,—
**And** earth was clothed in beauty; when the last,
The noble work of all, from dust He framed
Our bodies in His image,—when he placed
Within its temple-shrine of clay, the soul.—
**The** immortal soul,—in**fused by** His own truth,
Did He not show, 'tis this which gives to man
His high prerogative?  Why then declare
That he who thinks less of his worthless frame,
And lives a spirit, even in this world,
Lives not as well,—lives not as long. as he
**Who** drags **out** years **of** life, without one
        thought,—
One hope,—one wish beyond the present hour?

How shall **we** measure life? Not by the years,—
The months,—the days,—the moments **that we**
        pass
**On** earth.  By him whose soul is raised above
Base worldly things,—whose heart is fixed in
        heaven—
**His** life **is** measured by that soul's advance,—
**Its** cleansing from pollution and from sin,—
**The** enlargement of its powers,—the expanded
        field
Wherein it ranges,—till it glows and burns
With holy joys,—with high and heavenly hopes.

When in the silent night, all earth **lies** hushed
In slumber,—when the glorious stars shine out,
Each star a sun,—each sun a central light
Of some fair system, ever wheeling on
In one unbroken round,—and that again
Revolving round another sun,—while all
Suns, stars, and systems, proudly roll along,
In one majestic, ever-onward course,
In space uncircumscribed and limitless,—
Oh! think you then **the** undebased **soul**
Can calmly give itself to sleep,—to rest?

No! in the solemn stillness of the night,
**It** soars from earth,—it dwells in angels' homes,—
It hears the burning song,—the glowing chant,
That fills the sky-girt vaults of heaven with **joy!**
It pants, it sighs. to wing its flight from earth,
To join the heavenly choirs, and be with God.

And it is joy to muse the written page,
Whereon are stamped the gushings of the soul
Of genius ;—where, in never-dying light,
It glows and flashes as the lightning's glare;
Or where it burns with ray more mild,—more
　　**sure,**
And wins the soul, that half would turn away
From its more brilliant flashings.　These are
　　**hours**
Of holy joy,—of bliss, so pure, that earth
May hardly claim it.　Let his lamp grow dim,
And flicker to extinction; let his cheek
Be pale as sculptured marble,—and his eye
Lose its bright lustre,—till his shrouded frame
**Is** laid in dust.　Himself can never die!

His years, tis true, are few,—his life is long;
For he has gathered many a precious gem ;
Enraptured, he has dwelt where master minds
Have poured their own deep musings,—and his
　　heart

Has glowed with love to Him who framed us
    thus,—
**Who** placed within this worthless tegument
The spark of pure Divinity, which shines
With light unceasing.

**Yes**, his life is long,—
Long **to** the dull and loathsome epicure's,—
Long **to** the slothful man's—the grovelling herds
Who scarcely know they have a soul within,—
Long to all those who, creeping on to death,
Meet in the grave, the earth-worm's banquet-
    hall,—
And leave behind no monuments for good.
ANONYMOUS.

## MARCO BOZZARIS.

At midnight, in his guarded tent,
  The Turk was dreaming of the hour
When **Greece**, her knee in **su**ppliance bent,
  Should tremble at his power;
In dreams, through camp and court he bore
The trophies of a conqueror;
  In dreams, his song of triumph heard;
Then wore **his** monarch's signet ring;
Then pressed **that** monarch's throne—a king:
As wild his thoughts, and gay of wing,
  **As** Eden's garden bird.

At **midnight, in** the forest shades,
  Bozzaris ranged his Suliote band,
True as the steel of their tried blades,
  Heroes in heart and hand.
There had the Persian's thousands stood,
There had the glad earth drunk their blood,
  On old Platæa's day;
And now there breathed that haunted air
The sons of sires who conquered there,
With arm to strike, and soul to dare,
  **As** quick, as far, as they.

An hour passed on: the Turk awoke.
  That bright dream was his last.
He woke to hear his sentries shriek,
" To arms! they come! the Greek! the Greek!"
He woke, to die 'midst flame and smoke,
And shout, **and** groan, and sabre-stroke,
  And death-**shots** falling thick and fast
As lightnings from the mountain cloud,
And heard with voice as trumpet loud,
  Bozzaris cheer his band :
" Strike !—till the last armed **foe expires ;**
Strike !—for your altars and your fires ;
Strike !—for the green graves of your sires ;
  God, and your native land ! "

They fought like brave men, long and well ;
  They piled that ground with Moslem slain ;
They conquered ;—but Bozzaris fell,
  Bleeding at every vein.
His few surviving comrades saw
His smile when rang their loud hurrah
  And the red field was won,
Then saw in death his eyelids close,
Calmly as to a night's repose,—
  Like flowers at set of sun.

Come to the bridal chamber, Death !
  Come to the mother's, when she feels,
For the first time, her first-born's breath ;
  Come when the blessed seals
That close the pestilence are broke,
And crowded cities wail its stroke ;
Come in consumption's ghastly form,
The earthquake shock, the ocean storm ;
Come when the heart beats high and warm
  With banquet song, and dance, and wine ;
And thou art terrible :—the tear,
The groan, the knell, the pall, the bier,
And all we know, or dream, or fear,
  Of agony, **are thine.**

But to the hero, when his sword
  Has won the battle for the free,
Thy voice sounds like a prophet's word,
And in its hollow tones are heard
  The thanks of millions yet to **be.**
Come when his task of fame is wrought;
Come, with her laurel-leaf, blood-bought;
  **Come in** her crowning hour,—and then
**Thy sunken** eye's unearthly light,
**To** him is welcome **as** the sight
  Of sky and stars to prisoned men;
Thy grasp is welcome as the hand
Of brother in a foreign land;
**Thy** summons welcome as the cry
**That told the** Indian isles were nigh
  To the world-seeking Genoese,
When the land-wind, from woods of palm,
And orange-groves, and fields of balm,
  Blew o'er the Haytian seas.

Bozzaris! with the storied brave
  Greece nurtured in **her** glory's **time,**
Rest thee: there is no prouder grave,
  Even in her own proud clime.
She wore no funeral weeds for thee,
  Nor bade **the** dark hearse wave its plume
Like **torn branch** from death's leafless tree,
In sorrow's pomp and pageantry,
  The heartless luxury of the tomb;
But she remembers thee as one
Long loved, and for a season gone;
For thee her poet's lyre is wreathed,
Her marble wrought, her music breathed;
For thee she rings the birthday bells;
Of thee her babes' first lisping tells;
For thine her evening prayer is said,
At palace couch and cottage bed;
Her soldier, closing with the foe,
**Gives** for thy sake a deadlier blow;
His plighted maiden, when she **fears**

For him, the joy of her young years,
Thinks of thy fate, and checks her tears;
　And she, the mother of thy boys,
Though in her eye and faded cheek
Is read the grief she will not speak,
　The memory of her buried joys,—
And even she who gave thee birth,
Will, by their pilgrim-circled hearth,
　Talk of thy doom without a sigh;
For thou art Freedom's now, and Fame's:
One of the few, the immortal names
　That were not born to die.

Fitz Greene Halleck.

## THE NIGHT BEFORE CHRISTMAS.

'Twas the night before Christmas, when all
　　through the house
Not a creature was stirring, not even a mouse;
The stockings were hung by the chimney with
　　care,
In hopes that St. Nicholas soon would be there;
The children were nestled all snug in their beds,
While visions of sugar-plums danced through
　　their heads;
And Mamma in her kerchief, and I in my cap,
Had just settled our brains for a long winter's
　　nap—
When out on the lawn there arose such a clatter,
I sprang from my bed to see what was the matter.
Away to the window I flew like a flash,
Tore open the shutters and threw up the sash.
The moon, on the breast of the new-fallen snow,
Gave a lustre of mid-day to objects below;
When, what to my wondering eyes should ap-
　　pear,
But a miniature sleigh, and eight tiny reindeer,
With a little old driver, so lively and quick,
I knew in a moment it must be St. Nick.

More rapid than eagles his coursers they came,
And he whistled, and shouted, and called them
 by name:
" Now, Dasher! now, Dancer! **now,** Prancer!
 now, Vixen!
On, Comet! on, Cupid! on, Donder and Blit-
 zen!—
To **the top of** the porch, to the top of the wall!
Now, **dash away,** dash away, dash away all!"
As **dry** leaves that before the wild hurricane fly,
When they meet with an obstacle, mount to the
 sky,
So, up to the house-top the coursers they flew,
**With** the sleigh full of toys—and **St.** Nicholas
 **too.**
And **then** in a twinkling I heard on the roof
The prancing and pawing of each little hoof,
As I drew in my head, and was turning around,
Down the chimney St. Nicholas came with **a**
 bound.
He was dressed all **in fur from his** head to his
 foot,
And his clothes were all tarnished with ashes
 and soot ;
**A** bundle of **toys** he had flung on his back,
**And** he **looked** like a pedler just opening his
 pack.
His eyes **how** they twinkled! his dimples how
 **merry !**
His **cheeks were** like roses, his **nose** like a cherry ;
His droll little mouth was drawn up like a bow,
And the beard on his chin was as white as the
 snow.
The stump of **a** pipe he held tight in his teeth,
And the smoke, it encircled his head like **a**
 wreath.
**He** had a broad face and **a** little round belly
That shook, when he laughed, like a bowl full of
 jelly.

He was chubby and plump—a right jolly old elf;
And I laughed when I saw him, in spite of my-
    self.
A wink of his eye, and a twist of his head,
Soon gave me to know I had nothing to dread.
He spake not a word, but went straight to his
    work,
And filled all the stockings ; then turned with a
    jerk,
And laying his finger aside of his nose,
And giving a nod, up the chimney he rose.
He sprang to his sleigh, to his team gave a
    whistle,
And away they all flew like the down of a
    thistle ;
But I heard him exclaim, ere he drove out of
    sight,
" Happy Christmas to all, and to all a good-
    night ! "

CLEMENT C. MOORE.

## THE NIGHT AFTER CHRISTMAS.

'Twas the night after Christmas, when all through
    the house,
Every soul was abed, and still as a mouse,
The stockings so lately St. Nicholas' care,
Were emptied of all that was eatable there,
The darlings had been duly tucked up in their
    beds—
With very full stomachs and pains in their heads.
I was dozing away in my new cotton cap,
And Nancy was rather far gone in a nap,
When out in the Nursery rose such a clatter,
I sprang from my sleep, crying—" What is the
    matter ? "
I flew to each bedside, still half in a doze,
Tore open the curtains and threw off the clothes,
While the light of the taper served clearly to
    show

The piteous plight of those objects below ;
For what to the fond father's eyes should appear,
But the little pale face of each sick little dear ;
For each pet that had crammed itself full as a
    tick,
I knew in a moment now felt like Old Nick.
Their pulses were rapid, their breathings the
    same,
What their stomachs rejected I 'll mention **by**
    name—
Now Turkey, **now Stuffing,** Plumb Pudding of
    course,
And Custards, and Crullers, and Cranberry sauce,
Before outraged nature all **went** to the wall ;
Yes—Lollypops, Flapdoddle, Dinner and all.
Like pellets, which urchins from pop-guns let fly,
Went Figs, Nuts, and Raisins, Jams, Jelly, and
    Pie.
'Till each error of diet was brought to my view,
To the shame of Mamma and Santa Claus too.
I turned from the sight, **to my** bed-room **stepped**
    back,
And brought out a phial marked " Pulv. Ipecac,"
When my Nancy exclaimed—for their sufferings
    shocked her—
**" Don't you think** you had bet**ter,** love, run for
    the Doctor ? "**
I ran—and was scarcely back under my roof,
When I heard the sharp clatter of old Jalap's
    hoof,
I **might say** that I hardly had turned myself
    round,
When the Doctor came into **the room** with a
    bound.
**He** was covered with **mud** from his head to his
    foot,
And the suit he had on was his very worst suit ;
He had hardly had time to put *that* on his back,
And he looked like a Falstaff, half fuddled with
    sack.

His eyes how they twinkled!   Had the Doctor
  got merry ?
His cheeks looked like **Port,** and his breath
  smelt of *Sherry,*
He hadn't been shaved **for a** fortnight or so,
And the beard on his chin wasn't white as the
  snow.
But inspecting their tongues in despite of their
  teeth,
And drawing his watch from **his** waistcoat be-
  neath—
He felt of each pulse, saying :—"Each little **belly**
Must get rid "—here he laughed—" of the rest
  of that jelly."
I gazed on each chubby, plump, sick little elf,
And groaned when he said so, in spite of myself ;
But a wink of his eye when he physicked **our
  Fred,**
Soon gave me to know **I** had nothing to dread.
He didn't prescribe—but went straightway to
  work,
And dosed all the rest—gave **his** trousers a jerk,
And adding directions while blowing his nose,
He buttoned his coat—from his chair he arose,
Then jumped **in** his gig—gave old Jalap a
  whistle,
**And** Jalap dashed off as **if** pricked by a thistle ;
**But** the Doctor exclaimed, ere he drove **out of**
  sight,
" They 'll be well to-morrow—good-night ! Jones
  —good-night ! "

Anonymous.

## SWEEPING THE FLOOR.

Sweep the floor and the sweep the floor ;
  Sweep the dust, pick up the pin :
Make it clean from fire to door,
  Clean for father to come in.

Mother says that **God** goes sweeping—
  Looking, sweeping with a broom,
All the time that **we are** sleeping,
  For a shilling in the room.

Did he drop it out of glory,
  Walking far above the birds?
Or did mother make the story
  To set me thinking afterwards?

If I were the swept-for shilling
  I would hearken through the gloom—
Roll down fast and fall down willing,
  Right before the sweeping broom.

ANONYMOUS.

---

## THE TEACHER'S DREAM.

The weary teacher sat alone
  While twilight gathered on :
And not a sound was heard around,—
  The boys and girls **were** gone.

The weary teacher sat alone,
  Unnerved and pale was he ;
Bowed 'neath a yoke of care, he spoke
  In sad soliloquy :

" Another round, another round
  Of labor thrown away,
Another chain of toil and pain
  Dragged through a tedious day.

" Of no avail is constant zeal,
  Love's sacrifice is lost,
The hopes of morn, so golden, turn,
  Each evening, into dross.

" I squander on a barren field
  My strength, my life, my all :
The seeds I sow will never grow,
  They perish where they fall."

He sighed, and low upon his hands
  His aching brow he prest;
And o'er his frame ere long there came
  A soothing sense of rest.

And then he lifted up his face,
  But started back aghast,—
The room, by strange and sudden change,
  Assumed proportions vast.

It seemed a Senate-hall, and one
  Addressed a listening throng;
Each burning word all bosoms stirred,
  Applause rose loud and long.

The 'wildered teacher thought he knew
  The speaker's voice and look,
"And for his name," said he, "the same
  Is in my record book."

The stately Senate-hall dissolved,
  A church rose in its place,
Wherein there stood a man of God,
  Dispensing words of grace.

And though he spoke in solemn tone,
  And though his hair was gray,
The teacher's thought was strangely
    wrought:
  "I whipped that boy to-day."

The church, a phantasm, vanished soon;
  What saw the teacher then?
In classic gloom of alcoved room
  An author plied his pen.

"My idlest lad!" the teacher said,
  Filled with a new surprise—
"Shall I behold his name enrolled
  Among the great and wise?"

The vision of a cottage home
  The teacher now descried;

A mother's face illumed the place
　Her influence sanctified.

" A miracle ! a miracle !
　This matron, well I know,
Was but a wild and careless child,
　Not half an hour ago.

" And when she to her children speaks
　Of duty's golden rule,
Her lips repeat in accents sweet,
　My words to her at school."

The scene was changed again, and lo,
　The school-house rude and old ;
Upon the wall did darkness fall,
　The evening air was cold.

" A dream ! " the sleeper, waking, said,
　Then paced along the floor,
And, whistling slow **and** soft **and low,**
　He locked the school-house **door.**

And, walking home, his heart was **full**
　Of peace and trust and love and praise ;
And singing slow and soft and low,
　He murmured, "After many days."
W. H. VENABLE.

## LETTING THE OLD CAT DIE.

**Not** long ago, I wandered near
　**A** play-ground in the wood ;
And there heard words from a youngster's lips,
　That I never quite understood.

" Now let the old cat die ! " he laughed ;
　I saw him give a push,
Then gaily scamper away as he spied
　A face peep over the bush.

But what he pushed, or where he went,
　**I could** not well make out,

On account of the thicket of bending boughs
  That bordered the place about.

"The little villain has stoned a cat,
  Or hung it upon a limb;
And left it to die all alone," I said,
  "But I'll play the mischief with him."

I forced my way through the bending boughs,
  The poor old cat to seek,
And what did I find but a swinging child,
  With her bright hair brushing her cheek!

Her bright hair floated to and fro,
  Her little red dress flashed by;
But the loveliest thing of all, I thought,
  Was the gleam of her laughing eye.

Swinging and swinging, back and forth,
  With the rose light in her face,
She seemed like a bird and flower in one,
  And the forest her native place.

"Steady! I'll send you up, my child,"
  But she stopped me with a cry,
"Go 'way, go 'way! don't touch me, please;
  I'm letting the old cat die."

"You're letting him die!" I cried, aghast,
  "Why, where's the cat, my dear?"
And lo! the laugh that filled the wood
  Was a thing for the birds to hear.

"Why, don't you know" said the little maid,
  The sparkling, beautiful elf,
"That we call it letting the old cat die
  When the swing stops all by itself?"

Then swinging and swinging, and looking back,
  With the merriest look in her eye,
She bade me good-bye, and I left her alone,
  "Letting the old cat die."

ANONYMOUS.

## THE HOUSEKEEPER'S TRAGEDY.

**One** day as I wandered, I heard a complaining,
  **A**nd saw a poor woman, the picture of gloom;
She glanced at the mud on her doorstep ('twas
     raining),
  And this was her wail as she wielded her broom:

" Oh, life is a trial, and love is a trouble,
  **A**nd **beauty** will fade, and riches will flee,
And pleasures they dwindle, and prices they
     double,
  And nothing is what I could wish it to be.

" There's too much of worriment goes to a bonnet,
  There's **too** much of ironing goes **to** a **shirt** ;
There's **nothing** that pays for the time you **waste**
     on **it.**
  There's nothing that lasts us but trouble and
     dirt.

" In March it is mud, it's slush in December ;
  The midsummer breezes are loaded with dust ;
In Fall the leaves litter ; in muggy September
  The wallpaper rots and the candlesticks rust.

" There are worms in the cherries, and slugs in
     **the** roses,
  **And ants** in the sugar, and mice in the pies,
And **rubbish** of spiders no mortal supposes,
  **And** ravaging roaches, and damaging flies.

" **It's** sweeping at six, and it's dusting at seven ;
  **It's** victuals at eight, and it's dishes at nine ;
It's potting and panning from ten to eleven ;
  We scarce break our fast ere **we** plan how to
     dine.

" With grease and with grime from corner **to**
     centre,
  Forever **at** war and forever alert,
**No rest for** a day, lest the enemy enter—
  I spend my whole life in a struggle with dirt.

"Last night, in my dreams, I was stationed for-
    ever
On a little bare isle in the midst of the sea ;
My one chance of life **was a** ceaseless endeavor
    To sweep off the waves ere they swept **off** poor
    me.

" Alas ! 'twas no dream—again I behold it !
    I yield, I am helpless my fate to avert."
She rolled down her sleeves, her apron she
    folded,
    Then lay down and died, and **was buried in**
    dirt !

ANONYMOUS.

## "MOTHER'S FOOL."

" 'Tis plain enough to see," said a farmer's wife,
" These boys will make their mark in life ;
They were never made to handle a hoe,
And at once to a college ought to go.
There's Fred, he's little better than a fool,
But John and Henry must go to school."

" **Well**, really, wife," quoth Farmer **Brown**,
As he set his mug of cider down.
" Fred does more work in a day for me
Than both his brothers do in three.
Book larnin' will never plant one's corn,
Nor hoe potatoes, sure's you're born ;
Nor mend a rod of broken fence —
For my part, give me common sense."

But his wife was bound the roast to rule,
And John and Henry were sent to school,
While Fred, of course, was left behind
Because his mother said he had no mind.

Five years at school the students spent ;
Then into business each one went.
John learned to play the flute and fiddle,

And parted his hair, of course, in the middle;
While his brother looked rather higher than he,
And hung out a sign, " H. Brown, M.D."

Meanwhile, at home, their brother Fred
Had taken a notion into his head;
But he quietly trimmed his apple trees,
And weeded onions and planted peas,
While somehow, by hook or crook.
He managed to read full many a book.
Until at last his father said
He was getting " book larnin' " into his head;
" But for all that," added Farmer Brown,
" He's the smartest boy there is in town."

The war broke out, and Captain Fred
A hundred men to battle led,
And when the rebel flag came down,
Went marching home as General Brown.
But he went to work on the farm again,
And planted corn and sowed his grain;
He shingled the barn and mended the fence,
Till people declared he had common sense.

Now, common sense was very rare,
And the State House needed a portion there;
So the " family dunce " moved into town—
The people called him Governor Brown;
And his brothers, who went to the city school,
Came home to live with " mother's fool."

ANONYMOUS.

---

## MOLLY CAREW.

And what will I do?
Sure my love is all crost,
Like a bud in the frost;
And there's no use at all in my going to bed,
For 'tis *dhrames* and not sleep that comes into
my head,
And 'tis all about you,

My sweet Molly Carew—
**And** indeed 'tis a sin and **a shame!**
You're complater than nature
In every feature.
The snow can't compare
With your forehead so **fair,**
And **I** rather would see just one blink of your eye,
Than the prettiest star that shines out of the sky,
And by this and by that,
For the matter o' that,
You're more distant by far than that **same!**
But why should I spake
Of your forehead and eyes,
When **your** nose **it** defies
**Paddy** Blake, the schoolmaster, **to** put it **in
rhyme,**
**Tho'** there's one Burke, **he** says, that would call
it sumb-lime;
And then for **your** cheek,
Troth 'twould take him a week,
Its beauties to tell, as he'd rather;
Then your lips! O, machree!
In their beautiful glow,
**T**hey **a** pattern might be
For the cherries to grow.
'Twas an apple that tempted our mother, we know,
For apples were scarce, I suppose, long ago,
But **at** this time o' day,
' Pon my conscience I'll say
Such cherries might **tempt a** man's father!

By the man in the moon,
You taze me all ways
**That a** woman can plaze,
For you dance twice as high with that thief Pat
Magee
As when you take share of a jig, dear, with me.
Tho' the piper I bate,
For fear the owld cheat
**Wouldn't play** you your favorite tune.

And when you 're at mass,
My devotion you crass,
For 'tis thinking of you
I am, Molly Carew.
While you wear, on purpose, a bonnet so deep,
That I can't at your sweet purty face get a peep;
O, lave off that bonnet,
**Or** else I 'll lave on it
**The** loss of my wandering sowl!

Don't provoke me to do it;
For there's girls by the score
That loves me—and more,
And you'd look very quare if some morning
**you'd** meet
My wedding all marching in pride down **the**
street;
Troth, you 'd open your eyes,
And you 'd die with surprise
**To** think 'twasn't you was come to it!
And faith, Kitty Naile,
And her cow, I go bail,
Would jump if I 'd say,
"Kitty Naile, name the day."
And tho' **you're** fair and fresh as a morning in
May,
While she 's **short and** dark like a cold Winter's
day,
Yet **if** you don't repent
Before Easter, when Lent
Is over. I'll marry for spite,
And when I die for you,
My ghost will haunt you every night.

Samuel Lover.

---

## UP ABOVE AND DOWN BELOW.

Down below, the wild November, whistling
  Through the beech's dome of burning red,
And the Autumn, sprinkling penitential
  Dust and ashes on the chestnut's head.

Down below, a pall of airy purple
  Darkly hanging from the mountain side,
And the sunset from his eye-brows staring
  O'er the long role of the leaden tide.

Up above, the tree with leaf unfading,
  By the everlasting river's brink,
And the sea of glass beyond whose margin
  Never yet the sun was known to sink.

Down below, the white wings of the sea-bird
  Dashed across the furrows dark with mould,
Flitting like the memories of our childhood,
  Through the trees now waxen pale and old.

Down below, imaginations quivering
  Through our human spirits like the wind,
Thoughts that toss like leaves upon the woodland,
  Hopes like sea-birds flashed across the mind.

Up above, the host no man can number,
  In white robes, a palm in every hand,
Each some work sublime forever working
  ·In the spacious tracts of that great land.

Up above, the thoughts that know no anguish,
  Tender care, sweet love for us below,
Noble pity, free from anxious terror,
  Larger love, without a touch of woe.

Down below, a sad, mysterious music,
  Wailing through the woods and on the shore,
Burdened with a grand, majestic secret,
  That keeps sweeping from us evermore.

Up above, a music that entwineth,
  With eternal threads of golden sound,
The great poem of this strange existence,
  All whose wondrous meaning hath been found.

Down below, the Church to whose poor window
  Glory by the autumnal trees is lent,

And a knot of worshippers in mourning,
  Missing some one at the Sacrament.

Up above, the burst of hallelujah,
  And without the sacramental mist,
Wrapt around us like a sunlit halo,
  One great vision of the face of Christ.

Down below, cold sunlight on the tombstone,
  And the green, wet turf, with faded flowers;
Winter roses, once like young hopes burning,
  Now beneath the ivy dripped with showers.

And the new-made grave within the churchyard,
  And the white cap on that dear face pale,
And the watcher ever, as it dusketh,
  Rocking to and fro with that long wail.

Up above, a crowned and happy spirit,
  Like an infant in the eternal years,
Who shall grow in love and light forever,
  Ordered in his place among his peers.

O, the sobbing of the winds of Autumn!
  O, the desolate heart that grave above!
O, the white cap shaking as it darkens,
  Round that shrine of memory and love.

O, the rest forever, and the rapture!
  O, the hand that wipes the tears away!
O, the golden homes beyond the sunset,
  And the hope that watches o'er the clay!
Bishop Alexander.

---

## THE SPECKLED HEN.

Dear brother Ben, I take my pen
To tell you where, and how and when,
I found the nest of our speckled hen.
She never would lay in a sensible way,
Like other hens, in the barn on the hay;

But here and there and everywhere,
On the stable floor, and the wood-house stair,
And once on the ground her eggs I found.
But yesterday I ran away,
With mother's leave, in the barn to play.
The sun shone bright on the seedy floor,
And the doves so white were a pretty sight
As they walked in and out of the open door,
With their little red feet and their feathers
      neat,
Cooing and cooing more and more.
Well, I went out to look about
On the platform wide, where side by side
I could see the pig-pens in their pride ;
And beyond them both, on a narrow shelf,
I saw the speckled hen hide herself
Behind a pile of hoes and rakes,
And pieces of boards and broken stakes.
" Ah ha ! old hen, I have found you now,
But to reach your nest I don't know how,
Unless I could creep or climb or crawl
Along the edge of the pig-pen wall."
And while I stood in a thoughtful mood,
The speckled hen cackled as loud as she could,
And flew away, as much as to say,
" For once my treasure is out of your way."
I didn't wait a moment then ;
I couldn't be conquered by that old hen !
But along the edge of the slippery ledge
I carefully crept, for the great pigs slept,
And I dared not even look to see
If they were thinking of eating me.
But all at once, oh, what a dunce !
I dropped my basket into the pen,
The one you gave me, brother Ben ;
There were two eggs in it, by the way,
That I found in the manger under the hay.
Then the pigs got up and ran about
With a noise between a grunt and a shout.

And when I saw them rooting, rooting,
Of course I slipped and lost my footing,
And tripped, and jumped, and finally fell
Right down among the pigs pell-mell.
For once in my life I was afraid;
For the door that led out into the shed
Was fastened tight with an iron hook,
And father was down in the fields by the brook,
Hoeing and weeding his rows of corn.
And here was his Polly, so scared and forlorn.
But I called him, and called him, as loud as I
    could.
I knew he would hear me—he must and he
    should—
"O father! O father! (Get out, you old pig)
O father! oh! oh!" for their mouths are so
    big.
Then I waited a minute and called him again,
"O father, O father, I am in the pig-pen!"
And father did hear, and he threw down his
    hoe,
And scampered as fast as a father could go.
The pigs had pushed me close to the wall,
And munched my basket, eggs and all,
And chewed my sun-bonnet into a ball.
And one had rubbed his muddy nose
All over my apron, clean and white;
And they sniffed at me, and stepped on my
    toes,
But hadn't taken the smallest bite,
When father opened the door at last,
And oh, in his arms he held me fast.

E. W. Denison.

---

## LAY OF THE MADMAN.

Many a year hath passed away,
Many a dark and dismal year,
Since last I roamed in the light of day
Or mingled my own with another's tear.

Woe to the daughters and sons of men—
Woe to them all when I roam again !
**Here** have I watched in this dungeon cell
Longer than memory's tongue can tell ;
Here have I shrieked in my wild despair
When the damned fiends from their prison
　　came,
Sported and gamboled and mocked me here,
With their eyes of fire and their tongues of
　　flame,
Shouting for ever and aye my name !
And I strove in vain to burst my chain,
And longed to be free as the winds again,
**That I might s**pring in the wizard ring,
And scatter them back to their hellish den !
Woe to the daughters and sons of men—
**Woe to** them all when I rove again !

How long have I been in this dungeon here,
Little I know and nothing I care.
What to me is the day **or** night,
Summer's heat or autumn sere,
Springtide flowers or winter's blight,
Pleasure's smile or sorrow's tear ?
**Time** ! what care I for thy flight—
**Joy** ! I spurn thee with disdain ;
**Not**hing love I but this clanking chain ;
Once I broke from its iron hold,
Nothing I **said**, but silent and bold,
Like the shepherd that watches his gentle fold,
Like **the** tiger that crouches in mountain lair
Hours upon hours, so watched I here—
Till one of the fiends that had **come** to bring
Herbs from the valley and drink from the
　　spring,
Stalked through my dungeon-entrance in !
**Ha** ! how he shrieked to see me free !
**Ho** ! how he trembled and knelt **to** me !
**He**, who had mocked me many a day,
And barred me out from its cheerful ray !

Gods! how I shouted to see him pray!
I wreathed my hands in the demon's hair,
And choked his breath in its muttered prayer;
And danced I then, in wild delight,
To see the trembling wretch's fright!
Gods! how I crushed his hated bones
'Gainst the jagged walls and the dungeon
    stones;
And plunged my arm adown his throat,
And dragged to life his beating heart,
And held it up that I might gloat
To see its quivering fibres start!
Ho! how I drank of the purple flood,
Quaffed and quaffed again of blood,
Till my brain grew dark and I knew no more
Till I found myself on this dungeon floor,
Fettered and held by this iron chain!
Ho! when I break its links again!
Ha! when I break its links again,
Woe to the daughters and sons of men?

My frame is shrunk, my soul is sad,
And devils mock and call me mad;
Light of day or ray of sun,
Friend or hope, I've none—I've none.
The spider shrinks from my grasp away,
Though he's known me for many a day.
The slimy toad, with his diamond eye,
Watches afar, but comes not nigh.
The craven rat, with her filthy brood,
Pilfers and gnaws at my scanty food; .
And when I strive to make her play,
Snaps at my fingers and flees away.
They called me mad and left me here
To my burning thoughts and the fiends' de-
    spair;
Never to hear soft pity's sigh,
Never to gaze on mortal eye—
Doomed through life, if life it be,
To helpless, hopeless misery.

Oh! if a single ray of light
Could pierce the gloom of this endless night!
If the cheerful tones of a human voice
Could make the depths of my heart rejoice;
If a single thing had loved me here
I ne'er had crouched to the fiends' despair.

They come again, they tear my brain;
They tumble a dart through every vein.
Oh! could I break this cursed chain,
Then would I spring in the wizard ring
And scatter them back to their hellish den!
Ho! when I break its links again—
Ha! when I break its links again—
Woe to the daughters and sons of men!
Woe to them all when I roam again!

ANONYMOUS.

## SAVING MOTHER.

The farmer sat in his easy chair,
Between the fire and the lamp-light's glare.
His face was ruddy and full and fair;
His three small boys in the chimney nook
Conned the lines of a picture book;
His wife, the pride of his home and heart,
Baked the biscuit and made the tart,
Laid the table and steeped the tea,
Deftly, swiftly, silently;
Tired and weary, weak and faint,
She bore her trials without complaint,
Like many another household saint—
Content, all selfish bliss above
In the patient ministry of love.

At last between the clouds of smoke
That wreathed his lips, the husband spoke:

"There's taxes to raise, and int'rest to pay—
And ef there should come a rainy day,
'Twould be mighty handy, I'm bound to say,

T' have somethin' put by ; for folks must **die,**
And there's funeral bills, and gravestones to
    buy—
Enough to swamp a man, purty **nigh.**
Besides, there's Edward and Dick and Joe
To be provided for when we go.
So 'f I was you, I'll tell you what I'd do :
I'd **be savin'** of wood as ever I could—
Extra fires don't du any good—
I'd be savin' of soap, and **savin'** of ile,
And run up some candles once in a while ;
I'd be rather savin' of coffee an' tea,
       For sugar is high,
       And all to buy.

"And cider is good enough drink for me ;
I'd be kinder careful of my cloe's
And look out sharp how the money goes—
Gewgaws is useless, nature knows ;
       Extra trimmin'
       'S the bane of women.

" I'd sell off the best of the cheese and **honey**
And eggs is as good, nigh about, as money ;
And as to **the** carpet you wanted new—
I guess we can make the old one du.
**And as for** the washer, and sewin' machine,
**Them** smooth-tongued agents so pesky mean,
**You'd** better get rid **of** 'em slick and clean.
**What do** they know about women's work ?
**Do they** kalkilate women was born to **shirk ?"**

Dick and Edward and little Joe
Sat in the corner in a row.
They saw their patient mother go
On ceaseless errands to and fro ;
They saw that her form was bent and thin,
Her temples gray, her cheeks sunk in,
They saw the quiver of lip and chin—
And then, with a wrath he could not smother,
Outspoke the youngest, frailest brother—

"You talk of savin' wood and ile,
An' tea an' sugar all the while,
But you never talk of savin' mother!"

          ANONYMOUS.

---

## THE STRANGER AND HIS FRIEND.

A poor wayfaring man of grief
 Hath often crossed me on my way,
Who sued so humbly for relief
 That I could never answer " Nay."
I had not power to ask his name,
Whither he went, or whence he came;
Yet there was something in his eye
That won my love—I knew not why.

Once, when my scanty meal was spread,
 He entered.   Not a word he spake.
Just perishing for want of bread,
 I gave him all; he blessed it, brake
And ate;—but gave me part again.
Mine was an angel's portion, then;
For while I fed with eager haste,
That crust was manna for my taste.

I spied him where a fountain burst
 Clear from the rock; his strength was
   gone;
The heedless water mocked his thirst,
 He heard it—saw it hurrying on.
I ran to raise the sufferer up;
Thrice from the stream he drained my cup,
Dipped, and returned it running o'er;
I drank, and never thirsted more.

'Twas night; the floods were out—it blew
 A winter hurricane aloof;
I heard his voice abroad, and flew
 To bid him welcome to my roof;
I warmed, I clothed, I cheered my guest—
Laid him on my couch to rest;

Then made the earth my bed, and seemed
In Eden's garden while I dreamed.

Stripped, wounded, beaten nigh to death,
  I found him by the highway side;
I roused his pulse, brought back his breath,
  Revived his spirits, and supplied
Wine, oil, refreshments; he was healed.
I had, myself, a wound concealed—
But from that hour forgot the smart,
And peace bound up my broken heart.

In prison, I saw him next, condemned
  To meet a traitor's doom at morn;
The tide of lying tongues I stemmed,
  And honored him midst shame and scorn.
My friendship's utmost zeal to try,
He asked if I for him would die;
The flesh was weak, my blood ran chill,
But the free spirit cried, "I will."

Then, in a moment, to my view
  The stranger darted from disguise;
The token in his hand, I knew—
  My Saviour stood before mine eyes.
He spake; and my poor name he named—
"Of me thou hast not been ashamed;
These deeds shall thy memorial be;
Fear not; thou didst them unto me."

JAMES MONTGOMERY.

## WHAT THEY SAY ABOUT CUPID.

They say the boy-god Love was born
  Six thousand years ago;
That ever since he's been at work
  With his quiver and his bow.
Yet how many hearts he's pierced mean-
      while
I'm sure *I* do not know—Do you?

They say his arrows are sharp and sure,
  And never fly amiss;
That the twang of his bow-string, short and
      shrill,
  Sounds very much like a kiss;
But as I never have heard the sound,
  I cannot vouch for this—Can you?

They say his golden barbs fly best,
  And pierce the toughest heart,
While for the young and tender ones
  He wings a different dart.
I wonder which he would shoot at me,
  For I've never felt their smart—Have
  you?

They say he liketh best to shoot
  From the depth of a sparkling eye,
Or he hideth in a jetty curl,
  And *whiz!* his arrows fly.
But when I see them I stand aside,
  And laugh at them whizzing by—Don't
    you?

They say the wound is a curious one,
  'Twixt a pleasure and a pain,
That as soon as the wounded ones are healed
  They wish to be shot again.
I should not like to be wounded at all,
  For fear the scar would remain—Should
    you?

They say he aims at all alike,
  Of high and low degree—
Nor costly suit, nor ragged coat,
  Is proof to his archery.
But let him shoot as long as he may
I'll not with the wounded be—Will you?
                              ANONYMOUS.

## THE **OLD HAT.**

I had a hat—it was not all **a hat**—
**Part** of the brim was gone—yet **still** I wore
**It** on, and people wondered, **as I** passed.
Some turned to gaze—others just cast an eye,
**A**nd soon withdrew it, as 'twere in contempt.
**But** still, my hat, although so fashionless,
**In** complement **extern,** had that within,
Surpassing show—my **head** continued warm ;
Being sheltered from **the weather,** spite of **all**
The want (as has **been said)** of brim.

A change came o'er the color of my hat.
That which was black grew brown, and then
    men stared
**With** *both* their eyes (they stared with *one* **be**
    fore) ;
**The** wonder now was twofold—and it seemed
Strange, that things so torn, and old, should still
Be **worn,** by one who might——but **let** that pass !
I had my reasons, which might be revealed,
But for some counter reasons far more strong,
Which tied my tongue to silence. Time passed **on.**
Green spring, and flowery summer, autumn
    brown,
And frosty winter came, and went, and came—
And still, through all the seasons of two years,
In **park, in city,** yea, in routs and balls,
The **hat was** worn and borne. Then folks grew
    wild
With curiosity—and whispers rose,
And questions passed about—how one so trim
In coats, boots, pumps, gloves, trousers, could
    ensconce
His caput in a covering so vile.

A change came o'er the nature of my hat—
Grease-spots **appeared**—but still in silence, on
I wore it—and then family and friends
**Glared** madly at each other. There was one

Who said—but hold—no matter what was said,
A time may come, when I——away—away—
Not till the season's ripe, can I reveal
Thoughts that do lie too deep for common minds.
Till then the world shall not pluck out the heart
Of this, my mystery.   When I will—I will!—
The hat was now greasy, and old, and torn—
But torn—old—greasy—still I wore it on.

A change came o'er the business of this hat,
Women, and men, and children scowled on me ;
My company was shunned—I was alone!
None would associate with such a hat—
Friendship itself proved faithless, for a hat.
She that I loved, within whose gentle breast
I treasured up my heart, looked cold as death—
Love's fires went out—extinguished by a hat.
Of those that knew me best, some turned aside
And scudded down dark · lanes—one man did
      place
His finger on his nose's side, and jeered—
Others, in horrid mockery, laughed outright ;
Yea, dogs, deceived by instinct's dubious ray,
Fixing their swart glare on my ragged hat,
Mistook me for a beggar—and they barked.
Thus, women, men, friends, strangers, lover, dogs,
One thought pervaded all—it was my hat.

A change—it was the last—came o'er this hat.
For lo! at length, the circling months went round,
The period was accomplished—and one day
This tattered, brown, old, greasy coverture
(Time had endeared its vileness) was transferred
To the possession of a wandering son
Of Israel's fated race—and friends once more
Greeted my digits with the wonted squeeze :
Once more I went my way—along—along—
And plucked no wondering gaze—the hand of
      scorn
With its annoying finger—men and dogs,

Once more grew  pointless, jokeless, laughless,
    growlless :
And last, not least of rescued blessings, love—
Love smiled on me again, when I assumed
A bran new beaver of the Andre mould ;
And then the laugh was mine, for then came **out**
**The** secret of this strangeness—'twas a BET.

ANONYMOUS.

## ROUGH AND SMOOTH.

Old Farmer Rough was grim and gruff,
    And drove his men about,
With "here" and "there," and  oft  would
      swear
    **When** things went wrong, **no** doubt.
**Work** must be done by set of sun,
    **And** all in order, too,
Upon the farm, or else he'd storm
    Till everything looked blue.

A pleasant word was seldom heard
    From him.  "It is enough
From day to day their hire to pay,"
    Said surly Farmer Rough.
"To keep **my** rules as well as tools
    **In order, I** have found
Upon **a** stone—with strap and hone—
    **They** must be often ground."

'Twas **thus** he wrought, and thus he bought
    Rich treasures from the soil,
Believing still men worked with will
    Whom praises did not spoil.
But sad and grave, though strong and brave,
    With sinews firm and tough,
The laborers grew—**and** the women, too—
    Who worked for Farmer Rough.

When ill-luck came, with frost and flame,
    And swept his goods away,

When loss of health and loss of wealth
　Brought on an evil day,
Then Farmer Rough, so grim and gruff,
　Gave many a bitter groan,
To think that he, alas! should be
　Left friendless and alone.

But Farmer Smooth, who in his youth
　The benefits had learned
Of tools well oiled, from those who **toiled**
　For him affection earned.
He spoke them soft, and helped them **oft**
　With counsels wise and **true**,
And ne'er begrudged **to those who drudged**
　**The praise which was their due.**

And when the floods swept all his goods
　Away, and he was left
In sorry plight—all in one night
　Of smiling lands bereft—
Friends flocked around, in grief profound,
　And gave substantial aid;
And Farmer Smooth said, " In good sooth,
　Who gives is well repaid."
JOSEPHINE POLLARD.

------

## THE CLOWN'S BABY.

It was out on the Western frontier.
　The miners, rugged and brown,
Were gathered around the posters,
　The circus had come to town!
The great tent shone in the darkness,
　Like a wonderful palace of light,
And rough men crowded the entrance;
　Shows didn't come every night.

Not a woman's face among them,
　Many a face that was bad,
And some that were very vacant,
　And some that were very sad,

And behind a canvas curtain,
  In a corner of the place,
The clown with chalk and vermilion
  Was making up his face.

A weary-looking woman,
  **With a** smile that still was sweet,
Sewed on a little garment,
  With **a** cradle at her feet.
Pantaloon stood ready and waiting,
  It **was** time for **the** going on ;
But the clown in vain searched wildly—
  The " property baby " was gone.

He murmured, impatiently hunting,
  " It's strange that I cannot find.
**There!** I've looked in every corner ;
  It must have been left behind ! "
The miners were stamping and shouting,
  They were not patient men ;
The clown bent over the cradle—
  " I must take *you*, little Ben."

The mother started and shivered,
  But trouble and want were near ;
She lifted **her** baby gently ;
  " **Y**ou'll be very careful, dear ? "
" Careful ?  You foolish darling "—
  How tenderly it was said !
What a smile shone through the chalk and
      paint—
  "**I** love each hair of his head ! "

The noise rose into an uproar,
  Misrule for a time was king ;
The clown with a foolish chuckle,
  Bolted into the ring.
But as, with a squeak and a flourish,
  The **fiddles** closed their tune,
" You'll hold him as if he was made of glass?"
  Said the clown to the pantaloon.

The jovial fellow nodded;
  "I've a couple myself," he said,
"I know how to handle 'em, bless you;
  Old fellow, go ahead!"
The fun grew fast and furious,
  And not one of all the crowd
Had guessed that the baby was alive,
  When he suddenly laughed aloud.

Oh, that baby laugh! it was echoed
  From the benches with a ring,
And the roughest customer there sprang up
  With "Boys, it's the real thing!"
The ring was jammed in a minute,
  Not a man that did not strive
For "a shot at holding the baby"—
  The baby that was "alive!"

He was thronged by kneeling suiters
  In the midst of the dusty ring,
And he held his court right royally,
  The fair little baby king;
Till one of the shouting courtiers,
  A man with a bold, hard face,
The talk for miles of the country
  And the terror of the place,

Raised the little king to his shoulder,
  And chuckled, "Look at that!"
As the chubby fingers clutched his hair.
  Then, "Boys, hand round the hat!"
There never was such a hatful
  Of silver, and gold, and notes;
People are not always penniless
  Because they don't wear coats!

And then, "Three cheers for the baby!"
  I tell you those cheers were meant,
And the way in which they were given
  Was enough to raise the tent.

And then there was sudden silence,
  And a gruff old miner said,
"Come, boys, enough **of** this rumpus;
  It's time it was put to **bed**."

So, looking a little sheepish,
  But with faces strangely bright,
The audience, somewhat lingering,
  Flocked out into the night.
And the bold-faced leader chuckled,
  "He wasn't a **bit** afraid!
He's as game as he is good-looking;
  Boys, that was a show that paid!"
St. Nicholas.

## IF I SHOULD DIE **TO NIGHT**.

If I should die to-night
My friends would look upon my quiet face
Before they laid it in its resting place,
And deem **that** death had **left** it almost **fair**;
And, laying snow-white flowers against my hair,
Would smooth it down with tearful tenderness,
And hold my hands with lingering caress—
Poor hands, so empty and so cold to-night!

If I should die to-night
My **friends** would call to mind, **with** loving
  thought,
Some **kindly** deed the icy hand had wrought,
Some gentle word the frozen lips had said;
Errands **on** which the willing feet had sped—
The memory of my selfishness and pride,
My hasty words, would all be put aside,
And so I should be loved and mourned to-night.

If I should die to-night
Even hearts estranged would turn once more
  to me,
Recalling other days remorsefully.
The eyes that chill me with averted glance

Would look upon me as of yore, perchance,
And soften in the old familiar way,
For who would war with dumb unconscious clay?
So I might rest, forgiven of all to-night.

            O, friends!   I pray to-night,
Keep not your kisses for my dead, cold brow.
The way is lonely; let me feel them now.
Think gently of me; I am travel-worn;
My faltering feet are pierced with many a thorn.
Forgive!   O hearts estranged, forgive, I plead!
When dreamless rest is mine, I shall not need
The tenderness for which I long to night.

ANONYMOUS.

----

## RAIN ON THE ROOF.

When the humid shadows gather over all the
        starry spheres,
And the melancholy darkness gently weeps in
        rainy tears,
'Tis a joy to press the pillow of a cottage cham-
        ber bed,
And listen to the patter of the soft rain over-
        head.

Every tinkle on the shingles has an echo in the
        heart,
And a thousand dreamy fancies into busy being
        start ;
And a thousand recollections weave their bright
        hues into woof,
As I listen to the patter of the soft rain on the
        roof.

There in fancy comes my mother, as she used to
        years agone,
To survey the infant sleepers ere she left them
        'till the dawn.

I can see her bending o'er me, as I listen to the
 strain
Which is played upon the shingles by the patter
 of the rain.

Then my little seraph sister, with her wings and
 waving hair,
And her bright-eyed cherub brother—a serene,
 angelic pair—
Glide around my wakeful pillow with their
 praise or mild reproof,
As I listen to the murmur of the soft rain on the
 roof.

And another comes to thrill me with her eyes'
 delicious blue:
I forget, as gazing on her, that her heart was all
 untrue;
I remember that I loved her as I ne'er may love
 again,
And my heart's quick pulses vibrate to the patter of the rain.

There is naught in art's bravuras that can work
 with such a spell,
In the spirit's pure, deep fountains, whence the
 holy passions well,
As that melody of nature—that subdued, subdu-
 ing strain,
Which is played upon the shingles by the patter
 of the rain.

COATES KINNEY.

## AN ORDER FOR A PICTURE.

O good painter, tell me true,
 Has your hand the cunning to draw
 Shapes of things that you never saw?
Ay? Well, here is an order for you.

Woods and corn-fields, a little brown,—
　The picture must not be over-bright,
　Yet all in the golden and gracious light
Of a cloud, when the summer sun is down,
　Alway and alway, night and morn,
　Woods upon woods, with fields of corn
　　Lying between them, not quite sere,
And not in the full, thick, leafy bloom,
When the wind can hardly find breathing-room
　　Under their tassels,—cattle near,
Biting shorter the short green grass,
And a hedge of sumach and sassafras,
With bluebirds twittering all around,—
(Ah, good painter, you can't paint sound !)
　These and the house where I was born,
Low and little, and black and old,
With children, many as it can hold,
All at the windows, open wide,—
Heads and shoulders clear outside,
And fair young faces all ablush :
　Perhaps you may have seen, some day,
　Roses crowding the seif-same way,
Out of a wilding, wayside bush.

　Listen closer.　When you have done
　　With woods and cornfields and grazing herds,
　A lady, the loveliest ever the sun
Looked down upon, you must paint for me ;
Oh, if I only could make you see
　The clear blue eyes, the tender smile,
The sovereign sweetness, the gentle grace,
The woman's soul, and the angel's face
　That are beaming on me all the while,
　I need not speak these foolish words:
　Yet one word tells you all I would say,—
She is my mother : you will agree
　That all the rest may be thrown away.

Two little urchins at her knee
You must paint, sir ; one like me,

The other with a clearer brow,
And the light of his adventurous eyes
Flashing with boldest enterprise;
At ten years old he went to sea,—
God knoweth if he be living now;
He sailed in the good ship "Commodore,"—
Nobody ever crossed her track
To bring us news, and she never came back.
Ah, 'tis twenty long years and more
Since that old ship went out of the bay
With my great-hearted brother on her deck:
I watched him till he shrank to a speck,
And his face was toward me all the way.
Bright his hair was, a golden brown,
The time we stood at our mother's knee:
That beauteous head, if it did go down,
Carried sunshine into the sea!

Out in the fields one summer night
We were together, half afraid
Of the corn-leaves' rustling and of the shade
Of the high hills, stretching so still and far,—
    *    *    *    *    *
Afraid to go home, sir; for one of us bore
A nest full of speckled and thin-shelled eggs;
The other, a bird, held fast by the legs,
Not so big as a straw of wheat:
The berries we gave her she wouldn't eat,
But cried and cried, till we held her bill,
So slim and shining, to keep her still.

At last we stood at our mother's knee.
Do you think, sir, if you try,
You can paint the look of a lie?
If you can, pray have the grace
To put it solely in the face
Of the urchin that is likest me:
I think 'twas solely mine, indeed:
But that's no matter,—paint it so;
The eyes of our mother (take good heed),

Looking not on the nestful of eggs,
Nor the fluttering bird, held so fast by the legs,
But straight through our faces down to our lies,
And, oh, with such injured, reproachful surprise !
 I felt my heart bleed where that glance **went,**
   **as** though
A sharp **blade** had struck through it.

     **You, sir,** know
That you on the canvas are to **repeat**
Things that are fairest, things most **sweet,**
Woods and corn-fields and mulberry tree,—
The mother. the lads, with their bird, at her knee
 But, O, that look of reproachful **woe** !
High as the heavens your name I'll shout,
If you **paint** me the picture, and leave that out.
       Alice Cary.

---

## THE KITCHEN CLOCK.

[From " Thistle Drift." ]

Knitting is **the maid** o' the kitchen. Milly ;
Doing nothing, **sits** the chore boy, Billy:
" Seconds reckoned,
Seconds reckoned ;
**Every** minute,
Sixty in it.
Milly, Billy,
Billy, Milly,
Tick-tock, tock-tick,
Nick-nock, knock-nick,
Knockety-nick, nickety-nock,"—
  Goes the kitchen clock.

Closer to the fire is rosy Milly,
Every whit as close and cozy, Billy :
" Time's **a** flying,
Worth your trying;
Pretty Milly—
Kiss her, Billy !

Milly, Billy,
Billy, Milly,
Tick-tock, tock-tick,
Now—now, quick—quick!
Knockety-nick, nickety-nock,"—
     Goes the kitchen clock.

Something's happened, very red is Milly·
Billy boy is looking very silly:
" Pretty misses,
Plenty kisses;
Make it twenty,
Take a plenty.
Billy, Milly,
Milly, Billy,
Right-left, left-right,
That's right, all right,
Knockety-nick, nickety-nock,"—
     Goes the kitchen clock.

Weeks gone, still they're sitting, Milly, Billy;
O, the winter winds are wondrous chilly!
" Winter weather,
Close together;
Wouldn't tarry,
Better marry,
Milly, Billy,
Billy, Milly,
Two—one, one—two,
Don't wait, 'twon't do,
Knockety-nick, nickety-nock,"—
     Goes the kitchen clock.

Winters two have gone, and where is Milly?
Spring has come again, and where is Billy?
" Give me credit,
For I did it ;
Treat me kindly,
Mind you wind me.
Mister Billy,

Mistress Milly,
My—O, O—my!
By-by, by-by,
Nickety-nock, cradle-rock,"
    Goes the kitchen clock.
        JOHN VANCE CHENEY.

## THE PETRIFIED FERN.

In a valley, centuries ago
  Grew a little fern leaf, green and slender,
  Veining delicate, and fibers tender;
Waving, when the wind crept down so low.
  Rushes tall, and moss, and grass grew round it,
  Playful sunbeams darted in and found it,
  Drops of dew stole in by night and crown'd it.
But no foot of man e'er trod that way
Earth was young and keeping holiday.

Monster fishes swam the silent main,
  Stately forests waved their giant branches,
  Mountains hurled their snowy avalanches,
Mammoth creatures stalked across the plain;
  Nature reveled in grand mysteries,
  But the little fern was not of these,
  Did not number with the hills and trees;
Only grew and waved its wild, sweet way;
None ever came to note it day by day.

Earth, one time, put on a frolic mood,
  Heaved the rocks, and changed the mighty
     motion
  Of the deep strong currents of the ocean,
Moved the plain and shook the haughty wood,
  Crushed the little fern in soft, moist clay,
  Covered it and hid it safe away.
  O the long, long centuries since that day!
O the agony! O life's bitter cost
Since that useless little fern was lost!

Useless ? Lost ? There came a thoughtful man,
  Searching Nature's secrets, far and deep ;
  From a fissure in a rocky steep
He withdrew a stone, o'er which there ran
  Fairy pencilings, a quaint design,
. Veinings, leafage, fibers clear and **fine,**
  **And the fern's** life lay in every line !
So, **I think, God** hides some souls away,
Sweetly to surprise us, the last day.

ANONYMOUS.

## MALARIA.

Our baby lay in its mother's arms,
All sweet with its tiny dimpled charms ;
But little mouth and tongue were sore,
And of **its** food 'twould take no more.
The doctor hemmed and shook his head,
And looking **wise, he gravely** said,
" Malaria—'tis plainly seen—
Three times a day give him quinine ! "
Said grandmamma, " Dear me, that's new ;
When I was young we called it 'sprue !' "

Our **urchin, Tom,** ne'er off his feet,
One day his dinner could not eat ;
His **head** ached so, he was so ill,
**Poor mother's** heart with fear **did fill.**
**The** doctor felt his hands and head,
And looking wise, he gravely said,
" Malaria—'tis plainly seen—
Three times a day give him quinine !"
Said grandmamma, " That can't be so !
He has been smoking, sir, **I** know !"

Our lady Maud, at seventeen—
As bright a girl as e'er was seen—
One day turned languid, white, and frail,
And roses red did strangely pale.
The doctor felt her pulse and said,

While wisely he did shake his head,
" Malaria—'tis plainly seen—
Three times a day give her quinine ! "
Said grandmamma, " That can't be right !
Why, my good sir, she danced all night ! "

Our **pride, our eldest**, Harry dear,
One **night** did act so strange and queer
That mother, frightened, panting, said,
" Run for the doctor—he'll **be** dead ! "
The doctor came, and shook his head,
And looking at him, grandly **said**,
" **Malaria**—'tis plainly seen—
**Three times** a day give him quinine ! "
" What stuff ! " said grandmamma, " I'm
          thinking
That good-for-nothing boy's been drinking ! "

The head of the house, forever well,
One day fell **ill, and sad** to tell,
Could not arise, but loud did cry,
" If this keeps on, I'd rather die ! "
The doctor came, stood by the bed,
And looking solemn, gravely said,
" Malaria—'tis plainly seen—
**T**hree times a day, **give** him quinine ! "
Growled grandmamma, " Oh, fiddle dee dee!
He's only bilious—seems to me ! "

One day **our** grandpa—eighty-four—
Complained that he could see no more ;
That, at his age, it worried him
That his good eye-sight should grow dim.
" I've often seen it act that way,"
The doctor solemnly did say,
" Malaria—'tis plainly seen—
Three times a day, give him quinine ! "
But grandma said, " I never **see** !
Old man, you're growing old, like me ! "

Isabel H. Reid.

## THE HIGHWAY COW.

The hue of her hide was a dusky brown,
   Her body was lean and her neck was slim,
One horn turned up and the other down,
   She was keen of vision and long of limb;
With a Roman nose and a short stump tail,
And ribs like the hoops of a home-made pail.

Many a mark did her old body wear:
   She had been a target for all things known;
On many a scar the dusky hair
   Would grow no more where once it had grown;
Many a passionate, parting shot
Had left upon her a lasting spot.

Many and many a well-aimed stone,
   Many a brickbat of goodly size,
And many a cudgel swiftly thrown,
   Had brought the tears to her bovine eyes;
Or had bounded off from her bony back,
With a noise like the sound of a rifle crack.

Many a day had she passed in the pound,
   For helping herself to her neighbor's corn.
Many a cowardly cur and hound
   Had been tran-fixed on her crumpled horn;
Many a tea-pot and old tin-pail
Had the farmer boys tied to her time-worn tail.

Old Deacon Gray was a pious man,
   Though sometimes tempted to be profane,
When many a weary mile he ran
   To drive her out of his growing grain.
Sharp pranks she used to play
To get her fill and to get away.

She knew when the deacon went to town,
   She wisely watched him when he went by;
He never passed her without a frown
   And an evil gleam in each angry eye;
He would crack his whip in a surly way,
And drive along in his " one horse shay."

Then at his homestead she loved to call,
  Lifting his bars with her crumpled horn;
Nimbly scaling his garden wall,
  Helping herself to his standing corn,
Eating his cabbages one by one,
Hurrying home when her work was done.

Often the deacon homeward came,
  Humming a hymn from the house of prayer,
His hopeful heart in a tranquil frame,
  His soul as calm as the evening air,
His forehead as smooth as a well-worn plow,
To find in his garden that highway cow.

His human passions were quick to rise,
  And striding forth with a savage cry,
With fury blazing from both his eyes,
  As lightnings flash in a summer sky;
Redder and redder his face would grow,
And after the creature he would go,

Over the garden round and round,
  Breaking his pear and apple trees;
Tramping his melons into the ground,
  Overturning his hive of bees;
Leaving him angry and badly stung,
Wishing the old cow's neck was wrung.

The mosses grew on the garden wall,
  The years went by with their work and play,
The boys of the village grew strong and tall,
  And the gray-haired farmers passed away
One by one as the red leaves fall,
But the highway cow outlived them all.

All earthly creatures must have their day,
  And some must have their months and years;
Some in dying will long delay,
  There is a climax to all careers,
And the highway cow at last was slain,
In running a race with a railway train.

All into pieces at last she went,
  Just like the savings banks when they fail;
Out of the world she was swiftly sent,
  Little was left but her old stumpy tail.
The farmer's cornfields and garden now
Are haunted no more by the highway cow.

ANONYMOUS.

## PATIENT MERCY JONES.

    Let us venerate the bones
    Of patient Mercy Jones,
    Who lies underneath these stones.

This is her story as once told to me
By him who still loved her, as all men might see—
Darius, her husband, his age seventy years,
A man of few words, but, for her, many tears.

Darius and Mercy were born in Vermont;
Both children were christened at baptismal font
In the very same place, on the very same day—
(Not much acquainted just then, I dare say).
The minister sprinkled the babies, and said,
" Who knows but this couple some time may be
    wed,
And I be the parson to join them together,
For weal or for woe through all sorts of weather!

Well, they *were* married, and happier folk
Never put both their heads in the same loving
    yoke.
They were poor, they worked hard, but nothing
    could try
The patience of Mercy, or cloud her bright eye.
She was clothed with Content as a beautiful
    robe ;
She had griefs—who has not on this changeable
    globe ?—
But at such times she seemed like the sister of
    Job.

She was patient with dogmas, where light **never**
    dawns,
She was patient with people who trod on her
    lawns;
She was patient with folks who said blue skies
    were gray,
And dentists **and oxen** who **pulled the wrong**
    **way**;
She was patient with phrases **no husband should**
    utter,
She was patient with cream that **declined to**
    be butter;
She was patient with buyers **with nothing** to pay,
She was patient with talkers with nothing to say;
She was patient with millers, whose trade was to
    cozen,
And grocers who counted out ten to the dozen;
She was patient with bunglers and fault-finding
    churls,
And tall, awkward lads who came courting **her**
    girls;
She was patient with crockery no art could mend,
And chimneys that smoked every day the wrong
    end;
She was patient with reapers who never would
    sow,
And long-winded callers who never would go;
She was patient with relatives, when, uninvited,
They came. and devoured, then complained they
    were slighted;
She was patient with crows that got into the corn,
And other dark deeds out of wantonness born;
She was patient with lightning that burned up
    the hay,
She was patient with poultry unwilling to lay;
She was patient with rogues who drank cider too
    strong,
She was patient **with** sermons that lasted too
    long;

She was patient with boots that tracked **up** her
    clean floors,
She was patient with peddlars and other smooth
    bores ;
**She** was patient with children who disobeyed
    rules,
And. to crown all the rest, she was patient with
    fools.

**The** neighboring husbands all envied the **lot**
Of Darius, and wickedly **got** up a plot
To bring o'er his sunshine an unpleasant spot.
" You think your wife's temper a proof against
    fate,
But *we* know of something her smiles will abate.
When she gets out of wood, and for more is in-
    clined,
Just send home the *crookedest* lot you can **find ;**
Let *us* pick it out, let *us* go and choose it,
**And** we'll bet you a farm, when she comes for to
    use it,
Her temper will **crack like** Nathan Dow's cornet,
And she'll be **as mad** as an elderly **hornet.**"

Darius was piqued, and he said, with a ***vum :***
" I'll pay for the wood, if *you'll* send it hum ;
But depend **on** it, neighbors, no danger will come."

Home came the gnarled roots, and a crookeder
    **load**
**Never** entered the gate of **a** Christian abode.
**A** ram's horn was straighter than any stick in it,
It seemed to be wriggling about every minute ;
It would not stand up, it would not lie down,
It twisted the vision of one-half the town.
To *look* at such **fuel** was really a sin,
For the chance was **Strabismus** would surely set in.

Darius said nothing to Mercy about it :
It *was* crooked **wood**—even *she* could not doubt it;
But never a harsh word escaped from her lips,

Any more than if the old snags were smooth
    chips.
She boiled with them, baked with them, washed
    with them through
The long winter months, and none ever knew
But the wood was as straight as Mehitable Drew,
Who was as straight as a die, or a gun, or an
    arrow,
And who made it her business all male hearts to
    harrow.

When the pile was burned up, and they needed
    more wood,
"Sure now," mused **Darius**, "I *shall* catch it
    good;
She has kept her remarks all condensed for the
    spring,
And my ears, for the trick, now deserve well to
    sing;
She never *did* scold me, but now she will pout,
And say with *such* wood sheis nearly worn out."

But Mercy, unruffled, was calm like the stream
That reflects back at evening the sun's perfect
    beam;
And she looked at Darius, and lovingly smiled,
As she made this request with a temper unriled:
"We are wanting more fuel, I am sorry to say;
I burn a great deal too much every day,
And I mean to use less than I have in the
    past;
But get, if you can, dear, a load like the last;
I never had wood that I liked half so well—
Do see who has nice *crooked* fuel to sell:
There's nothing that's better than wood full of
    knots,
It fays so complete round the kettles and pots,
And washing and cooking are really like play
When the sticks nestle close in so charming a
    way." JAMES T. FIELDS.

# THE NEGLECTED PATTERN.

A weaver sat one day at his loom,
  Among the colors bright,
With the pattern for his copying
  Hung fair and plain in sight.

But the weaver's thoughts were wandering
  Away on a distant track,
As he threw the shuttle in his hand
  Wearily forward and back.

And he turned his dim eyes to the ground,
  And his tears fell on the woof,
For his thoughts, alas! were not with his home,
  Nor the wife beneath its roof.

When her voice recalled him suddenly
  To himself, as she sadly said:
"Ah! woe is me! for your work is spoiled,
  And what will we do for bread?"

And then the weaver looked and saw
  His work must be undone;
For the threads were wrong, and the colors
    dimmed
Where the bitter tears had run.

"Alack, alack!" said the weaver,
  "And this had all been right
If I had not looked at my work, but kept
  The pattern in my sight!"

Ah! sad it was for the weaver,
  And sad for his luckless wife;
And sad it will be for us if we say,
  At the end of our task in life,

The colors that we had to weave
  Were bright in our early years;
But we wove the tissue wrong, and stained
  The woof with bitter tears.

We wove a web of doubt and fear—
  Not faith, and hope, and love,
Because we looked at our work, and not
  At our Pattern up above.

PHŒBE CARY.

---

## UNDER THE SNOW.

It was Christmas Eve in the year fourteen,
  And as ancient dalesmen used to tell,
The wildest winter they had ever seen,
  With the snow lying deep on moor and fell.

When Wagoner John got out his team,
  Smiler and Whitefoot, Duke and Gray,
With the light in his eyes of a young man's
    dream,
  As he thought of his wedding on New Year's
    Day,

To Ruth, the maid with the bonnie brown hair,
  And eyes of the deepest, sunniest blue,
Modest and winsome and wondrous fair,
  And true to her troth, for her heart was true

"Thou's surely not going," shouted mine host.
  "Thou'll be lost in the drift as sure as thou's
    born.
Thy lass winnot want to wed wi' a ghost,
  And that's what thou'll be on Christmas morn.

"It's eleven long miles fra Skipton toon,
  To Blueberg hooses and Washburn dale,
Thou had better turn back and sit thee doon,
  And comfort thy heart wi' a drop o' good ale."

Turn the swallows flying south,
  Turn the vines against the sun,
Herds from rivers in the drouth,
  Men must dare or nothing's done.

So what cares the lover for storm or drift,
  Or peril of death on the haggard way?
He sings to himself like a lark in the lift,
  And the joy in his heart **turns** December to
    May.

But **the** wind from the north brings a deadly chill,
  Creeping **into** his heart, and the drifts **are**
    deep,
Where the thick of the storm strikes Blueberg
    hill,
  He is weary and falls on a pleasant sleep,

And dreams he is walking by Washburn side,
  Walking **with** Ruth on a summer's day,
Singing that song to his bonnie bride,
  His own life forever and aye.

Now **read** me this riddle, how **Ruth** should hear
  That song of a heart in the clutch of doom.
It **stole** on her ear, distant and **clear**,
  As if her **lover was in the room.**

And read me this riddle, how Ruth should **know,**
  As she bounds to throw open the heavy **door,**
**Th**at her lover is lost in the drifting snow,
  **Dy**ing **or dead** on the great wild moor.

"Help! help!"  "Lost! lost!"
  Rings **through** the night as she rushes away,
Stumbling, **blinded,** and tempest-tossed,
  Straight to the drift where her lover lay.

**And swift** they leap after her into the night,
  Into the drifts by Blueberg hill.
Pullan, Ward, Robinson, each with his light,
  To find her there, holding him, white and still.

"He was dead in the drift, then?"
  I **hear them** say,
As I listen and **wonder,**
  Forgetting to play,
Fifty years syne come Christmas Day.

"Nay, nay, they were wed," the dalesman cried,
　" By Parson Carmalt on New Year's Day,
Bonnie Ruth were me great-great-grandsire's
　　bride,
　And Ma'ster Frankland gave her away."

" But how did she find him under the snow ?"
　They cried with a laughter touched with tears,
" Nay, lads," he said, softly, " we can never know,
　No, not if we live a hundred years."

There's a sight o' things gan
To the making o' man.
Then I rushed to my play
With a whoop and away,
Fifty years syne come Christmas Day.
ROBERT COLLYER.

---

## TO WHOM SHALL WE GIVE THANKS ?

A little boy had sought a pump
　From whence the sparkling water burst,
And drank with eager joy the draught
　That kindly quenched his thirst.
Then gracefully he touched his cap—
　" I thank you, Mr. Pump," he said,
" For this nice drink you've given me."
　This little boy had been well bred.

Then said the pump : " My little man,
　You're welcome to what I have done ;
But I am not the one to thank—
　I only help the water run."
" O, then," the little fellow said
　(Polite he always meant to be),
" Cold water, please accept my thanks,
　You have been very kind to me."

" Ah !" said cold water, " don't thank me ;
　Far up the hillside lives the spring
That sends me forth with generous hand,
　To gladden every living thing."

"I thank the spring, then," said the boy,
  And gracefully he bowed his head;
"O, don't thank me, my little man,"
  The spring with silvery accents said.

"O, don't thank me—for what am I
  Without the dew and summer rain?
Without their aid I ne'er could quench
  Your thirst, my little boy, again."
"O, well," then said the little boy,
  "I'll gladly thank the rain and dew."
"Pray, don't thank us—without the sun
  We could not fill one cup for you."

"Then, Mr. Sun, ten thousand thanks
  For all that you have done for me."
"Stop!" said the sun, with blushing face,
  "My little fellow, don't thank me.
'Twas from the ocean's mighty stores
  I drew the draught I gave to thee."
"O, ocean, thanks," then said the boy.
  It echoed back, "Not unto me.

"Not unto me, but unto Him
  Who founded the depths in which I lie;
Go, give thanks, my little boy,
  To Him who will thy wants supply."
The boy took off his cap and said,
  In tones so gentle and subdued,
"O God! I thank Thee for this gift,
  Thou art the giver of all good!"

MRS. LEVI WADE.

---

## WHAT CONSTITUTES A STATE?

What constitutes a state?
Not high-raised battlement or labored mound,
  Thick wall or moated gate;
Not cities proud with spires and turrets crowned;
  Not bays and broad-armed ports,

Where, laughing at the storm, rich navies **ride** ;
　Not starred and spangled courts,
Where low-browed baseness wafts perfume **to**
　　　pride,—
　No ; men, high-minded men,
With powers as far above **dull** brutes endued
　In forest, brake, or den,
As beasts excel cold rocks and brambles **rude**,—
　Men who their **duties** know,
But know their rights,and knowing,dare maintain,
　Prevent the long-aimed **blow**,
And crush the tyrant while they rend **the** chain ;
　These constitute a **state** ;
And sovereign law, **that** state's collected will,
　O'er thrones and globes elate
Sits empress, crowning good, repressing ill.
　Smit by her sacred **frown**,
The fiend, dissension, like a vapor sinks ;
　And e'en the all-dazzling crown
Hides his faint **rays,** and at her bidding shrinks.

Sir William Jones.

THE GAME OF LIFE.

There's a game much **in** fashion—I think **it's**
　　called *Euchre*
(Though I never have played for pleasure or
　　lucre),
In which, when **the** cards are in certain condi-
　　tions,
The players appear to have changed their posi-
　　tions,
And one of them cries in a confident tone,
" I think I may venture to ' go it alone ! ' "

While watching the game, 'tis a whim of the
　　bard's
A moral to draw from that skirmish of cards,
And to fancy he finds in the trivial strife,

Some excellent hints for the battle of Life;
Where—whether the prize be a ribbon **or**
    throne—
**The** winner is he who can **"go it alone!"**

When great Galileo proclaimed that **the world**
**In** a regular orbit was ceaselessly whirled,
And got—not a convert—for all of his pains,
But only derision and prison and chains,
" It moves, *for all that!*" was his answering
    tone,
For he knew, like the earth, **he** could "go it
    alone!"

**When** Kepler, with intellect piercing afar,
Discovered the laws of each planet and star,
And doctors, who ought to have lauded his name,
Derided his learning and blackened his fame,
**"I** can wait," he replied, " till the truth you shall
    own";
**For** he felt in his heart **he could** "go it alone!"

**Alas!** for the player who **idly** depends,
In the struggle of life, upon kindred or **friends;**
Whatever the value of blessings like these
They can **never** atone for inglorious ease,
Nor comfort the coward **who** finds with a groan,
**That his clutches have left** him to " go it alone!"

There's something, no doubt, in the hand you
    may hold.
Wealth, family, culture, wit, beauty and **gold,**
The fortunate owner may fairly regard
As, each in its way, a most excellent card;
Yet the game may be lost, with all these for your
    own,
Unless you've the courage to "go it alone!"

In battle **or** business, whatever the game,
In **law or love,** it is ever the same;
In the struggle for power, or the scramble for
    pelf,

Let this be your motto, "RELY ON YOURSELF!"
For, whether the prize be a ribbon or throne,
The victor is he who can "go it alone!"

JOHN G. SAXE.

## THE BEST COW IN PERIL.

Old Farmer B is a stingy man,
He keeps all he gets, and gets all he can.
By all his friends he is said to be
As tight as the bark on a young birch tree.
He goes to church, and he rents a pew,
But the dimes he gives to the Lord are few.
If he gets to heaven with the good and great
He will be let in at the smallest gate.

Now Farmer B, besides drags and plows,
Keeps a number of fine calves and cows.
He makes no butter, but sends by express
The milk to the city's thirstiness.

"What do city folks know about milk?
They are better judges of cloth and silk.
Not a man who buys, I vow, can tell
If I water it not or water it well—
If they do not know, then where's the sin?
I'll put the sparkling water in."
Thus talked to himself, old Farmer B.
How mean is he, young and old can see.

One night it was dark, oh, fearfully dark—
The watch dog never came out to bark—
Old Farmer B in his bed did snore,
When rap, rap, rap, nearly shattered the door,
And a voice cried out, in a hasty breath :
"Your best cow, neighbor, is choking to death!"

Clipping off the end of a rousing snore,
Farmer B bounded out on the bedroom floor,
And the midnight voice was heard no more.
He pulled on his pants, he knew not how,
For his thoughts were all on the choking cow ;
He flew to the yard like a frightened deer,

For his stingy soul was filled with fear ;
Looking around by his lantern's light,
He found that the cows **were** there all right.

"**I** will give a dime," cried Farmer **B**,
"**To** know who played that trick **on** me.
**May** the hand be stiff, and the knuckle sore
**That** knocked to-night at my farm-house door."

**And** now, a scowl **on** his face and a shaking
    head,
Farmer B again sought his nice warm bed.
No good thoughts came—they were o'er-
    powered—
The little good nature he had had soured.

When he went to water his **milk** next day,
The midnight voice seemed **again to** say,
As he pumped away with panting breath :
"**Your** best cow, neighbor, is choking **to death!**"
**The meaning** of this he soon found **out,**
For a stone **was driven in the old** pump's **spout.**

Old Farmer B, when he drives in town,
Now meets his neighbors with savage frown,
They smile, and ask, as they kindly bow,
"How **getteth along** the best cow now ?"

Anonymous.

---

## THE STARS.

When the radiant morn of creation broke,
And the world in the smile of God awoke,
And the empty realms of darkness and death,
Were moved through their depth by his mighty
    breath,
And orbs of beauty and spheres of flame
From the void abyss **by** myriads came,—
In **the** joy of youth, as they darted away,
Through **the widening** wastes of space to play,
Their silver **voices in chorus** rung,
And this was the song the bright ones sung:

"Away, away, through the wide, wide sky,
The blue fair fields that before us lie,—
Each sun, with the worlds that round him roll,
Each planet, poised on her turning pole;
With her isles of green, and her clouds of white,
And her waters that lie like fluid light.

"For the source of glory uncovers his face,
And the brightness o'erflows unbounded space;
And we drink as we go to the luminous tides
In our ruddy air and our blooming sides;
Lo, yonder the living splendors play;
*Away*, on our joyous path, *away!*

"Look, *look*, through our glittering ranks afar,
In the infinite azure, star after star.    [pass!
How they brighten and bloom, as they swiftly
How the verdure runs o'er each rolling mass!
And the path of the gentle winds is seen,
Where the small waves dance, and the young
   woods lean.

"And see where the brighter day-beams pour,
How the rainbows hang in the sunny shower;
And the morn and eve, with their pomp of hues,
Shift o'er the bright planets and shed their dews;
And 'twixt them both, o'er the teeming ground,
With her shadowy cone the night goes round!

"Away, away! in our blossoming bowers,
In the soft air wrapping these spheres of ours,
In the seas and fountains that shine with morn,
See, love is brooding, and life is born,
And breathing myriads are breaking from night,
To rejoice, like us, in motion and light.

"Glide on in your beauty, ye youthful spheres,
To weave the dance that measures the years;
Glide on, in the glory and gladness sent,
To the farthest wall of the firmament,—
The boundless, visible smile of Him,
To the veil of whose brow your lamps are dim."

W. C. BRYANT.

## PLEASANT WEATHER.

Thank God for pleasant weather!
  Chant it, merry rills!
And clap your hands together,
  Ye exulting hills!
Thank him, teeming valley,
  Thank him, fruitful plain,
For the golden sunshine,
  And the silver rain.

Thank God, of good the giver!
  Shout it, sportive breeze!
Respond, O tuneful river,
  To the nodding trees.
Thank him, bud and birdling,
  As ye grow and sing;
Mingle in thanksgiving,
  Every living thing.

Thank God, with cheerful spirit,
  In a glow of love,
For what we here inherit,
  And our hopes above.
Universal Nature
  Revels in her birth,
When God, in pleasant weather,
  Smiles upon the earth.

ANONYMOUS.

---

## THE STREET MUSICIANS.

One day through a narrow and noisome street
Where naught but squalor and poverty greet
The passer-by, I chanced to stray.
'Twas a mellow and bright October day,
A genial autumn sun shone down
On rich and poor in that crowded town;
And over the house-tops a deep blue sky
Greeted each beggar's upturned eye,
While the very heavens seemed to smile

His hunger and weariness to beguile.
Bare-headed children, ragged and free,
Over the curb-stones romped in glee.
Lazily by, a policeman walked ;
Shop-men stood in their doors and talked ;
Now and then, with a glance downcast,
Some wreck of a sot went staggering past,
With a trembling form and a visage wan ;
Yet the current of life went flowing on ;
And the sky was blue, and the sunlight fell
On the happy ones, and the sad as well.
But hark ! through that narrow and crowded
    street,
Of a sudden there poured a melody sweet,
A volume of soft harmonious sound
Strangely contrasting with all around ;
And I paused to listen, while each sweet note,
Pure as a warbling from robin's throat,
Seemed to float on the idle air
To attic, and cellar, and crazy stair,
And carry a whisper of peace and rest
Wherever it went on its pathway blest.

    " Sweet and low, sweet and low,
      Wind of the western sea,
    Low, low, breathe and blow,
      Wind of the western sea !
    Over the rolling waters go,
    Come from the dying moors, and blow,
      Blow him again to me ;
        While my little one, while my pretty
        one sleeps."

'Twas a strolling minstrel band of four
Who, standing before a groggery door,
With puffed out cheeks and beating feet
Were playing there in that busy street,
Vagabonds, they, no doubt ; in fact
Their garb was ragged, the trumpets cracked,
And they looked like men who seldom knew

What 'twas to own a dollar or two.
Yet, spite of this, as I listened there,
To the sweet soft notes of the plaintive air
That came from those minstrels, ragged and odd
I thought, "'Tis a message sent from God,
Bringing reminders pure and sweet,
To the poor sad souls in this narrow street."
Then the little children over the way
Looked and wondered and stopped their play,
And the officer paused in his weary walk,
While the gossiping shop-men ceased to talk;
And from tenement windows all about,
There was many a weary face peeped out
And smiled at the joy that had suddenly come
To cheer its povert**y-stric**ken **home.**
**Out of** the groggery, reeling, came
**Into** the sunlight (oh, for shame!)
One whose visage and mien bespoke
A dreadful bondage to liquor's yoke—
A soul of honor and pride bereft,
Yet, there were traces o**f manh**ood left.
And as the music reached his ear
**He,** staggering, paused—then lingered near,
**A**bashed **and** doubting—then gave a start,
**For the** melody sweet had touched his heart;
Those **strains, so** plaintive and soft and low,
Recalled the lullab**y,** long ago,
That his mother in tones so sweet **and** mild
Had sung to him as a little child.

"Sleep and rest, sleep and rest,
    Father will come to thee soon;
  Rest, rest, on mother's breast,
    Father will come to thee soon;
  Father will come to his babe in the nest,
  Silver sails all out of the west
    Under the silver moon.
      **Sleep,** my little one, sleep my pretty
      **one, sleep."**

Then, over him like a torrent, came
The sense of his present sin and shame,
And the tears came pouring down his cheek.
" Oh God !" he cried, " I am frail and weak !"
And he hid his face and murmured a prayer
Out of the depths of his dark despair.
(God grant his penitent prayer was heard !)
He turned away and without a word,
But with steady step, and a figure bowed,
Was lost in the hurrying, passing crowd.
The music ceased and I went my way,
But I ne'er shall forget that sunny day
When I heard that music so soft and sweet,
Wafted down through the narrow street.

George L. Catlin.

## THE PRETTY PICTURES.

I am a little peasant girl ;
　My father's very poor,
No rich and handsome things have we—
　No carpet on our floor;

And yet, this morning, when I woke,
　I saw, to my surprise,
Four pretty pictures in my room,
　Alike in shape and size.

The first was of a lake so clear,
　With woods encircled round:
Thro' which there sprang a frightened deer,
　Pursued by many a hound.

The second is a quiet stream,
　Which through the valley winds;
Tall trees and shrubs are on the brink,
　And flowers of various kinds.

The next a little hamlet seems,
　With its neat church and spire ;
Behind it hills and mountains rise
　Up to the clouds and higher.

The last is a vast waterfall,
  Which a broad lake supplies;
Masses of water tumble down,
  And clouds of spray arise.

These pictures all will fade away—
  I know it to my sorrow;
But mother says she thinks I'll have
  Four other ones to-morrow.

Who gives them to me, do you ask?
  And how much do they cost?
The giver I have never seen,
  The painter is—JACK FROST.

ANONYMOUS.

---

## THE KAISER.

The Kaiser's hand from all his foes
Had won him glory and repose;
Richly through his rejoicing land
Were felt the blessings of his hand;
And when at eve he sought his rest,
A myriad hearts his slumbers blessed.

In midnight's hush a tempest broke;—
Throughout his realm its myriads woke.
And by the lightning's rapid flash,
And 'mid the thunder's bellowing crash,
In faith to heaven their prayers they spake,
For Christ's and for the Kaiser's sake.

But with a start, and with a pang,
Up from his couch the Kaiser sprang;
What! feareth he who never feared
When bloody deaths through hosts careered?
What! can the tempest's passing sound
That heart of battles thus confound?

No! no! But in its deepest deep
It wakes a cry no more to sleep;
And there! and there! in wrath begin

The pangs—the power of secret sin.
A blow is dealt,—a strife is stirred,—
Without, the storm may pass unheard !

And, therefore, from his palace door
He passed into the loud uproar ;
In wildest wind, and blackest night,
He passed away in sudden flight :
'Mid lightning, rain, and thunder's roll
He went,—a fire within his soul.

The Kaiser went in storm and night,
But ne'er returned in peace and light ;
Astonished thousands asked his lot,
Love sought, and sought, but found him not.
But conscience did what conscience would,
And sealed its errand—blood for blood !

W. Howitt.

## A FEVER DREAM.

A fever scorched my body, fired my brain !
Like lava, in Vesuvius, boiled my blood
Within the glowing caverns of my heart.
I raged with thirst, and begged a cold clear
    draught
Of fountain water.  'T was with tears denied.
I drank a nauseous febrifuge, and slept ;
But rested not—harassed with horrid dreams
Of burning deserts, and of dusty plains—
Mountains disgorging flames—forests on fire—
Steam, sunshine, smoke, and boiling lakes—
Hills of hot sand, and glowing stones that seemed
Embers and ashes of a burnt-up world !
Thirst raged within me.  I sought the deepest
    vale,
And called on all the rocks and caves for water ;—
I climbed a mountain, and from cliff to cliff
Pursued a flying cloud, howling for water :—
I crushed the withered herbs, and gnawed dry
    roots,

Still crying, Water! water!—while the cliffs
   and caves,
In horrid mockery, re-echoed "Water!"
The baked plain gaped for moisture,
And **from** its arid breast heaved smoke, that
   seemed
The breath **of** furnace—fierce, volcanic fire,
Or hot monsoon, that raises Syrian sands
To **clouds.** **A**mid the forests we espied
A faint and bleating **herd.** **S**udden, a shrill
And horrid **shout arose of—**"Blood! blood!
   blood!"
**We** fell upon them with **the** tiger's thirst,
**A**nd drank up all the blood that was **not** human!
**We were** dyed in **blood!** Despair returned ;
**The cry of blood was** hushed, and dumb con-
   fusion reigned.
Even then, when hope **was** dead !—past hope—
I **heard a** laugh ! and saw **a** wretched man
Rip his own veins, and, **bleeding,** drink
With eager joy. The **example** seized on **all :—**
Each fell upon himself, tearing his veins,
**Fiercely** in search of blood ! And some there
   **were,**
**Who, having emptied** their **own** veins, did seize
**Upon their neighbor's** arms, and slew them **for**
   their blood !—
  " Rend, O ye lightnings ! the sealed firmament,
And flood a burning world. Rain ! rain ! pour !
   **pour !**
Open ye windows of high heaven ! and pour
The mighty deluge. Let us drown and drink
**Lu**xurious death ! **Ye** earthquakes, split the
   globe,
The solid rock ribbed globe !—and lay all bare
**Its** subterranean rivers and fresh seas ! "
  **Thus raged** the multitude. And many fell
In fierce convulsion ;—many slew themselves.
And now, I saw the city all in flames—

The forest burning—and the very earth on fire!
I saw the mountains open with a roar
Loud as the seven apocalyptic thunders,
And seas of lava rolling headlong down,
Through crackling forests fierce, and hot as hell,
Down to the plain;—I turned to fly—and waked!

JOHN M. HARNEY.

## BERNARDINE DU BORN.

King Henry sat upon his throne,
  And, full of wrath and scorn,
His eye a recreant knight surveyed—
  Sir Bernardine du Born.
And he that haughty glance returned,
  Like lion in his lair,
And loftily his unchanged brow
  Gleamed through his crisped hair.

" Thou art a traitor to the realm !
  Lord of a lawless band !
The bold in speech, the fierce in broil,
  The troubler of our land !
Thy castles and thy rebel towers
  Are forfeit to the crown ;
And thou beneath the Norman ax
  Shall end thy base renown !

" Deign'st thou no word to bar thy doom,—
  Thou with strange madness fired ?
Hath reason quite forsook thy breast ?"
  Plantagenet inquired.
Sir Bernard turned him toward the king,
  And blenched not in his pride ;
" My reason failed, most gracious liege,
  The year Prince Henry died."

Quick, at that name, a cloud of woe
  Passed o'er the monarch's brow ;
Touched with that bleeding chord of love,
  To which the mightiest bow.

And backward swept the tide of years;
  Again his first-born moved—
The fair, the graceful, the sublime,
  The erring, yet beloved.

And ever, cherished by his side,
  One chosen friend was near,
To share in boyhood's ardent sport,
  Or youth's untamed career;
With him the merry chase he sought,
  Beneath the dewy morn,
With him in knightly tourney rode
  This Bernardine du Born.

Then in the mourning father's soul
  Each trace of ire grew dim,
And what his buried idol loved
  Seemed cleansed of guilt to him ;—
And faintly through his tears he spoke,
  " God send his grace to thee !
And, for the dear sake of the dead,
  Go forth, unscathed and free."

Sigourney.

## THE DEATH-FIRE.

Beneath the ever dense and leafy gloom
Of the hushed wilderness, a lurid flame
Crept, like a serpent, gorged with kindling
    blood,
Around the knotted trunk of an old forest oak ;
Then upward and abroad it fiercely spread,
Through the dusk pine-tops and the clinging
    vines,
Till the dark forest crimsoned with the glare.
Strong winds swept through the hot and crack-
    ling boughs,
While scintillating sparks—a fiery rain—
Fell from the arrowy flames that darted through
The black and smoky air.

In double ranks around that flaming tree,
Sat fierce-browed warriors, like a crowd of
        fiends
Sent forth to hold their orgies on the earth.
Their shafted arrows, and the sinewy bow,
The tomahawk, and club, and keen-edged knife,
Flashed back the fire, and there all hotly gleamed
In the tall grass, that coiled all crisply back,
Grew stiff and died on the scorched earth.
The sparkling river, flowing with sweet chime,
So cool and tranquil in its verdant banks,
In gentle contrast with the flaming trees,
And the red demons crouching underneath,
Mocked the devoted victims.
        One was a girl, so gently fair,
        She seemed a being of upper air,
        Lured by the sound of the water's swell,
        To the haunt of demons dark and fell!
        Shackled by many a galling thong,
        But in Christian courage firm and strong,
        Stood a brave man, with his eye on fire,
        As he bent its glance on the funeral pyre;—
        Yet his bosom heaved and his heart beat quick;
        His labored breath came fast and thick;
        His cheek grew pale, and drops of pain
        Sprang to his brow like beaded rain,
        As he felt the clasp of his pallid bride,
        Where she clung in fear to his pinioned side.
        A savage shout—a fierce, deep yell—
        Rings through the forest cove and dell;
        The wood is alive on either hand
        With the rushing feet of that murderous band.
        One start from the earth—one feeble cry,
Like the moan of a fawn when the hounds are
        nigh—
And she sinks to the ground with a shuddering
        thrill,
And lies at his feet all cold and still.
With the mighty strength of his stern despair,

Like a lion roused in his guarded lair,
The youth has rended his bonds apart—
The bride is snatched to his throbbing heart!
With a bound he clears the savage crew,
And plunges on toward the bark canoe.
He nears the bank—a fiendish scream
From the baffled foes rings o'er the stream;
He springs to the barque;—away, away!—
It is lost from sight in the flashing spray!

ANN S. STEPHENS.

## SONG, FROM THE LADY OF THE LAKE.

Soldier, rest! thy warfare o'er,
  Sleep the sleep that knows not breaking;
Dream of battle-fields no more,
  Days of danger, nights of waking.
In our isle's enchanted hall,
  Hands unseen thy couch are strewing;
Fairy strains of music fall,
  Every sense in slumber dewing.
Soldier, rest! thy warfare o'er,
Dream of fighting fields no more;
Sleep the sleep that knows not breaking,
Morn of toil, nor night of waking.

No rude sound shall reach thine ear,
  Armor's clang, or war-steed's champing,
Trump nor pibroch summon here,
  Mustering clan, or squadron tramping.
Yet the lark's shrill fife may come,
  At the day-break, from the fallow,
And the bittern sound his drum,
  Booming from the sedgy shallow.
Ruder sounds shall none be near,
Guard's nor warder's challenge here,
Here's no war-steed's neigh and champing,
Shouting clans, or squadrons stamping.

Huntsman, **rest!** thy chase **is** done,
  **While our** slumb'rons spells assail ye,
Dream not with the rising sun,
  Bugles here shall sound reveille.
Sleep! the deer is in his den;
  Sleep! thy hounds are by thee lying;
Sleep! nor dream, in yonder glen,
  How the gallant steed lay dying.
Huntsman, **rest!** thy chase is done,
Think not of the rising sun,
For at dawning to assail ye,
**Here no** bugles **sound** reveille.

WALTER SCOTT.

## SMALL THINGS.

Who dares to scorn the meanest thing,
The humblest weed that grows,
While pleasure spreads its joyous wing
On every breeze that blows?
The simplest flower that, hidden, blooms
The lowest on the ground,
Is lavish of its rare perfumes,
And scatters sweetness round.

The poorest friend upholds a part
Of life's harmonious plan;
The weakest hand may have the art
To serve the strongest man.
The bird that highest, clearest sings,
To greet the morning's birth,
Falls down **to** drink, with folded wings,
**Love's rapture on** the earth.

From germs too small for mortal sight
Grow all things that are seen,
**Their** floating particles of light
Weave nature's robe of green.
The motes that fill the sunny rays
Build ocean, earth, and sky,—
The wondrous orbs that round us blaze
Are motes to Deity!

**Life,** love, devotion, closely twine,
Like tree, and flower, and fruit;
They ripen by a power divine,
Though fed by leaf and **root.**
And he, who would be truly **great,**
Must venture to be small;
**On** airy columns rests the dome
**That,** shining, circles all.

Small duties **grow** to mighty deeds,
Small words to thoughts of power;
Great forests **spring from tiny** seeds,
As moments make the **hour.**
And life, howe'er it lowly **grows,**
The essence to it given,
Like odor from the breathing rose,
Floats evermore to Heaven.

F. BENNOCH.

## THE FLOWER AND THE SONG.

A blossom grew in lonely **glen,**
Far from the busy **walks of men;**
Its petals opened, pearly white,
**Unnoticed,** yet all fair and bright.
"In vain," it sighed, " I oped my cup,
**And** held **it** to the daylight up;
Its beauty blessed no loving **eye,**—
**Unvalued** and alone, I die."
Low bent **its** head, its white leaves shrank,
**Fell on the** moss-beds green and dank,
**Died in** the valley,—not a trace
Was left of all its peerless grace.

But on the flower's deserted stem
The seeds remained; and, soft on them
Fell early dew and sunny rays,
Till ripe they stood in autumn days;
**And,** nurtured in a warmer clime,
They graced another summer-time.
Those fairer flowers not nameless died,

Neglected in their beauty's pride;
But poets praised their splendor rare,
And maidens twined them in their hair;
And knights, in triumph's golden hours,
Adorned their shields with those bright
   flowers.

A poet mused on glorious themes—
A wondrous radiance filled his dreams;
He strove, in language, to express
His fancy's blooming loveliness.
But he was all unknown to fame,
The world had never heard his name;
It hurried on its busy way,
Nor listened to his graceful lay.
"In vain," he said, "my song was sung,—
A rose upon the river flung;
A pearl let fall on angry seas,—
A flute-note dying on the breeze."

The nameless poet passed away,
A youth perused his thrilling lay;
It stirred his genius' latent fire—
That flute-note woke upon his lyre;
That pearl shone like a star to him,
To guide him on his pathway dim;
That last rose bloomed again, to be
His crown of immortality.
Then not in vain that song was sung,
Although upon the poet's tongue
It died;—an echo caught the strain,
Which never can be mute again.

               ANONYMOUS.

## THE PHILOSOPHY OF SPORT.

Bear lightly on their foreheads, Time!
   Strew roses on their way;
The young in heart, however old,
   That prize the present day,
And, wiser than the pompous proud,
   Are wise enough to play.

I love to see a man **forget**
  **His** blood is growing cold,
And leap, or swim, or gather flowers,
  Oblivious of his gold,
And mix with children in their sport,
  **Nor** think **that** he is old.

**I love** to see the man of care
  Take pleasure in a toy ;
**I love** to see him row or ride,
  And tread **the** grass with joy,
Or hunt the flying cricket-ball
  As lusty **as a** boy.

**All** sports that spare the humblest **pain,**
  That **neither** maim nor kill—
That **lead us to** the quiet field,
  Or to the wholesome hill,
Are duties which the **pure of** heart
  **R**eligiously fulfil.

Though some may laugh **that full-grown** men
  May frolic in the wood,
Like children let adrift from school,—
  Not **mine** that scornful mood ;—
I honor human happiness,
  And **deem it** gratitude.

And, though perchance the Cricketer,
  Or Chinaman that flies
His Dragon-**kite** with boys and girls,
  **May** seem to some unwise,
**I see no** folly in their play,
  **But** sense that underlies.

The road of life **is** hard enough—
  Bestrewn with snag and thorn ;
I would not mock the simplest joy
  That made it less forlorn ;
But fill **its** evening path with flowers
  As fresh as those of morn.

'T is something, when the moon has **passed,**
    To brave the touch of Time—
**And** say, " Good friend, **thou** harm'st me not,
    **My** soul is in its prime ;
Thou canst not chill **my** warmth of heart ;—
    I carol while I climb."

Give us but health, and peace of mind,
    Whate'er our clime or clan,
We'll **take** delight in simple things,
    Nor deem that sports unman ;
And **let** the proud, who fly no kites,
    Despise **us if they can** !

C. Mackay.

### SPEECH **OF** SEMPRONIUS FOR WAR.

My voice is still for war.
**Gods!** can a Roman senate long debate
**Which of** the two to choose—slavery or death ?
**No ;** let us rise at once, gird on our swords,
And, at the head of our remaining troops,
Attack the foe ; break through the thick **array**
Of his thronged legions, and charge home upon
    him.
**Perhaps some** arm more lucky than the rest
**May reach** his heart, and **free the** world from
    bondage.
**Rise,** fathers, rise ! 'tis Rome demands your help;
**Rise,** and revenge her slaughtered citizens,
Or share their fate ! The corpse of half her senate
Manure the fields of Thessaly, while we
Sit here, deliberating in cold debates,
If we should sacrifice our lives to honor,
Or wear them out in servitude and chains.
**Rouse** up, **for** shame ! our brothers of Pharsalia
Point at their wounds, and cry aloud, " To battle !"
Great Pompey's shade complains that we are
    slow,
And Scipio's ghost walks unrevenged amongst us !

Joseph Addison.

## THE STORY OF THE GENTIANS.

In the beautiful age of fairy mirth,
When the Angel of Flowers dwelt on the earth,
At the close of a sultry summer day,
There passed through the forest a weary Fay.
All day he had journeyed, and now, o'erworn,
With the water spent in his drinking-horn,
He longed for a draught of refreshing dew,
And then to slumber the long night through.
"O! is there a kindly flower," he said,
"That its cup of dew for my sake will shed?"
"I will!" cried a dear little Gentian flower,
That was nodding to sleep in a jessamine bower,
"I'll give thee the dew Night has given to me;
May it prove refreshment and strength to thee!"
The Fairy drank it, and sank to rest
In a sky-lark's deserted, grassy nest.
The Angel of Flowers at the sunrise came,
When the mountains were tipped with hues of
    flame;
Taking his way by the jessamine bower,
Where nestled the generous Gentian flower,
"Little blossom," he said, "thy love I have
    seen,
And thou shalt be fairer than thou hast been.
No prettier charm for thee can I devise
Than a fringe on the lids of those violet eyes."
He vanished; and sudden a wondrous change
Came over the flower; the Bee thought it
    strange
When he came again, and he slowly flew
To its hidden depths through that fringe of
    blue.
But a sister Gentian was standing by,
With envy and jealousy in her eye;
With a flush of anger and look of pride,
"My buds shall not open to-day!" she cried.
The Angel of Flowers was hovering near,
And her passionate words he chanced to hear:

" Thou must **keep** thy vow, though it bring **thee**
　　pain,
Thou may'st never open thy buds again ! "
O ! nevermore may the flower look up,
Never catch **the** dew in her deep-blue cup ;
And **the tears come** oft in her close-shut eyes,
Turned blindly up toward the beautiful skies ;
While her sister raises, **with** happy love,
Her azure-fringed eyes to **the blue** above ;
And sometimes she looks in the smiling **eye**
Of the kind Flower-Angel passing by ;
And the blind one knows by the falling tear
That the pitying Spirit is hovering near.
Anonymous.

---

## DARKNESS.

I had a dream, which was not *all* a dream.
The bright sun was extinguished, and the stars
Did wander, darkling, in the eternal space,
Rayless, and pathless, and the icy **earth**
Swung blind, and blackening, in the moonless
　　air ;
Morn came, and went—and came, and brought
　　no day ;
And men forgot their passions, in the dread
Of this their desolation ; and all hearts
Were chilled into a selfish prayer for light.
　　　　　　　　　　　　Some lay down,
And hid their eyes, and wept ; and some did
　　rest
Their chins upon their clenched hands, and
　　smiled ;
And others hurried to and fro, and fed
Their funeral piles with fuel, and looked up,
With mad disquietude, on the dull sky,
The pall of a past world ; and then again,
With curses, cast them down upon the dust,
And gnashed their teeth, and howled.

The wild birds shrieked,
And, terrified, did flutter on the ground,
And flap their useless wings: the wildest brutes
Came tame, and tremulous; and vipers crawled
And twined themselves among the multitude,
Hissing, but stingless—they were slain for food.
The meager by the meager were devoured;
Even dogs assailed their masters—all save one,
And he was faithful to a corse, and kept
The birds, and beasts, and famished men at bay,
Till hunger clung them, or the dropping dead
Lured their lank jaws; himself sought out no
      food,
But, with a piteous and perpetual moan,
And a quick desolate cry, licking the hand
Which answered not with a caress—he died.
    The crowd was famished by degrees; but two
Of an enormous city did survive,
And they were enemies; they met beside
The dying embers of an altar-place,
Where had been heaped a mass of holy things,
For an unholy usage: they raked up,
And, shivering, scraped, with their cold skeleton
      hands,
The feeble ashes, and their feeble breath
Blew for a little life, and made a flame,
Which was a mockery: then they lifted
Their eyes, as it grew lighter, and beheld
Each other's aspects: saw, and shrieked, and died,
Even of their mutual hideousness they died,
Unknowing who he was upon whose brow
Famine had written *fiend.* The world was void;
The populous and the powerful was a lump—
Seasonless, herbless, treeless, manless, lifeless:
A lump of death—a chaos of hard clay.
The rivers, lakes, and ocean, all stood still,
And nothing stirred within their silent depths;
Ships, sailorless, lay rotting on the sea,

And their masts fell down piecemeal; as they
 dropped,
They slept, on the abyss, without a surge:
The waves were dead; the tides were in their
 grave;
The moon, their mistress, had expired before;
The winds were withered in the stagnant air,
And the clouds perished: darkness had no need
Of aid from them; *she* was the *universe.*
         LORD BYRON.

---

## BERNARDO AND KING ALPHONSO.

With some good ten of his chosen men,
 Bernardo hath appeared,
Before them all in the palace hall,
 The lying king to beard;
With cap in hand and eye on ground,
 He came in reverend guise,
But ever and anon he frowned,
 And flame broke from his eyes.

"A curse upon thee," cried the king,
 "Who com'st unbid to me!
But what from traitor's blood should spring,
 Save traitor like to thee?
His sire, lords, had a traitor's heart,—
 Perchance our champion brave
May think it were a pious part
 To share Don Sancho's grave."

"Whoever told this tale,
 The king hath rashness to repeat,"
Cries Bernard,—"here my gage I fling
 Before the liar's feet.
No treason was in Sancho's blood,—
 No stain in mine doth lie:
Below the throne, what knight will own
 The coward calumny?

"Ye swore upon your kingly faith,
  To set Don Sancho free;
But curse upon your paltering breath!
  The light he ne'er did see:
He died in dungeon cold and dim,
  By Alphonso's base decree;
And visage blind, and mangled limb,
  Were all they gave to me.

"The king that swerveth from his word
  Hath stained his purple black:
No Spanish lord shall draw his sword
  Behind a liar's back.
But noble vengeance shall be mine;
  And open hate I'll show;—
The king hath injured Carpio's line,
  And Bernard is his foe!"

"Seize—seize him!" loud the king doth scream:
  "There are a thousand here;
Let his foul blood this instant stream;—
  What! caitiffs, do you fear?
Seize—seize the traitor!" But not one
  To move a finger dareth:
Bernardo standeth by the throne,
  And calm his sword he bareth.

He drew the falchion from its sheath,
  And held it up on high:
And all the hall was still as death:—
  Cries Bernard, " Here am I;
And here's the sword that owns no lord,
  Excepting heaven and me:
Fain would I know who dares its point,—
  King, conde, or grandee."

Then to his mouth his horn he drew,—
  It hung below his cloak;
His ten true men the signal knew,
  And through the ring they broke.

With helm on head, and blade in **hand**,
  The knights the circle break,
And back the lordlings 'gan to stand,
  And the false king to quake.

" Ha ! Bernard !" quoth Alphonso,
  " What means this warlike guise ?
Ye know full well I jested ;—
  Ye **know** your worth I prize !"
But Bernard turned upon his heel,
  And, smiling, passed away.
Long rued Alphonso and Castile
  The *jesting* of that day !

J. G. LOCKHART.

### THE MANIAC.

Stay, jailer, stay, **and** hear my woe !
  She is not mad who kneels to thee ;
For what I'm now, too well I know,
  And what I was, and what should be.
I'll rave no more in proud despair ;
  My language shall be mild, though sad :
But **yet** I firmly, truly swear,
  I **am** not mad, I am not mad.

My tyrant **husband** forged the tale
  Which chains me in this dismal cell ;
My fate unknown my friends bewail—
  Oh ! jailer, haste **that** fate to tell :
Oh ! haste my father's heart to cheer :
  His heart at once 'twill grieve and glad
To know, though kept a captive here,
  I am not mad, I am not mad.

He smiles in scorn, and turns the key ;
  He quits the grate ; I knelt in vain ;
His glimmering lamp, still, still I **see**—
  'Tis gone ! and all is gloom again.

Cold, bitter cold !—No warmth ! no light !—
　Life, all thy comforts once I had ;
Yet here I'm chained, this freezing night,
　Although not mad ; no, no, not mad.

'Tis sure some dream, some vision vain ;
　What ! I,—the child of rank and wealth,—
Am I the wretch who clanks this chain,
　Bereft of freedom, friends, and health ?
Ah ! while I dwell on blessings fled,
　Which never more my heart must glad,
How aches my heart, how burns my head ;
　But 'tis not mad ; no 'tis not mad.

Hast thou, my child, forgot, ere this,
　A mother's face, a mother's tongue ?
She'll ne'er forget your parting kiss,
　Nor round her neck how fast you clung ;
Nor how with her you sued to stay ;
　Nor how that suit your sire forbade ;
Nor how—I'll drive such thoughts away ;
They'll make me mad, they'll make me mad.

His rosy lips, how sweet they smiled !
　His mild blue eyes, how bright they shone !
None ever bore a lovelier child :
　And art thou now forever gone ?
And must I never see thee more,
　My pretty, pretty, pretty lad ?
I will be free ! unbar the door !
　I am not mad ; I am not mad.

Oh ! hark ! what mean those yells and cries ?
　His chain some furious madman breaks ;
He comes,—I see his glaring eyes ;
　Now, now, my dungeon-grate he shakes.
Help ! help !—He's gone !—Oh ! fearful woe,
　Such screams to hear, such sights to see !
My brain, my brain,—I know, I know,
　I am not mad, but soon shall be.

Yes, soon ;—for, lo you !—while I speak—
　　Mark how yon demon's eyeballs glare !
He sees me ; now, with dreadful shriek,
　　He whirls a serpent high in air.
Horror !—the reptile strikes his tooth
　　Deep in my heart, so crushed and sad ;
Ay, laugh, ye fiends ;—I feel the truth ;
　　Your task is done—I'm mad ! I'm mad !

LEWIS.

---

### THE AMERICAN PATRIOT'S SONG.

Hark ! hear ye the sounds that the winds on their
　　pinions
Exultingly roll from the shore to the sea,
With a voice that resounds through her bound-
　　less dominions ?
'Tis Columbia calls on her sons to be free !

Behold on yon summits, where heaven has
　　throned her,
　　How she starts from her proud inaccessible
　　　seat ;
With nature's impregnable ramparts around her,
　　And the cataract's thunder and foam at her
　　　feet !

In the breeze of her mountains her loose locks
　　are shaken,
　　While the soul-stirring notes of her warrior-
　　　song
From the rock to the valley re-echo—"Awaken,
　　Awaken, ye hearts that have slumbered too
　　　long !"

Yes, despots ! too long did your tyranny hold us,
　　In a vassalage vile, ere its weakness was known ;
Till we learned that the links of the chain that
　　controlled us
Were forged by the fears of its captives alone.

That spell is destroyed, and no longer availing,
  Despised as detested—pause well ere ye dare
To cope with a people whose **spirit** and feeling
  Are roused by remembrance and steeled by
    **despair.**

Go, tame the wild torrent, or stem with a straw
  The proud surges that sweep o'er the strand
    that confines them;
**But** presume not again to give freemen **a law,**
  **Nor** think with **the chains** they have broken
    to bind them.

To hearts **that the** spirit of **liberty** flushes,
  Resistance **is** idle,—and numbers a dream;—
They burst **from** control, as the mountain-stream
    rushes
  From its fetters **of ice, in** the warmth of the
    beam.

Anonymous.

## THE STREET OF **BY**-AND-BYE.

"By the street of 'By-and-Bye,' one arrives at the house
of 'Never.'"—*Old Saying.*

O! shun **the** spot. my youthful friends, **I** urge
    you **to beware;**
Beguiling is **the pleasant way,** and softly breathes
    the air;
Yet none have **ever** passed **to** scenes ennobling,
    great, and high,
Who **once** began to linger **in the street of** By-
    and-Bye.

How varied **are** the images arising to my sight
Of those who wished to shun the wrong, who
    loved and prized **the** right;
Yet from the silken bonds of sloth they vainly
    **strove to** fly,
**Which** held them gently prisoned in the street
    **of** By-and-Bye.

A youth aspired to climb the height of Learning's lofty hill;
What dimmed his bright intelligence—what
  quelled his earnest will?
Why did the object of his quest still mock his
  wistful eye?
Too long, alas! he tarried in the street of By-
  and-Bye.

"My projects thrive," the merchant said; "when
  doubled is my store,
How freely shall my ready gold be showered
  among the poor!"
Vast grew his wealth, yet strove he not the
  mourner's tear to dry;
He never journeyed onward from the street of
  By-and-Bye.

"Forgive thy erring brother, he had wept and
  suffered long,"
I said to one, who answered—"He hath done me
  grievous wrong;
Yet will I seek my brother, and forgive him, ere
  I die;"
Alas! Death shortly found him in the street of
  By-and-Bye!

The wearied worldling muses upon lost and
  wasted days,
Resolved to turn hereafter from the error of his
  ways,
To lift his grovelling thoughts from earth, and
  fix them on the sky;
Why does he linger fondly in the street of By-
  and-Bye?

Then shun the spot, my youthful friends; work
  on, while yet you may;
Let not old age o'ertake you as you slothfully
  delay,

Lest you should gaze around you, and discover
   with a sigh,
You have reached the house of "**Never**" by the
   street of By-and-Bye !

**Mrs.** Abdy.

## PARTING OF DOUGLAS AND MARMION.

Not far advanced was morning day,
When Marmion did his troops array,
  To Surrey's camp to ride ;
He had safe-conduct for his band,
Beneath the royal seal and hand,
  And Douglas gave a guide ;
The ancient Earl, with stately grace,
Would Clara on her palfrey place,
And whispered, in an under tone,
" Let the hawk stoop, his prey is flown."
The train from out the castle drew ;
But Marmion stopped to bid adieu :—
  " Though something I might plain," he said,
  " Of cold respect to stranger guest,
  Sent hither by your king's behest,
  While in Tantallon's towers I staid,
  Part we in friendship from your land,
  And, noble Earl, receive my hand."—
But Douglas round him drew his cloak,
Folded his arms, and thus he spoke :
" My manors, halls, and bowers, shall still
Be open, at my sovereign's will,
To each one whom he lists, howe'er
Unmeet to be the owner's peer.
My castles are my king's alone,
From turret to foundation stone,—
The hand of Douglas is his own,
And never shall in friendly grasp,
The hand of such as Marmion clasp."

Burned Marmion's swarthy cheek like fire,
And shook his very frame with ire,
  And—" This to me ! " he said,—

" An 't were not for thy hoary beard,
Such hand as Marmion's had not spared
　To cleave the Douglas' head !
And, first, I tell thee, haughty peer,
He, who does England's message here,
Although the meanest in her state,
May well, proud Angus, be thy mate ;
And, Douglas, more I tell thee here,
　Even in thy pitch of pride,
Here in thy hold, thy vassals near,
(Nay, never look upon your lord,
And lay your hands upon your sword,)
　I tell thee, thou'rt defied !
And if thou said'st, I am not peer
To any lord in Scotland here,
Lowland or Highland, far or near,
　Lord Angus, thou hast lied !"
On the Earl's cheek the flush of rage
O'ercame the ashen hue of age ;
Fierce he broke forth—" And dar'st thou then
To beard the lion in his den,
　The Douglas in his hall ?
And hop'st thou hence unscathed to go ?—
No, by St. Bride of Bothwell, no !—
Up draw-bridge, grooms—what, warder, ho !
　Let the portcullis fall."—
Lord Marmion turned,—well was his need,
And dashed the rowels in his steed,
Like arrow through the archway sprung,
The ponderous grate behind him rung :
To pass there was such scanty room,
The bars, descending razed his plume.

The steed along the draw-bridge flies,
Just as it trembled on the rise ;
Not lighter does the swallow skim
Along the smooth lake's level brim.
And when Lord Marmion reached his band,
He halts, and turns with clenched hand,
And shout of loud defiance pours,

And shook his gauntlet at the towers.
"Horse! horse!" the Douglas cried, "and
    chase!"
But soon he reined his fury's pace:
"A royal messenger he came,
Though most unworthy of the name.—
Saint Mary mend my fiery mood!
Old age ne'er cools the Douglas blood;
I thought to slay him where he stood.—
'Tis pity of him, too," he cried;
"Bold can he speak, and fairly ride:
I warrant him a warrior tried."—
With this his mandate he recalls,
And slowly seeks his castle halls.

WALTER SCOTT.

## THE MUMMY.

And thou hast walked about (how strange a
    story!)
  In Thebes' streets three thousand years ago,
When the Memnonium was in all its glory,
  And time had not begun to overthrow
Those temples, palaces, and piles stupendous,
Of which the very ruins are tremendous.

Speak! for thou long enough hast acted dummy,
  Thou hast a tongue, come let us hear its tune:
Thou'rt standing on thy legs above ground,
    Mummy!
  Revisiting the glimpses of the moon;
Not like thin ghosts or disembodied creatures,
But with thy bones and flesh, and limbs and
    features.

Tell us—for doubtless thou canst recollect,
  To whom should we assign the sphynx's fame?
Was Cheops or Cephrenes architect
  Of either pyramid that bears his name?
Is Pompey's pillar really a misnomer?
Had Thebes a hundred gates, as sung by Homer?

Perhaps thou wert a Mason, and forbidden
  By oath to tell the mysteries of thy trade,
Then say what secret melody was hidden
  In Memnon's statue, which at sunrise played?
Perhaps thou wert a priest—if so, my struggles
Are vain ;—Egyptian priests ne'er owned their
      juggles.

Perchance that very hand, now pinioned flat,
  Has hob-a-nobbed with Pharaoh, glass to
      glass ;
Or dropped a half-penny in Homer's hat,
  Or doffed thine own to let Queen Dido pass,
Or held, by Solomon's own invitation,
A torch at the great temple's dedication.

I need not ask thee if that hand, when armed,
  Has any Roman soldier mauled and knuckled,
For thou wert dead, and buried, and embalmed,
  Ere Romulus and Remus had been suckled :—
Antiquity appears to have begun
Long after thy primeval race was run.

Since first thy form was in this box extended,
  We have, above ground, seen some strange
      mutations;
The Roman empire has begun and ended ;
  New worlds have risen—we have lost old
      nations,
And countless kings have into dust been hum-
      bled,
While not a fragment of thy flesh has crumbled.

Didst thou not hear the pother o'er thy head
  When the great Persian conqueror, Cambyses,
Marched armies o'er thy tomb, with thundering
      tread,
  O'erthrew Osiris, Orus, Apis, Isis,
And shook the pyramids with fear and wonder,
When the gigantic Memnon fell asunder?

**If** the tomb's secrets may not be confessed,
The nature of the private life unfold ;—
**A** heart has throbbed beneath that leathern
       breast,
   **And** tears adown that dusky cheek have
       rolled :—
**Have** children climbed those knees, and kissed
       that face ?
What was thy name and station, age and race ?

Statue of flesh—immortal **of the dead!**
   Imperishable type of evanescence !
Posthumous man, who quitt'st thy narrow bed,
   And standest undecayed within our presence,
Thou **wilt hear nothing** till the judgment morn-
       ing,
**When** the great trump shall thrill thee with its
       warning.

Why should **this worthless** tegument endure,
   If its undying guest be lost forever?
Oh, let us keep the **soul** embalmed and **pure**
   In living virtue ; that when both must sever,
Although corruption may our frame consume,
Th' immortal **spirit** in the skies may bloom.
Smith.

---

## THE OLD OAKEN BUCKET.

How **dear to** my heart are the scenes of my
       childhood !
   When fond recollection presents them to
       view ;
The orchard, the meadow, the deep tangled
       wild-wood,
   And every loved spot which my infancy
       knew ;
**The** wide spreading pond, and the mill that
       stood by it,
   The bridge, and the rock where the cataract
       fell ;

The cot of my father, the dairy-house nigh it,
  And e'en the rude bucket which hung in the
     well;
    The old oaken bucket — the iron-bound
      bucket—
    The moss-covered bucket, which hung in
      the well.

That moss-covered vessel I hail as a treasure;
  For often at noon, when returned from the
     field,
I found it the source of an exquisite pleasure,
  The purest and sweetest that nature can yield.
How ardent I seized it with hands that were
     glowing,
And quick to the white pebbled bottom it fell;
Then soon, with the emblem of truth overflow-
     ing,
    And dripping with coolness, it rose from the
     well;
    The old oaken bucket—the iron-bound
      bucket—
    The moss-covered bucket arose from the
     well.

How sweet from the green mossy brim to re-
     ceive it,
  As poised on the curb, it inclined to my lips!
Not a full, blushing goblet could tempt me to
     · leave it,
  Though filled with the nectar that Jupiter sips.
And now, far removed from that loved situation,
  The tear of regret will intrusively swell,
As fancy reverts to my father's plantation,
  And sighs for the bucket which hangs in the
     well;
    The old oaken bucket—the iron-bound
      bucket—
    The moss-covered bucket which hangs in
     the well.     Samuel Woodworth.

## THE MUSIC OF THE WAVES.

When moonlight's soft and tender charm
  Is brightening all the sea,
When all the earth lies still and calm
  In night's serenity,
I love to stand upon the shore
  Which Ocean gently laves,
And hear the sound I love so well—
  The music of the waves.

I love to think how, everywhere,
  On many a distant strand,
That music fills the breezy air,
  Along the shelly sand;
How, far away, its low notes roll
  Through lonely, echoing caves,
Where naught but listening stars can hear
  The music of the waves.

God woke the ocean's organ tone
  E'en at creation's birth;
And still, though thousand years are flown,
  Its loud notes ring on earth;
Ay, still it sounds, eternally,
  If Ocean smiles or raves;
In sleep or madness ceaseth not
  The music of the waves.

But not in dull monotony
  That tireless voice sings on;
The music of the changing sea
  Hath many a varied tone.
It sometimes seems a requiem
  O'er many nameless graves,
Whose silent inmates hear no more
  The music of the waves.

And oft in very happiness
  It breaks upon the shore,
The gladness striving to express
  With which its heart brims o'er.

As changeful as the rainbow foam
　With which the shore it laves,
Rings on, in varied beauty still,
　The music of the waves.

ANONYMOUS.

## TRUEST WISDOM.

"Receive instruction and not silver; and knowledge,
rather than choice gold. For wisdom is better than
rubies; and all the things that may be desired are not to
be compared to it."—Prov. viii. 10, 11.

'Tis the part of truest wisdom,
　Well to store the youthful mind;
He who works the mines of learning
　Will more precious jewels find,—
Worth far more than sparkling diamonds
　Or than pearls from Persian seas—
"Pearls of wisdom" with pure luster
　Dim the flashing light of these.

'Tis the time, ere care or sorrow
　Fill the weary world-worn heart,
Choicest lore from books to borrow,
　Acting well the student's part.
Heed thou, then, what says the Scripture,—
　Take it to thy inmost heart—
Knowledge has more worth than silver,
　Even in life's crowded mart.

Skill is stronger far than sinews,
　Science aids in every art;
All improvements, world-wide blessings,
　From some studious brain take start.
Toil, then, onward, ardent ever,
　Fearless scale each towering height,
Where mysterious clouds are resting,
　Hiding still thy goal from sight;

For amid life's whirl and bustle
　Comes no more the quiet hour,
When thou canst, in peace, be gaining
　Knowledge, which is highest Power.

Be, then, strong and struggle nobly,
  **A**dd, with patience, line to line
Of its truthful, earnest lessons
  While the days of youth are thine.

**So s**halt thou, **when** age is shedding
  Thick **its** snows upon thy head,
And the path of life seems lengthened
  To thy weary, faltering tread,
Find within thy **mind's** deep coffers
  Better wealth **than** countless **gold**—
Gems of knowledge rich and sparkling—
  Diamond thoughts of price untold.

ANONYMOUS.

## "I CAN !"

" I CAN !" **Yes,** sir—we know you can !
  **We** read **it in your eye,**
There is a mystic **talisman**
  Flashing all **gloriously !**
Speak it **out** boldly, **let it** ring,
  There is a volume **there,**
There's meaning in the eagle's wing ;
  **Then** soar, and do, and dare !

" I CAN !" climbs to the mountain top,
  And **plows t**he billowy main,
It lifts **the hammer in the** shop ;
  And **drives t**he saw **and plane ;**
'Tis fearless **in** the **battle** shock,
  And always leads the **van**
**Of** young America's brave sons,—
  They never quailed nor ran.

" I CAN !" **He is a** fiery youth,
  And WILL a brother twin,
And, arm in arm, **in** love and truth,
  They'll either die or win ;
Shoulder to shoulder, ever ready,
  All firm and fearless still
The brothers labor—true and steady—
  " I CAN," and brave " I WILL !"

"I can" e'en on his pleasure trips
  Travels by telegraph,
He plumes the snowy wing of ships,
  And never works by half;
His music is the humming loom,
  And shuttles are his dances,
Then clear the way and quick give room
  For the noble souled "I can," sirs!

"I can!" Yes, sir—we know you can!
  'Tis lithe in every limb,
To your blood 'tis a busy fan,
  How can the flame burn dim?
It tensely draws your sturdy nerves,—
  No bow's without a string,
And when nor bow nor bow-string swerves
  An arrow's on the wing.

I've got to "sixthly," and would make
  A personal "application"
In four heads; listen every one
  Of this our Yankee nation;
*Banish from you every can't,*
  *And show yourself a man,*
*And nothing will your purpose daunt,*
  *Led by the brave "I can!"*

Anonymous.

## A NEW THEORY OF FROST: OR THE STORY OF THE FROST-KING.

The cold winter-wind rushed noisily forth,
  Blew merrily far and free,
From its home in the frozen caves of the
      North,
  Away over land and sea;
Away, away, o'er the stiffening earth,
  And the icy ocean-tide,
With a rushing sound, and a noisy mirth,
  Resistlessly, far and wide.

The Frost-King sat on a lofty seat,
  In his glorious palace hall;
A carpet of snow was spread for his feet,
  In his hand was an icicle tall.
Gorgeous and brilliant the Northern Lights
     bright,
Flashed from the pillars around,
In rosy, and purple, and emerald light,
  And danced o'er the carpeted ground.

Fringes of icicles hung from the roof,—
  Hung from the seat of the throne;
And there, in the midst of the beautiful hall,
  Sat the merry Frost-King, alone.
Then he thought to himself, and he spoke out
     aloud,—
  "The South Wind has just come back;
And he brings such tales of the kingdoms proud
  That he passed on his homeward track ;—

"I too, must go from my beautiful home,
  And journey the wide world through;
I will see for myself, as I onward roam,
  If the stories he tells are true."
Then his servants fastened his icy car
  To the North Wind, fleet and strong,
And away right merrily, free and far,
  The North Wind bore him along.

And, speeding away like the arrowy light,
  He came to visit us, here ;
He wanders about in the starry night,
  And looks at the houses queer,
At the green pine tree, and the hemlock free,
  With branches drooping and low,
At the withered leaf, and the naked tree,
  All crusted and sparkling with snow.

But the merry Frost-King grows weary and sad,
  For he longs for his home once more ;
For the music of icebergs, crashing glad
  Away from the rocky shore :

He waits to go back with the soft South Wind ;
   But, far in the sunny South-land,
Its fleet, fair horses, I know we should find,
   Are fastened, and quietly stand.

No longer merry, but weary and worn,
   He wanders about in the night,
Homesick, and longing so much to return
   To his beautiful palace of light ;
And he thinks of naught but his far-away home ;
   Of his ice-towers, floating free ;
Of his fringe-hung roof, and his icicled dome,
   Where the light plays gloriously.

He remembers a bay, where a brave little bark,
   That he fought for, and won, at last,
From her daring crew, in the winter dark,
   In his icy chains is fast.
And he longs to go back to his trophy of war,
   And fasten her tighter still,
Lest the lawless sea-currents should bear her far
   Away, in spite of his will.

And when he looks in at the windows bright,
   As he wearily wanders past,
And sees our home by the dancing fire-light,
   His tears fall heavy and fast ;
And he sighs, " No home is so dear as my hall,
   Let me show you my beautiful land ! "
And then on the pane, with his fingers small,
   He draws with a trembling hand.

And he draws his glorious northern home,
   His palace and crystal hall,
His icebergs grand, and his icicled dome,
   And a snow-wreath over all :
And the little bark in the ice-bound bay,—
   The prize that is fairly his own,—
With her tapering masts, pointing, night and
     day,
   To the polar star, alone.

But sometimes the tears of the little Frost-King
  Fall as fast as his finger moves,
And drop on the picture, and blot every thing
  He may draw of the land he loves ;
And palace, throne, icebergs, all melt into one,—
  A broad stretching frost-sheet of **white :**
Then he sighs yet again, and more sadly goes on
  **To** the next pane, all gleaming and bright.

**Thus** he wearily wanders **along** the street,
  Through the starry winter night ;
**We** can not hear the sound of his feet,
  **Or** mark his figure slight.
But **when we see,** by the morning sun,
  His **beautiful** pictures around,
We **know he has** been here, **and drawn every**
      one,
  Though we **heard** not **a voice or sound.**

Then pity, oh ! pity the **sad Frost-King !**
  And hope, that the days **to** come
The South Wind's horses **may** swiftly bring,
  And carry him back to his home.
And study the pictures he leaves for you all,
  And find his palace and throne,
**And** the icicled wall, and **the icebergs** tall,
  **And his ship in** the **bay,** alone.
A. E. Brackett.

---

## THE MAIN TRUCK, OR A LEAP FOR LIFE.

**Old** Ironsides * at anchor lay,
  In **the** harbor of Mahon ;
**A** dead calm **rested** on the bay,—
  The waves to **sleep** had gone ;
When little Hal, **the** Captain's son,
  A lad both **brave and** good,
In **sport,** up shroud **and** rigging ran,
  **And on the** main truck† stood !

---

* The United States frigate Constitution.
† The topmost point of the main mast.

A shudder shot through every vein,—
  All eyes were turned on high!
There stood the boy, with dizzy brain,
  Between the sea and sky;
No hold had he above, below;
  Alone he stood in air:
To that far height none dared to go,—
  No aid could reach him there.

We gazed, but not a man could speak!
  With horror all aghast,
In groups, with pallid brow and cheek,
  We watched the quivering mast.
The atmosphere grew thick and hot,
  And of a lurid hue;
As riveted unto the spot,
  Stood officers and crew.

The father came on deck:—he gasped,
  "O God! thy will be done!"
Then suddenly a rifle grasped,
  And aimed it at his son.
"Jump, far out, boy, into the wave!
  Jump, or I fire," he said;
"That only chance your life can save;
  Jump, jump, boy!"  He obeyed.

He sunk,—he rose,—he lived,—he moved,—
  And for the ship struck out.
On board we hailed the lad beloved,
  With many a manly shout.
His father drew, in silent joy,
  Those wet arms round his neck,
And folded to his heart his boy,—
  *Then fainted on the deck.*

ANONYMOUS.

www.ingramcontent.com/pod-product-compliance
Lightning Source LLC
Chambersburg PA
CBHW031022120726
47905CB00007B/2006